The
Spinster's
SECRET

EMILY
LARKIN

www.emilylarkin.com

Publisher's Note: This is a work of fiction. Names, characters, places, and incidents are a product of the author's imagination. Locales and public names are sometimes used for atmospheric purposes. Any resemblance to actual people, living or dead, or to businesses, companies, events, institutions, or locales is completely coincidental.

The Spinster's Secret / Emily Larkin. – 2nd ed.

ISBN 978-0-9951428-2-4

Cover Design: JD Smith Design

A NOTE TO READERS

The word bâtman occurs several times in this novel. A bâtman was an enlisted soldier who performed his normal regimental duties, but also acted as an officer's valet. For this, he received extra pay. It wasn't uncommon for a bâtman to follow his officer into civilian life, as Edward's bâtman has done.

*C*HAPTER 1

*H**is Lordship swiftly divested me of my gown, placing hot kisses on the skin he bared. "You are a goddess," he breathed, as he untrussed my bosom . . .*

Matilda Chapple glanced at the window. Outside the overcast sky was darkening towards dusk. If she hurried, she could mail this installment of Chérie's *Confessions* before night fell.

Seizing me in his arms, he carried me to the bed, she wrote hastily. *He pushed aside the froth of my petticoats with impatience. In less than a minute he had made his entrance and slaked his lust upon my . . .*

Mattie halted, the quill held above the page, and squinted at her draft. What was that word? Feverish? Fevered? Fervent?

. . . upon my fevered body.

Mattie continued swiftly copying. Finally, she finished: *We lay sated in the sunlight. For my part, I was as pleased by his lordship's manly vigor as he was so evidently pleased by my feminine charms. I foresaw many pleasant months ahead as his mistress.*

And on that note, dear readers, I shall end this latest confession from my pen.

Chérie.

Mattie laid down the quill. She glanced at the window

again, hastily blotted the pages, and folded them. She sealed the letter with a wafer and wrote the address of her publisher clearly. Then she folded another letter around it and sealed that, too, writing the address of her friend Anne on it: *Mrs. Thos. Brocklesby, Lombard Street, London.*

Done.

Mattie bundled up the draft and hid it with the others in the concealed cupboard in the wainscoting. She crammed a bonnet on her head, threw a thick shawl around her shoulders, and grabbed the letter.

There was still an hour of daylight left, but deep shadows gathered in the corridors of Creed Hall. The stairs creaked as she hurried down them. The entrance hall was cave-like, dark and chilly and musty.

"Matilda!"

Mattie swung around, clutching the letter to her breast.

Her uncle stood in the doorway to his study, leaning heavily on a cane. "Where are you going?"

Mattie raised the letter, showing it to him. "A letter to a friend, Uncle Arthur. I'm taking it down to the village."

Her uncle frowned, his face pleating into sour, disapproving folds. "I sent Durce with the mail an hour ago."

"Yes, Uncle. I hadn't quite finished—"

"Durce can take it tomorrow."

"I should like to send it today, Uncle. If I may."

Uncle Arthur's eyebrows pinched together in a scowl. The wispy feathers of white hair ringing his domed skull, the beak-like nose, made him look like a gaunt, bad-tempered bird of prey. "Mr. Kane will be arriving soon."

"I'll only be twenty minutes. I promise." Mattie bowed her head and held her breath. *Please, please, please . . .*

Her uncle sniffed. "Very well. But don't be late for our guest. We owe him every courtesy."

"No, Uncle." Mattie dipped him a curtsy. "Thank you."

Outside, the sky was heavy with rain clouds. The air was

dank and bracingly cold, scented with the smell of decaying vegetation. Mattie took a deep breath, filling her lungs, feeling her spirits lift, conscious of a delicious sense of freedom. She walked briskly down the long drive, skirting puddles and mud. On either side, trees stretched leafless branches towards the sky. Once she was out of sight of the Hall's windows, Mattie lengthened her stride into a run. She spread her arms wide, catching the wintry breeze with her shawl. It felt as if she was galloping, as if she was flying, as if she was *free*.

At the lane, she slowed to a walk and turned right. The village of Soddy Morton was visible in the hollow a mile away.

Mattie crossed the crumbling stone bridge. The brook rushed and churned below, brown and swollen, its banks cloaked in winter-dead weeds. She blew out a breath. It hung fog-like in front of her. Icy mud splashed her half boots and the hem of her gown, but a feeling of joy warmed her. She didn't see the bleak landscape—the bare fields, the bare trees, the heavy, gray sky. Instead, her imagination showed her a cheerful boarding house with a cozy kitchen and a view of the sea through the windows.

Mattie inhaled deeply, almost smelling the tang of the ocean, almost tasting sea salt on her tongue.

Her grip tightened on the letter. Soon she would be free of Uncle Arthur, free of Creed Hall, free of Soddy Morton and Northamptonshire. Every word that she wrote and every confession that she mailed to London brought the dream of owning a boarding house closer.

Soon it wouldn't be a dream, it would be reality.

Edward Kane, lately of the Royal Horse Guards, tooled his curricle over the low bridge to the clatter of iron-shod hooves on stone and halted at his first glimpse of Creed Hall.

It crouched to his left at the crest of the hill, built of stone so dark it almost looked black, crowded by leafless trees. He grimaced. What had Toby called it? The dungeon.

"Ugly," his bâtman, Tigh, commented from his seat alongside Edward.

Edward grunted agreement. A gust of wind whistled across the bare fields, and with it, the first icy drops of rain. He shivered, and urged the horses up the driveway. Guilt—a familiar companion since Waterloo—seemed to wrap more closely around him with each step the weary horses took. The Hall disappeared, then came into sight again, looking even more grim and inhospitable. He drew the curricle to a halt in front of the frowning, iron-studded door, handed the reins to Tigh, and clambered down. "Take it round to the stables."

"Yes, sir."

Edward rubbed his aching thigh. Guilt settled more heavily on him as he limped up the steps. Creed Hall loomed above him. It was ugly, but even so, it was Toby's home. *It should be him here, not me.*

The door opened on grating hinges before he reached it. "Mr. Kane."

Edward stepped inside, shivering. He handed his hat to the elderly butler, shrugged out of his fur-lined driving coat, and peeled off his gloves. Oil paintings hung on the dark-paneled walls, barely discernible in the gloom.

"Sir Arthur is in the library, sir," the butler said, receiving the gloves and managing not to stare at Edward's butchered hands. Or perhaps he didn't notice the lack of fingers in the dimness. "If you would follow me, sir?"

Edward followed.

The library was almost as dark as the entrance hall. The curtains were drawn against the dusk, but a lone candle burned on a side table and a meager fire smoked in the grate. A figure sat in a winged leather armchair beside the fireplace, shrouded in shadow.

"Mr. Kane, sir," the butler said, and departed.

Edward bowed towards the armchair. "Sir Arthur?"

Sir Arthur levered himself from the armchair. Edward tried to find some points of similarity between his host and Toby. Height, leanness, a long face, but there it stopped. Arthur Strickland was thin to the point of emaciation, his high, domed skull bare except for a few wisps of white hair, his skin withered into pale, desiccated folds. Where Toby had liked to laugh, it appeared that Arthur Strickland preferred to frown. Lines of disapproval were engraved on his face, pinching between the feathery eyebrows and deeply bracketing his mouth.

Sir Arthur held out his hand, leaning heavily on his ebony cane, noticed the three fingers missing from Edward's right hand, and hesitated.

"It doesn't hurt, sir," Edward said. *Not much.*

Strickland shook hands with him, a dry, limp clasp. "Waterloo?"

"Yes."

Interest sharpened in the old man's eyes.

Edward braced himself for the inevitable questions, but instead Sir Arthur said, "Sherry?"

"Please."

Strickland rang for a servant. Edward sat silently while the butler bustled into the library, poured two small glasses of sherry, and left. Sir Arthur's gaze was on his face. Edward watched the old man trace the scars, saw him note the missing ear. Finally the perusal ended. "Waterloo as well?"

Edward nodded. He sipped his sherry. It was mouth-puckeringly dry.

Strickland sighed. He leaned back in his armchair. "My son . . . you were with him when he died?"

"Yes, sir."

Sir Arthur glanced at the fire, blinked several times, swallowed, and brought his gaze back to Edward. "Would you mind . . . telling me?"

A rush of memory ambushed Edward. For a brief moment

he was back at Waterloo. The smells of blood and cordite filled his nose. Toby's shout rang in his ears—*Get up, Ned!*—as vivid, as clear, as if the battle had been yesterday, not five months ago.

Muscles clenched in Edward's stomach. He gulped a fortifying mouthful of sherry. "Not at all." He looked away from the old man's face and began his tale.

There was silence for a long time after Edward had finished, then Arthur Strickland cleared his throat. "Thank you."

Edward nodded.

The old man stood slowly. "We dine at six."

Edward glanced at the clock on the mantelpiece. Half past five.

"My sister's nurse-companion dines with us. I hope you don't mind?"

"Not at all."

He gave Strickland a few minutes to make his way slowly from the library, leaning on his cane, then summoned the butler with a jerk of the bell rope and followed the man up creaking stairs and along dark, chilly corridors to his bed-chamber. The mutton smell of tallow candles hung in the air.

The fire in his room was as meager as the one in the library. The four-poster bed loomed like a crêpe-shrouded mausoleum, hung with dark green velvet. His valise had been unpacked and his few clothes neatly put away. The package of Toby's effects lay on the dresser. Edward turned away from it. He'd deal with that later. He'd had all the memories he could cope with for the moment.

Tigh bustled in, stocky and middle-aged, his face weather-beaten beneath bristling eyebrows. He carried a jug of steaming water. "It's colder than a nun's monosyllable in 'ere, sir."

Edward grunted agreement. He stripped out of his traveling clothes and dressed quickly in pantaloons and a fresh shirt. He washed his face and ran a comb through his hair. He didn't bother looking in the mirror; no trick of styling his hair would hide the jagged remnants of his left ear or mask the scars that disfigured his cheeks and brow. The neckcloth took several minutes of concentration; the lack of fingers on his right hand made it hard to form the exact creases. He almost gave up and let Tigh do it, but it was an independence he'd fought hard to regain—tying his own neckcloth—and he gritted his teeth and persevered, while outside the rain drummed heavily down.

A glance at his pocket watch showed that it wanted five minutes to the hour. Edward donned his white waistcoat, shrugged into the black long-tailed coat Tigh held out, nodded his thanks to the bâtman, and retraced his steps to the ground floor. The corridors were dim, lit with the barest number of candles.

At the foot of the stairs he paused and looked around. A door stood ajar opposite the library. Faint light and the sound of women's voices came from within.

Edward walked over and touched the door with his fingertips. It swung open. The conversation inside halted.

"Er . . . good evening," he said, as the room's two occupants turned to stare at him.

Their reaction was one he still hadn't become accustomed to. Both ladies were well bred enough not to recoil, but he saw the startled widening of their eyes, the stiffening of their faces as they took in his appearance.

There was a moment of silence while they examined each other. His brain mentally cataloged them: one pretty and petite, one tall and plain. He knew what they saw: a hulking brute of a man with a scarred face.

Both ladies were dressed in the gray of half-mourning. The plain one was brown-haired and built on robust lines, with a deep bosom and wide hips. The pretty one looked as if she'd stepped out of a poem, except that her golden hair, blue eyes, and milk-white complexion were entirely real. A line flicked through Edward's mind: *Her tresses gold, her eyes like glassy streams, her teeth are pearl, the breasts are ivory.*

His gaze swung between the two ladies. The larger one had to be the nurse-companion, sturdily competent, which meant that the ethereal little blonde was Toby's cousin, Matilda Chapple. He focused his attention on her and bowed. "Miss Chapple?"

"I am Miss Chapple."

Edward's gaze jerked back to the brunette.

"You must be Mr. Kane." Her voice was a low contralto.

"Yes, ma'am." Edward bowed again.

Miss Chapple smiled warmly. "Welcome to Creed Hall." She advanced across the room towards him, holding out her hand, a friendly gesture. She was even taller than he'd thought, all of six foot.

Edward held out his own hand. Miss Chapple saw the missing fingers, hesitated for a brief fraction of a second, and then clasped it. Her handshake was as warm and welcoming as her smile. "Toby spoke often of you."

"And he spoke often of you."

"He did?" He saw something in Miss Chapple's eyes—a dark flicker of grief—before she released his hand. "He was the best of cousins." She turned towards the pretty blonde. "May I present Mrs. Dunn?"

He was shaking hands with Mrs. Dunn when the *thump thump* of a cane heralded Arthur Strickland's arrival. Strickland entered the parlor leaning on the ebony cane, an elderly woman on his arm. "My sister," he said. "Lady Marchbank."

Lady Marchbank was as cadaver-like as her brother. She was dressed entirely in black, from her black lace cap to the black hem of her gown. *A female grim reaper,* was Edward's involuntary thought. He squashed it hastily and bowed. The resemblance between brother and sister was strong: the tall, stooped postures; the long, bony faces; the wrinkles folded into deep, disapproving lines.

A clock struck six somewhere in the house, a ponderous sound. "I should inform you, Mr. Kane, that we dine plainly at Creed Hall," Strickland announced as the last echo died away. "And for the sake of our digestion we preserve the strictest silence."

Mattie studied Mr. Kane surreptitiously while she ate. Goliath, Toby had called him, and she understood how he'd come by that name. He was an uncommonly large gentleman, taller than she was by a good half foot, and solidly built. He looked as if he could carry the weight of a coach-and-four on those broad shoulders.

Mr. Kane had dark hair and a tanned face crossed with pink scars. She knew his age: thirty. The same age Toby would be if he were alive.

Mattie traced the scars scoring across his brow, bisecting an eyebrow, curving down his cheek. She examined his left ear. Most of it was missing. Her gaze dropped to his hands. They bore scars similar to those across his face. Three fingers were missing on his right hand, and one on his left.

Had his sword been cut from his hand? Did that account for the missing fingers?

She imagined him weaponless, trying to ward off an attack . . .

Her ribcage tightened. Mattie looked away from Mr. Kane's battered hands and forced herself to think of something else. Outside, rain came down in torrents. A cold wind leaked through the cracks in the window casement. The clink of cutlery was loud in the silence: the scrape of a knife across a plate, the tiny clatter of fork tines as her uncle speared a piece of boiled mutton.

What did Mr. Kane think of so silent a meal? Perhaps he was grateful. He didn't look like a man skilled at small talk, a man who could turn a pretty phrase as easily as he could tie his own shoelaces. He looked like a fighter.

A fighter who'd lost a battle and had almost died.

Her gaze crept back to him. Mr. Kane seemed undismayed by the food. *I'll have no sauces in my house,* her uncle was fond of announcing. *No spices. Food boiled in plain water is all that one requires.*

Pig swill, Toby had called it the last time he'd been home. He had gone down to the village inn to eat his dinner—and smuggled back a roasted chicken and a plum pie for her afterwards.

Grief tightened Mattie's throat. She looked down at her plate and blinked back tears. *I miss you, Toby.*

After dinner, the ladies retired to the drawing room. Arthur Strickland poured two small measures of port. Edward sat back and braced himself for more questions about Waterloo.

"When did you return to England?" Strickland asked, sipping his port.

"Last month."

Strickland glanced at Edward's ear, his hands. "I hadn't realized you were so seriously injured."

"I wasn't," Edward said, ignoring the broken leg that had kept him immobilized for months. "A friend of mine lost an arm. He contracted fever and almost died. I stayed with him until he was well enough to travel."

"Gareth Locke," Strickland said.

Edward nodded, and tasted the port. Too sweet.

"Tobias's friend."

"Yes."

The three of them—Gareth and Toby and himself—had been inseparable since their first day at school. They'd gone through Harrow and Oxford together, had caroused together, soldiered together, almost died together.

And now we are two.

Edward looked down at his port. The color reminded him of blood—and with that thought came another rush of memory: the blood-and-smoke smell of the battlefield, the din of cannons, the soft sobbing of a dying soldier.

Toby hadn't wept. He'd died instantly. And lain alongside Edward for all of that terrible day . . .

Edward's stomach clenched. For a moment he thought he was going to bring his dinner back up. He shook his head, breaking the memory.

"I hear Locke inherited a baronetcy from his uncle," Strickland said.

Edward's stomach settled back into place. "Yes."

"Lucky man."

Edward remembered the expression on Gareth's face when he'd bid him farewell yesterday. He shook his head again. "I think he'd have preferred to keep his arm." *And his sweetheart.* Not even a baronetcy had been enough to reconcile Miss Swinthorp to marriage with a one-armed man. A brief statement had appeared in the newspapers two days after Gareth's return to London, announcing the termination of their engagement.

Stupid bitch. Edward clenched his right hand. Even after five months, a dull twinge of pain accompanied the movement.

He unclenched his hand and looked down at it, at the stumps of three of his fingers, and felt the familiar sense of disbelief, the familiar pang of loss. Would it ever fade? Or would he always mourn his missing fingers?

At least he'd not had a sweetheart to be repulsed by his injuries.

Strickland grunted, and then struggled to his feet, leaning on the cane. "Please join us in the drawing room."

Edward stood. "It would be my pleasure, sir."

Strickland made his way slowly to the door. Edward followed. They traversed the corridor at a snail's pace. "My niece reads to us in the evenings," Strickland said, stopping outside a paneled door.

"How delightful," Edward said, remembering her contralto voice. "Poetry?"

"Sermons," the old man said, opening the door.

Sermons? Edward almost balked. *If you can face Napoleon's army on a battlefield, you can face an evening of sermons,* he told himself, and he squared his shoulders and followed his host into the drawing room.

Like every other room he'd seen in this house, it was a bleak chamber, paneled in dark wood. The furniture was stiff, the fire too small for the grate. All three ladies had shawls draped around their shoulders. He thought he saw Mrs. Dunn shiver as she bent over her embroidery frame.

Edward chose a mahogany armchair. Despite its apparent sturdiness, the chair creaked beneath his weight. He shifted slightly, trying to make himself more comfortable. The chair creaked again, more loudly. He took that as a warning and stilled.

Miss Chapple presided over the teapot. "Tea, Mr. Kane?"

"Please."

The *clink* of china was loud as she placed teacups on saucers and poured for himself and her uncle, not because she was clumsy—the movement of her fingers was deft and unhesitating—but because the room was so silent. "Milk?" she asked. "Sugar?"

Edward shook his head. Milk and sugar were things he'd learned to do without on campaign.

He accepted his cup and sipped. The tea was weak and tepid—but it rid the sweet taste of port from his mouth.

Her duties as hostess done, Miss Chapple stood and took

a place to one side of the fireplace, where she didn't block the meager heat. Edward drained his teacup and cast a longing glance at the door. Could he claim tiredness as an escape?

Not when it was barely half past seven.

He sighed, and placed the teacup back in its saucer.

Miss Chapple opened the leather-bound book. She looked at Edward. "I shall be reading from *Sermons to Young Women*," she told him. "By the Reverend James Fordyce. Are you familiar with the work, Mr. Kane?"

"Er . . . no." He sat back in the armchair, making it creak again, and composed his face into an expression of interest.

"Sermon Two," Miss Chapple said. "On Modesty of Apparel." She glanced at Mrs. Dunn briefly, as if some silent message passed between them, and then began to read aloud: "Let me recall the attention of my female friends to a subject that concerns them highly . . ."

Edward stopped paying attention. He gazed at the fire and allowed Miss Chapple's voice to flow over him. She had a surprisingly attractive voice, low and melodic, lulling him towards sleep . . .

He jerked back to full attention. The clock on the mantel-piece had advanced twenty minutes. Miss Chapple still read from the book of sermons: "Is not a constant pursuit of trivial ornament an indubitable proof of a trivial mind?"

Edward glanced swiftly around. Had anyone noticed he'd fallen into a doze?

No.

Lady Marchbank was listening with fierce attention, her lips pursed in approval. Arthur Strickland was watching his niece, nodding as she spoke, agreeing with Fordyce.

"Will she that is always looking into her glass, be much disposed to look into her character?"

Mrs. Dunn, blonde and pretty, was also listening intently, her eyes fixed on Miss Chapple's face, but . . .

Edward narrowed his eyes. Mrs. Dunn's lips moved silent-ly, as if she was counting under her breath. He glanced at her hands. Her fingers tapped against her knee as she listened—tiny, almost indiscernible movements.

Was she counting something?

Edward returned his gaze to Miss Chapple. He scanned her from head to toe. She was extremely plain, her brown hair pulled back severely from her face and her mannishly tall figure garbed in an unflattering gray gown.

Edward's gaze lingered on her breasts for a fleeting moment before he wrenched them away. *She's reading a sermon,* he admonished himself. And she was Toby's cousin. His favorite cousin.

Edward observed Miss Chapple more thoughtfully. Toby had spoken highly of her. There must be something more to her than was visible at first glance.

He closed his eyes for a brief moment. When he opened them again, the clock hands had advanced another fifteen minutes.

Edward sat up straight, blinking. He uncrossed his legs and crossed them the other way. The armchair uttered a creaking groan.

"The less vanity you betray," Miss Chapple read, "the more merit we shall always be disposed to allow you."

He focused his attention on her, trying to guess her age. She was well past girlhood. Somewhere in her twenties, but precisely where was hard to determine; her skin was as smooth as that of a girl in her teens.

Edward studied her, trying to see a resemblance to Toby and finding none. Miss Chapple's hair was an indifferent mid-brown, her nose unremarkable and quite unlike Toby's jutting beak. An ordinary face, although he thought she might have dimples when she smiled. The only feature of note was her mouth, which was too large for beauty. But a lush mouth could never be a fault in a woman.

Miss Chapple's figure was as generous as her mouth; she had none of Toby's leanness. The gray gown was overlarge, as if attempting to hide her abundant curves; it only succeeded in making her look heavier than she was. Edward found himself glancing at her breasts again, and looked abruptly away, fastening his gaze on Mrs. Dunn. Her lips moved infinitesimally as her fingers tapped lightly against her knee. What was she counting?

He watched Mrs. Dunn's fingers and listened to Miss Chapple. ". . . has been thought the most common—"

Mrs. Dunn's forefinger tapped once on her knee.

". . . the rankest—"

Another tap.

". . . and the most noxious—"

Another tap.

". . . weed that grows in the heart of a female—"

Another tap.

Edward suppressed a grin. She was counting the *the*s. He settled back more comfortably in the armchair, ignoring the creak it made, and turned his attention to Miss Chapple again. How much longer could the wretched sermon be? Miss Chapple's voice was as soporific as a lullaby . . .

The jerk of his head dropping forward woke him. The clock told him he'd lost another five minutes. Edward glanced around. No one had noticed. He swallowed a yawn and managed not to rub his eyes.

". . . that leads the world," Miss Chapple said, a note of finality in her voice. She closed the book and glanced at Mrs. Dunn. Her eyebrows quirked a silent question, her lips twitched fractionally, a dimple showed briefly in her right cheek, and then all expression smoothed from her face and she was dull and drab and nondescript again.

"Excellent," Strickland said, in his dry, cracked voice. "Excellent. Don't you agree, Mr. Kane?"

"Yes," Edward said, his tone heartfelt. It was indeed excellent that the sermon was over.

Mattie wrote by the light of one sputtering tallow candle, huddled in her blanket. *He removed my garters and my stockings swiftly, and then his hands skimmed higher.*

And then what?

She laid down the quill and flicked through the pages of the countess's diary, searching for a description of a similar moment. Ah, here was one that would work. *Heat flushed beneath my skin and a wild eagerness began to rise in me.*

Mattie dipped the quill in ink and copied the sentence. The hour was approaching midnight, everyone long asleep, but the house was far from silent. Hail battered against the windowpanes, the shutters rattled and banged, and wind whistled down the chimney, stirring the ashes in the grate and making the candle flame flicker.

She closed the diary and continued with her story: *His hands roamed across my body, and there was such strength in his touch, such gentleness, that I couldn't help trusting him. That I, a courtesan, should trust a man, seemed incredible, and that it should be this man, with his fierce pockmarked face and his brutal reputation, seemed even more incredible. But trust him I did, and I yielded eagerly to his passion.*

Mattie wrote for another hour, until the candle was in danger of guttering, before finally laying down her quill. She looked at the pile of pages with satisfaction. One final chapter and Chérie's *Memoir* would be finished. A whole book—the history of Chérie's time as a courtesan—for which her publisher would pay a *lot* more than he did for each confession.

And when she was paid, she could leave Creed Hall.

Mattie hugged the blanket tightly around herself, shivering, building the dream again: a boarding house beside the sea. There would be no dark paneling, no fires that were too small for their grates. The boarding house would be bright and cheerful and *warm*.

She yawned and stretched, catching the blanket as it slithered from her shoulders. "Freedom," she said aloud, to the rattling, banging, whistling accompaniment of the storm.

CHAPTER 2

Edward woke at dawn. He listened for rain against the windowpanes, but heard only silence.

He climbed out of bed. His leg was stiff, as it always was in the mornings. He limped across the room and opened the shutters. A gray sky and bare winter trees met his eyes. Everything was sodden—the trees, the straggling lawn, the sweep of the driveway dotted with puddles—but it wasn't raining. A few more hours, and he could leave. In fact, even if it *did* start raining again, he was leaving. He'd rather endure a march over the Spanish Alps than a second night at Creed Hall.

Edward shivered. His breath hung in front of his face, mist-like. There was no ice in the water in his basin, but it was still too damned cold. *You're getting soft,* he chided himself.

He looked at the fireplace. No fire burned there, and no water steamed in his wash jug. He pulled the bell rope. A few minutes later a harried young housemaid brought hot water and laid a fresh fire. The sideways glances she cast him while she crouched at the grate were apprehensive. Edward wasn't sure whether it was his scarred face or his gender that frightened her. *I can't force myself on you, even if I were a man who would want to do such a thing.* He turned away from her and looked out the window again. Waterloo had taken his ability to bed a woman, to sire a child, to truly be a man. His mouth tightened. *I am a eunuch, without being castrated.*

Tigh bustled into the room, Edward's cleaned and polished boots under his arm. "Not enough servants," he said, as he shut the door after the departing housemaid. "Should have twice as many in a house this size. And as for the food!"

Edward grunted and stepped away from the window.

"I et better in Spain," Tigh grumbled as he stropped the razor blade. He glanced up, his eyes twinkling beneath bristling eyebrows. "Remember those rats, sir?"

Edward shoved his self-pity aside. He grinned at the bâtman. "How could I forget?"

"Mighty tasty, they were," Tigh said, laying the sharpened razor and a towel beside the wash basin. "Mighty tasty."

Edward whistled under his breath while he shaved. He'd be back in London by evening, sitting down to a hearty meal—roasted capons, perhaps, or venison pie—in front of a roaring fire.

He glanced at the fire the housemaid had lit. It consisted of a bare handful of coal. His gaze drifted to the oilskin-wrapped packet lying on the dresser and the whistle died on his tongue. Before he left, he had to open that packet and distribute its contents.

Edward looked down at the water in the basin, at the scum of soap and the dark flecks of his whiskers. *It should be Toby here. Not me.*

Edward had the breakfast parlor to himself. The toast was cold and the eggs had been poached until the yolks were hard, but the sausages were flavorsome. Edward ate five of them before pushing his plate away.

He stayed seated for a moment, examining the room—the

heavy moldings on the ceiling, the dark paneling, the stiff furniture, the view out the single, narrow window at leafless trees. Two other windows in the room had been bricked up and painted over; Arthur Strickland was avoiding paying window tax.

He remembered a comment Toby had once made: *My father's so mean he doesn't dot his i's, to save ink.* At the time, Edward had laughed and thought it a joke; now he wasn't so certain.

Creed Hall was even grimmer in daylight than it had been at night. Lord, how had Toby managed to grow up here and retain his sense of humor?

The housemaid who'd relaid his fire brought a fresh pot of tea. Edward poured himself a cup, and after a moment's hesitation, added sugar. Creed Hall needed something to sweeten it. "When does your master rise?"

"Before dawn, sir."

Of course he does. Strickland wasn't the sort to relax abed. "Where would I find him?"

"In his study, sir."

Edward drank his tea—the sugar failed to make the room any more cheerful—pushed back his chair, and wandered out into the corridor. Faintly, he heard the sound of voices.

He headed in the direction of the noise, passing the drawing room and the library, and arrived at a door that was open. A thin, peevish voice, raised in complaint, was clearly audible. "A mess! An absolute mess!" Edward had no difficulty recognizing its owner: Arthur Strickland.

"Well, get going, man! There's no time to waste!"

"Yes, sir."

Edward moved back as someone emerged from the room. In the gloom of the corridor, the man didn't see him. He strode down the corridor towards the back reaches of the house, dressed in a bulky coat and bringing the smell of outdoors with him—wet clothes and mud.

Edward stepped into the doorway and glanced inside,

seeing a desk and bookcases. He had found Strickland's study.

Arthur Strickland sat behind the desk, scowling at a small pile of letters. He glanced up, saw Edward, and beckoned him irritably inside.

"Something's wrong, sir?"

"The bridge has washed out." Strickland picked up a letter, holding it fastidiously by one corner. Water dripped onto the desk.

Edward advanced further into the room. "What's that?"

"Soddy Morton's mail," Strickland said, releasing the letter. It landed with a wet *splat* on top of the pile. "The innkeeper's boy takes it to Gripton each morning, to catch the Mail."

"What happened?"

"He rode into the creek. Fool of a boy must be blind!" Strickland shoved the letters aside.

"Was he hurt?" Edward asked, walking across to the desk. He picked up one of the letters. It dangled limply, dripping. The address was unreadable. "Or the horse?"

Strickland didn't answer the question. He poked at the sodden pile. "A mess," he muttered irritably. "An absolute mess."

The wafer slowly slid from the letter Edward was holding, falling with a faint *plop* onto the desk. The letter unfolded. The crossed writing was smeared and illegible. "These will have to be returned to their senders."

"I know that!" Strickland snapped.

Edward put down the letter. "I have something for you, sir. I'll just fetch it." And once he'd handed over Toby's possessions, he'd depart—broken bridge or not. He'd drive the curricle across country if he had to. *Just get me out of here.*

He took the stairs two at a time back to his bedchamber, grabbed the packet on the dresser, and undid the string. His haste slowed, though, once the parcel's contents lay exposed: letters, a pocket watch, a signet ring.

Emotion ambushed him, grief and guilt entwined. His chest tightened, making breathing difficult.

Edward squeezed his eyes shut. He inhaled a shallow breath, wrestling the emotions back into the shadows.

Soldiers died. Toby had known that. They'd all known it.

He took a deeper breath, expanding his lungs, and then opened his eyes and looked at Toby's belongings again. This time, the grief stayed locked tightly away. The guilt was there, though, as it always was, a smothering weight.

After a moment Edward picked up the pocket watch. The silver was cool and smooth.

The stumps of his missing fingers framed the watch—little finger and ring finger gone, middle finger chopped off at the first knuckle, forefinger missing its tip. The hand of a soldier.

He felt the familiar sense of disbelief—*that's not my hand*—and on its heels, a surge of loss.

Edward hissed out a breath, annoyed with himself, and gathered up the rest of the items for Arthur Strickland. Surely the day must soon come when he'd see his hands and recognize them as his own? When he'd not mourn the missing fingers?

He went downstairs. It was the house that was affecting him—so grim and cold and cheerless. No wonder his mood was dark.

Strickland sat where Edward had left him, behind the desk. He'd spread the letters out. Some were still sealed, others lay limply open. "Just look at that!" the old man said, looking up as he entered. "Ruined!"

Edward made no reply.

Strickland turned his attention to a letter. "Fool boy. Must have been blind or drunk . . ." His voice stopped.

"Sir?" Edward said. "I have some items belonging to—"

"Quiet." Strickland didn't look up.

Edward took a slow breath. *He's an old man.* He swallowed his annoyance, advanced to the desk, and laid Toby's belongings on one corner, away from the damp pile of mail. "I'll leave them here for you, sir."

"Look at this!" Strickland thrust a wet letter at him. His thin face was flushed with outrage. "This . . . this is *filth*!"

Edward took the letter. It was several pages long. The ink was smeared, but still readable.

Dear reader, in answer to your request, here is a further confession from my pen.

Edward raised his eyebrows. What the hell?

Previously, I told of my first encounter with Lord S. Now, if you are willing to be the recipient of another confession, I should like to share some details of my time as Lord S.'s mistress.

"Filth!" Strickland said again, struggling to his feet. "Disgusting filth!"

Edward ignored him. His gaze skipped down the page:

For some time we wandered, exchanging fond touches and kisses, until presently we came upon a little folly built in the form of a Roman temple, perfectly round, with a pantiled roof and a colonnade. A pretty wilderness of trees surrounded it, and at its marble feet ran a sparkling brook. Lord S. led me inside the folly, wherein a fine, large divan tossed with pillows stood squarely in a shaft of sunlight.

The page ended. Edward tried to peel the corner up to read the next page. He couldn't. The sheets of paper were stuck together. He tried the next page.

. . . until finally his passion was spent. We lay entwined, sunlight warm on our skin. From outside came the sound of birdsong and the ripple of running water. After several minutes Lord S. roused himself and suggested that we refresh ourselves with a swim.

Taking me by the hand he led me outside and coaxed me into the brook. We sported in the water for some time, until Lord S.'s passion was manifestly aroused again.

Edward read swiftly to the bottom of the page. "Filth!" he heard Strickland mutter while he paced the study, his cane thudding angrily with each step. "Filth!"

Alas, the next two pages were stuck together. Edward tried to peel them apart, but the limp paper disintegrated into shreds. Only the final sentence was legible: *And on that note, dear readers, I shall end this latest confession from my pen.*

Chérie.

He set the pages together again, disappointed.

"Here!" A thump of the cane. "In Soddy Morton!" Another thump. "To find such *filth*!"

Edward nodded his agreement. Soddy Morton was the last place he'd have expected the notorious Chérie to reside. "She's thought to live in London."

Strickland swung around and pinned him with a fierce glare. "You're familiar with the writer?"

"Uh . . . I have heard of her, sir." And he'd read the last three installments of her confessions. "She claims to be a courtesan by the name of Chérie. Her confessions are quite popular in London." That was an understatement; Chérie's *Confessions* had taken London by storm. *Well, half of London,* Edward amended. *The male half.*

"She must be stopped!" Strickland shook his cane at him. His face was mottled with rage. "I won't have such depravity in Soddy Morton!"

Edward looked down at Chérie's letter. It was addressed to a publishing house in London. Of a sender's address, there was no sign.

"I won't have it!" Strickland said again. He thumped the cane on the floor to emphasize this statement, and then bent over wheezing.

"Sir?" Edward dropped the letter and strode across to him.

"Can't breathe—" Strickland gasped.

Edward half-carried the man to an armchair. Strickland collapsed into it, his face an alarming shade of puce.

"Sir?" Edward went down on one knee and swiftly loosened the man's neckcloth. "Calm yourself. There's no need to be in such a taking."

With the neckcloth loosened, Strickland's breathing became easier. "I won't have it," he wheezed. "Not in Soddy Morton. Not on my doorstep!"

Edward suppressed a shrug. Chérie's *Confessions* weren't something he'd wish a lady to read, but they were harmless enough entertainment for gentlemen.

Breath whistled in Strickland's throat. His face was alarmingly flushed.

"I'll ring for a servant, sir. You should rest in bed."

"No," the old man said stubbornly, wheezing. "I must find her."

Edward resisted the urge to roll his eyes. He stood and glanced around the study. A decanter of sherry sat on a narrow sideboard. He strode across, poured a healthy slug into a glass, and brought it back to Strickland.

The man took the glass. "I won't have such filth in my village," he muttered. "I shall find her!"

"If you find her, sir, what do you hope to achieve?" Chérie had every right to live in Soddy Morton if she wished. Although God only knew why anyone would choose to do so.

"I'll run her out of the village!"

Edward looked down at the old man. How had someone this pinched and disapproving sired a son like Toby? "How?"

"I'm Justice of the Peace here." Triumph gleamed in Strickland's eyes. "I'll see her prosecuted." He sipped the sherry. His hand trembled as he held the glass, but his high color was fading and his breathing was steadier.

"On what charge, sir?"

Strickland shrugged. "Whatever I wish."

Edward bit his tongue. *I don't think that's how your authority is supposed to be used.*

Strickland swallowed the last of the sherry.

"More, sir?"

Strickland shook his head.

Edward took the glass and placed it on the sideboard. When he turned back, he saw the old man struggle feebly to stand. "You should be abed, sir."

Strickland sagged back into the armchair. "I won't have that woman in the village one more day than is necessary!" His face twisted into an expression of frustration and pain—and then, to Edward's dismay, tears filled the old man's eyes. "If my son were still alive, he'd help me find her."

Perhaps. And then Toby would have taken off to London with her. He'd had a way with the ladies.

The guilt that had ridden on Edward's shoulders for the past five months seemed to grow heavier, pushing down on him until his knees almost buckled. He looked away. A gray sky and a skeletal oak tree were visible through the window.

The window blurred and tilted sideways as memory swamped him. For a second he wasn't standing in a dark-paneled study; he was lying dazed on a muddy field in Belgium. *Ned?* Toby appeared above him, frantic. *Ned! Get up! Get—* Blood sprayed hot across his face.

The muscles in Edward's belly, in his chest, in his throat, clenched at the memory. He smelled Toby's blood in the study, tasted it on his tongue—

Edward blinked and shook his head. The window straightened and came back into focus. The smell of blood evaporated. He cleared his throat and looked down at Strickland.

The old man bowed his head. "Why did he have to die?" The words were quiet, barely audible—and heartbroken. A tear leaked down Strickland's pale, wrinkled cheek.

Edward fished in his pocket for a handkerchief and silently held it out.

The old man wiped his eyes. "Why did he have to die?" he whispered again. "My only child."

He died trying to save me. The guilt had its arms around him now, like a gnarled hag riding on his back, hugging so tightly he could scarcely breathe. Edward cleared his throat again. "I'll find Chérie for you."

Strickland blinked and raised his head, his eyes still bright with tears. "What?"

"I'll find Chérie," Edward said more loudly, trying to ignore the sinking sensation in his chest.

"You will?" Strickland stared up at him, his expression dumbfounded, and then he lowered the handkerchief.

"Yes. I give you my word of honor."

"Mr. Kane . . ." A smile creased the old man's face and for

the merest fraction of a second Edward saw a likeness to Toby. Strickland reached out and clasped one of Edward's hands with both of his. His fingers were cold, dry, shaking faintly. "Thank you, Mr. Kane. Thank you."

The man's tremulous gratitude was embarrassing. Edward cleared his throat again. "You're welcome, sir." He disengaged his hand and rang the bell, and stood back and watched the butler and Strickland's manservant help the old man from the room.

In the gloomy silence of the empty study, his own words echoed in his ears: *I'll find Chérie.*

Edward grimaced. *Idiot.* Toby wouldn't have wanted him to help Strickland in this—running a woman out of the village that was her home. Toby had had none of his father's grim, narrow morality; if Toby had set out to find Chérie, it would have been to toast her health and her continued confessions—and charm his way into her bed.

Edward sighed, and walked across to the window. The view was desolate: heavy sky, dripping trees, sodden driveway.

But was Chérie a woman? For all anyone knew, the *Confessions* were written by a man.

Edward grunted a laugh. He turned away from the window. He'd given his word of honor to *find* Chérie, and he'd do just that: find the author of the *Confessions* and warn her—or him—to get out of Soddy Morton.

And then he'd get the hell out of here himself.

"Mr. Kane?"

Edward looked up from his perusal of Chérie's confession. Miss Chapple stood in the doorway to the study, dressed in a gray gown that was even drabber than the one she'd worn last night. "Griggs says that my uncle has had a turn."

"Yes." He stood and thrust the damp pages of the confession into his pocket. "He had a little difficulty breathing. But don't worry, Miss Chapple. I'm sure he'll be fine once he's rested."

Her gaze focused on the letters on the desk, amid their little puddle of water. A faint frown furrowed her brow. "What are those?"

"Soddy Morton's mail. The bridge washed away last night."

She stepped into the room. "Mail *to* Soddy Morton, or from?"

"From," Edward said.

"Oh!" She advanced towards the desk with quick steps. "I sent a letter . . ."

"Then by all means, take it." He gestured at the pile. "You'll have to rewrite it, I'm afraid."

Miss Chapple began to go through the waterlogged letters, peeling them apart.

"I understand the innkeeper is your postmaster?"

She nodded.

"Then I shall return these to him." *And ask him about the letter to the London publisher.* A spark of hope flickered in his breast. Chérie might take no more than an hour to find. He could be on his way back to London by noon. "What's his name?"

"Potts," Miss Chapple said. "Is this all of them?" She had reached the bottom of the pile. The final letter was little more than ink-smeared pulp.

Edward shrugged. "I believe so."

Miss Chapple frowned. She began to go through the letters again.

"Your letter's missing?"

"Missing? Oh, no! It's just . . . I thought there would have been more mail than this."

"Uh . . . no," Edward said, aware of the confession in his pocket. "That's all of them." *Except one.*

Miss Chapple extracted a letter from the pile. She didn't

look pleased. The furrow between her eyebrows was deeper. "Here's mine." She held it up. The letter had lost its wafer. The page hung open, limp and dripping, the ink smeared in long, illegible trails. "Thank you," she said, and left the study, still frowning.

Mattie sat hunched over the little mahogany escritoire in her bedchamber, her lower lip caught between her teeth, writing as fast as she could. The quill scratched busily over the paper. *Taking me by the hand he led me outside and coaxed me into the brook. We sported in the water for some time, until Lord S.'s passion was manifestly aroused again.*

Two more pages, and then the final sentence: *And on that note, dear readers, I shall end this latest confession from my pen.*

Chérie.

Mattie blew out a breath. Done. She laid down the quill and flexed her cramped fingers. Now all that remained was a letter to Anne, in which to hide the confession. And this time, she'd seal it with wax. Lots of wax.

Mattie frowned while she gathered the pages together and folded them. What had happened to the confession she'd sent yesterday?

The thought of someone finding it—or worse, of Uncle Arthur discovering her secret—was enough to make her heart clench in her chest. The roof over her head, the clothes she wore, the food she ate, were all at Uncle Arthur's generosity. A cold generosity, perhaps, without the gift of love to leaven it, but generosity nonetheless; to repay him with distress of any kind would be unspeakable.

"He will never know," Mattie told herself firmly as she sealed the letter with a large dollop of wax. The missing confession was lost in the creek. Washed away, and long since disintegrated. She had nothing to worry about. In a month's time she'd have enough money to leave Creed Hall without causing Uncle Arthur any distress at all.

Strickland kept no riding horses in the stables, and taking the curricle into Soddy Morton wasn't an option unless Edward wished to detour sixteen miles via Gripton, which he didn't. He debated riding one of his carriage horses, then decided to walk. Carriage horses made poor riding mounts.

His boots were heavy with mud by the time he reached the village, but the exercise had eased the ache in his thigh. He wasn't limping as he strode down the High Street, past cottages built of the same dark gray limestone as Creed Hall, a smoke-stained forge, and a whipping block and stocks across from the market cross.

Soddy Morton wasn't large. It boasted only one inn, a plaster and timber building with low eaves and a slate roof. Edward used the boot scraper at the door and went inside.

The innkeeper was in the taproom, a stout man with the ruddy complexion of a drinker. He was leaning on the counter, a tankard of ale in his fist, conversing with his sole customer—a blacksmith, by his leather apron and burn-flecked forearms.

Both men turned to look at Edward when he entered. He saw shock flicker across the innkeeper's face—the widening of his eyes, the startled blink—as the man took in the scars.

"Mr. Potts? My name is Kane. I'm staying at Creed Hall."

The innkeeper put down his tankard and straightened. "What can I do for you, sir?"

"I understand you're Soddy Morton's postmaster." Edward laid the soggy bundle of letters on the counter. "This is this morning's mail. It was retrieved from the creek on Sir Arthur Strickland's property."

The innkeeper lost his smile. He reached for the letters and swiftly counted them. "One's missing," he said, lifting his head.

Edward blinked. There were *two* letters missing—the one Miss Chapple had taken, and the confession from Chérie, now resting snugly in his breast pocket. "One?"

The innkeeper nodded. "Fifteen letters, there was." He counted them again. "Now there's only fourteen." He scowled at Edward, as if the scars on his face branded him for a criminal.

"Miss Chapple has taken a letter."

The man grunted. His scowl faded slightly.

"Are you certain there were fifteen?"

"Aye," the innkeeper said. "Wrote it in the ledger, I did. Fifteen."

Edward touched his breast pocket, feeling the thick wedge of damp paper. It didn't make sense, unless . . .

He examined the letters lying on the counter. Nine were unsealed. Had Chérie's confession been concealed inside one of them?

Edward extracted the damp confession from his pocket. It was folded to show only the address. "Do you recognize this?" he said, laying it on the counter. "It was, er . . . also found on Sir Arthur's property."

The innkeeper's gaze fastened on the stumps of Edward's missing fingers.

"The address, as you see, is in London."

The innkeeper stopped staring at Edward's hand. He peered at the address. "Lunnon?" He shook his head. "Only two letters to Lunnon yesterday. That weren't one of 'em."

"Are you certain?"

"I allus write in the corner, see?" The innkeeper pointed at the letters Edward had returned.

Edward frowned and reexamined Chérie's letter. The man was correct; there was nothing to show whether the postage had been paid or not. *How did I miss that?* "Do you perhaps recognize the handwriting?"

The innkeeper shook his head. "All smeared like that? Could be anyone's."

Edward uttered a silent curse. This wasn't going to be as easy as he'd hoped. "Do you think it could have been inside one of those?" He indicated the wet letters lying on the counter.

The innkeeper shrugged. "No way of knowing."

"Except asking the senders."

The innkeeper returned his stare, his expression stolid.

"I appreciate that you're a busy man, Mr. Potts. I would be happy to undertake that task for you."

The innkeeper's eyes narrowed suspiciously. "You would?"

No. But I've given my word of honor, fool that I am. "I have time on my hands."

The innkeeper's gaze went to Edward's butchered fingers again.

Edward repressed the urge to hide his hands in his pockets. Instead, he held them where the innkeeper could see them clearly. "Waterloo."

"You fought at Waterloo?" A note of respect crept into the man's voice.

No, I lay all day in the mud, while men died around me. "Yes," Edward forced himself to say. "Royal Horse Guards."

"Mr. Tobias's regiment." The innkeeper said, straightening. Halfway down the counter, the blacksmith turned his head and stared at Edward.

"Yes."

"We were right sorry to hear about Mr. Tobias. He were very well liked in these parts, he were."

"Liked to have a good laugh, Mr. Tobias did," the blacksmith said, raising his tankard in a toast. "God rest his soul."

"Yes," Edward said. "He did like to laugh." He looked down at the letters, feeling the weight of guilt on his shoulders. "I'll just make a note of the senders, Mr. Potts. If I may?"

He waited while the man fetched paper and ink and a quill, and then quickly jotted down the names of the people who'd sent the opened letters. The writing was smudged beyond legibility in two cases, but the innkeeper was certain of the names. "Mr. Humphries, the curate," he said. "And Widow Weeks. She writes to her daughter every week."

Edward looked at the list once it was complete. Nine names. One of whom had to be Chérie. *Probably not the curate,* he thought. But he didn't cross the man's name out.

He asked for another sheet of paper and sat down in a corner of the taproom to compose a brief letter to Gareth. *I need a favor,* he wrote. *Can you send me as many of Chérie's confessions as you can lay hands on?* He thought for a moment, and added a postscript. *And I'd appreciate it if you'd have your man pack up a week's worth of my clothes and send them to Creed Hall. I shall be here longer than I anticipated.*

The door from the yard swung open and someone entered the taproom. Edward looked up. It was Miss Chapple. Her gown was muddy almost to the knee.

The innkeeper abandoned his tankard and his conversation with the blacksmith again.

Edward read what he'd written. He crossed out *week,* and wrote *a few days* instead. There were only nine names on his list. If he was lucky, Chérie would be the first person he approached; if he was unlucky, she'd be the ninth. Either way, it would scarcely take a week.

Miss Chapple's voice was a low, contralto murmur in the background. Edward folded the letter, pushed back his chair, and walked across to where she stood. "Miss Chapple."

She started and spun around, her eyes wide. "Mr. Kane! What . . . what are you doing here?"

"I brought back the mail."

"Oh." She swallowed. "My uncle's footman could have done that. He comes in each day."

Edward shrugged. "I wanted to see Soddy Morton." He pushed the folded letter across the taproom counter. "You have a wafer?"

The innkeeper did. Edward watched his letter sealed, and then turned to Miss Chapple. "What brings you here?"

"Like you, a letter. I write to a friend in London every week." She nodded to the innkeeper. "Thank you, Mr. Potts."

After Miss Chapple had departed, Edward entered into negotiations for the hire of a mount from the innkeeper's stable. Only one horse was up to his weight.

"His name's Trojan," the ostler informed him as he tightened the girths. "Acos he's so big. But he's as gentle as a babe."

"Trojan." Edward smoothed his hand down the gray gelding's neck. "What's his pace like?"

"He don't like to go fast."

Edward glanced at the sky. The hills in the distance had disappeared behind a haze of rain. "He'll have to, unless he wants to get wet." He swung up into the saddle and tossed a coin to the ostler.

Trojan was an amiable beast, but the ostler had been correct: he didn't like to go fast. With effort, Edward urged the gelding into a slow trot. Miss Chapple was halfway back to the Hall before they caught up with her.

"Oh, no!" she said, when he reined in and dismounted. "Pray don't walk, Mr. Kane. It's so muddy!"

"I'm used to mud, Miss Chapple." Edward matched his stride to hers. "I apologize for not informing you that I intended to visit the village. I could have spared you the exertion."

"You would have deprived me of a pleasure," she said. "I like to walk."

"You do?" Edward said, avoiding a puddle.

"The exercise is refreshing." Miss Chapple cast him a sideways glance beneath her dowdy bonnet, in the manner of one imparting a secret. A dimple flickered in her cheek. "And . . . I confess that I like to leave the Hall."

The mud sucked at his boots, reminding him of Waterloo. The reek of the battlefield filled his nose between one step and the next: cannon smoke, blood, death. Edward shoved the memory aside. "Do you never ride?" And then he remembered the emptiness of Strickland's stables. "Your uncle keeps no riding horses?"

"He thinks it an unnecessary luxury."

Edward suppressed a grunt. Such parsimony seemed entirely in keeping with what he'd seen of Arthur Strickland.

"If you'd like to ride, I can offer you Trojan as a mount. I have it on good authority that he's as gentle as a baby, for all his size."

Miss Chapple glanced past him at the big gray gelding. Her expression became wistful. "I should love to."

"Then please do," Edward said. "I'll be at Creed Hall for a few more days. I'll tell the groom you may ride Trojan as often as you wish."

Miss Chapple shook her head. "Thank you, Mr. Kane. Your offer is most generous. But I have no riding habit—and even if I did, my uncle doesn't keep a sidesaddle."

"Ah," Edward said. He walked in silence for several seconds, then asked: "How long have you lived at Creed Hall?"

"Ten years," Miss Chapple said. "My uncle was kind enough to take me in when my parents died."

They turned up a farm lane, passed a barn, and set off across an open field. The mud became deeper, sucking greedily at their boots.

Creed Hall was dimly visible on the crest of the hill, a dark, angular shape, surrounded by winter-bare trees. A bleak place to call home. "You must be lonely here," Edward said involuntarily.

She glanced at him. "Not now that Mrs. Dunn lives with us."

Which meant that she had been lonely before that. Edward felt a stirring of pity for her. "Has Lady Marchbank lived with you long?"

"Three years," Miss Chapple said, holding her skirts up above her ankles as she strode through the mud. "Since she was widowed."

They came to a gate and a stile. "My uncle plans to turn Creed Hall into a school for missionaries' children," Miss Chapple said, climbing the stile.

"He does?" Edward led Trojan through the gate and latched it again.

Miss Chapple nodded. "He wishes to provide missionaries' children with a free and rigorous education."

Edward followed her gaze, trying to imagine Creed Hall full of children. It looked like a prison atop the hill, grim and dark, jutting from the leafless trees that encircled it. *Poor creatures.*

Miss Chapple tipped her face up to the sky. "It's starting to rain."

"Would you like to shelter?" He looked back at the barn. "I can ride ahead and fetch . . ." What? No carriage could plow its way through these boggy fields. "An umbrella?"

Laughter sprang into her face, bringing a glimpse of dimples. "Thank you for the offer, Mr. Kane, but a little rain won't hurt me. I shan't melt away."

They set off across the next field. It was novel to walk with so tall a female. He didn't have to bend his head to speak to her or shorten his stride to match hers. "Do you have any brothers or sisters, Miss Chapple?"

She shook her head. "I counted Toby as my brother."

As did I.

Edward cleared his throat. "He always said you were his favorite cousin."

Miss Chapple glanced at him from beneath the brim of her bonnet. "You think that high praise? I was Toby's only cousin, Mr. Kane. That was his way of a joke."

"Oh." Edward blinked, and then frowned. He trudged through the mud, thinking back to the times he'd heard Toby mention Miss Chapple. "A joke, perhaps, but I believe the sentiment was truly meant. He always said . . . you made him laugh."

Her lips twisted into a sad smile. "He made me laugh, too. High Toby." Her expression altered, her eyes narrowing. "Was it you who held up that coach with him, or was it Sir Gareth?"

Edward missed a step. "Uh . . . what?"

"A coach," Miss Chapple said. "He held one up on a lark. Oh, years ago! When he was up at Oxford."

"He told you about that?"

Miss Chapple nodded. "He said it was my fault, because it was I who first called him High Toby." She snorted, an expressive puff of sound that reminded him of Toby. "So was it you, Mr. Kane, who went with him, or Sir Gareth?"

Edward opened his mouth to lie, encountered surprisingly astute gray eyes, and spoke the truth: "It was me."

Miss Chapple shook her head and tutted. "I am shocked, Mr. Kane. Truly shocked!" Her cheeks dimpled.

Edward felt himself flush. "We were young and very foolish."

Miss Chapple's dimples became more pronounced. "Toby said the occupant was a fat little clerk who threw a ledger at him."

"Hit him on the head." He had a flash of memory: moonlight, the clerk's shrill vituperation, the pages of the ledger fluttering whitely. "Knocked him off his horse."

Miss Chapple laughed. "He didn't tell me that!"

Edward grinned and shrugged. "I'm not surprised. It was an ignominious moment."

They walked a few paces in silence, apart from the squelch of mud and patter of raindrops. Edward's grin faded. He glanced sideways at Miss Chapple. "I wouldn't do such a thing now."

She met his glance. "Of course not."

They went through another gate. One more field remained, bare and fallow, and then the wooded rise to Creed Hall. "You do a lot of walking?" he asked Miss Chapple as they strode across the paddock. Her cheeks were pink with exertion, but she wasn't out of breath.

"Every day," she said cheerfully. "A circuit of the park."

"Creed Hall has a park?"

"Woods and a lake."

By the time they reached the far side of the field, the rain was coming down heavily. It didn't fall straight down from the sky, but came at them slanting, striking their faces beneath the brims of their hats. The drops were hard and stingingly cold, almost sleet.

They paused at the bottom of the rise, beneath the shelter of a large, gnarled oak. Water dripped from its branches. Miss Chapple wiped her face with a corner of her cloak. "Toby always used to say that Creed Hall was the ugliest building in England."

Edward followed her gaze. The Hall was visible through the trees. The narrow windows and frowning roof hadn't been designed with beauty in mind. More than half the windows were bricked over, giving the impression that its inhabitants were trying to shut out the world.

"Toby didn't like coming here." Miss Chapple said. "The last time he visited, he left after only two days." He heard sadness in her voice, saw it in the way she pressed her lips together for a brief second. "He was meant to stay for a week."

"Why did he leave?"

"They argued." She pulled a face. "Uncle Arthur wanted Toby to resign his commission and become a curate. He said the curate's position in Soddy Morton was coming open. Toby said he'd rather hang himself."

Edward grunted. It sounded exactly like something Toby would have said. He looked up at Creed Hall again and grimaced. "I should hate to live here."

Miss Chapple hesitated, and then said, "I consider myself very fortunate to be at Creed Hall."

"Er . . . of course you do." Water trickled down his cheek. He wiped it away with a wet sleeve.

"My father suffered a reversal on the 'Change shortly before he died. If my uncle hadn't taken me in, I might have ended up in the poorhouse." Miss Chapple's light tone and the upward twist of her lips turned the last sentence into a joke.

Edward glanced up at Creed Hall again. Better than a poorhouse, yes . . . but it was a grim, lonely place to call home.

Pity stirred in his chest again.

They began to climb, trudging through leaf mold and mud. The wood felt like a cemetery—the bare skeletons of trees, the mounds of dead leaves. Even the muffled clop of Trojan's hooves seemed funereal. Rain dripped off the brim of Edward's hat. The ascent made his leg ache. He began to limp.

"Mr. Kane? Are you all right?"

Absurdly, he felt himself flush, as if the limp was something to be ashamed of. "I broke my leg at Waterloo."

Miss Chapple halted. "Should you be walking?"

Edward halted, too. "Waterloo was more than five months ago."

"That's not an answer," she said tartly. "If the injury hurts, then you shouldn't be walking."

Edward shrugged. "It doesn't hurt much."

Miss Chapple snorted. "Get up on that horse you hired," she told him, "and *ride*."

Edward grinned. He was beginning to like Miss Chapple. "You remind me of my brigade major."

Her face became expressionless. "Your brigade major?"

Edward kicked himself mentally. *Idiot*. "I . . . uh, it was a compliment, Miss Chapple. Lithgow was a grand chap." *And he was a man, you lummock.*

Miss Chapple's eyebrows lifted briefly in silent skepticism. "You should ride, Mr. Kane," she said, turning away from him and beginning to climb the hill again. "There's no need for you to keep me company."

Edward grimaced and followed her, tugging Trojan's reins. After three steps his leg began to protest again. "I didn't mean what you think, Miss Chapple." What *did* she think? That he thought her bossy? Man-like?

She stopped and looked back at him. "Mr. Kane, you don't need to explain yourself."

"Yes," Edward said, halting alongside her. "I do. It wasn't my intention to insult you."

"I'm not insulted."

Yes, you are.

"What I meant was . . . It was a joke, Miss Chapple. I beg your pardon. I . . . I've been around men too much. I've lost the knack of speaking with ladies."

Her eyebrows rose again. "You've lost the knack of speaking with ladies?"

"Yes."

"And tell me, Mr. Kane, what does the knack of speaking with ladies entail?" Her voice was light, polite—but something in her inflection told him he'd strayed onto dangerous ground.

"Uh . . ." Edward said, aware that he'd blundered again. Pretty compliments? No, she might take that as an insult against her sex. Mincing one's words? No, that could be taken as an insult, too. "Uh . . ."

Miss Chapple's mouth tucked in at the corners, as if she was suppressing a smile. "It's all right, Mr. Kane. You don't need to answer. And for heaven's sake, get up on that horse of yours and ride!"

*C*HAPTER 3

*E*dward rode the last few hundred yards; it seemed the most prudent thing to do. He didn't wish to annoy Miss Chapple any more than he already had.

He turned Trojan over to the elderly groom and hurried around to the main entrance as fast as his aching leg would allow, catching up with Miss Chapple on the doorstep. Her bonnet was bedraggled, her gown wet and filthy, her cheeks flushed with exertion.

"How do you feel?" she asked, taking off the bonnet and shaking water from it. "Perhaps you should rest?"

"I'm not an invalid," Edward said, as the door opened.

They stepped into the gloomy entrance hall. Miss Chapple turned to the butler. "Griggs, can you please send a pot of hot tea to Mr. Kane's bedchamber?"

"To the library," Edward said, firmly.

Miss Chapple frowned and opened her mouth.

"I hope you'll join me," he said.

Miss Chapple closed her mouth. She lifted her shoulders in a slight shrug. "Very well."

Fifteen minutes later, having changed her wet clothes for dry ones, Mattie went downstairs. The library was chilly. A small fire burned grudgingly in the grate.

Mr. Kane stood at one of the windows looking out at the rain. He blocked most of the weak daylight. Outlined against the window, he looked giant-like, too tall and broad to be a mere man. The moniker Toby had given him—Goliath—fitted perfectly.

Mattie pulled her shawl tightly about her shoulders and advanced into the room. A floorboard creaked. Mr. Kane turned his head.

"How do you feel?" she asked.

"Very well," Mr. Kane said. "And you?"

"I'm not the one who recently broke a leg," Mattie said, sitting in one of the leather armchairs beside the fireplace. Griggs had already brought the tea. The tray sat on the little oak tripod table.

"No." Mr. Kane smiled faintly and sat opposite her.

A short, awkward silence fell. Mattie busied herself pouring the tea. Mrs. Whatley, the cook, had placed a plate of plum cake on the tray. The slices were small. Mattie handed Mr. Kane his tea—no milk, no sugar—and a piece of cake. He thanked her politely.

Mattie cast around for a topic of conversation. "How long have you been back in England, Mr. Kane?"

"A month. I would have come into Northamptonshire sooner, but I visited my parents first."

"Of course you should have visited them first! They must have been terribly worried about you."

"Yes." He touched what remained of his left ear, a gesture she thought he was unaware of.

What had his parents' emotions been when they'd first seen him? The missing fingers, the missing ear, the scars slicing across his face. Had they been distressed by his injuries—or merely relieved he'd survived?

Mr. Kane lowered his hand. "I have something for you."

He reached inside his coat and withdrew a sheaf of letters. "Your letters to Toby. I thought you might like them back."

Mattie's throat constricted. For a moment she couldn't speak. She put her teacup and saucer on the table. "He kept them?"

Mr. Kane nodded.

Mattie took the letters. She opened one—*Dearest Toby, it's now spring and the woods are full of primroses and birdsong*—and folded it again. She placed the bundle on the table alongside her teacup and cleared her throat. "Thank you, Mr. Kane."

"You're welcome."

She looked across at him, seeing the scars, the marks of warfare scored into his skin. He'd clearly come close to death at Waterloo. A question hovered on her tongue. *Carpe diem,* Toby had always said. Seize the day.

Mattie took a deep breath. "Mr. Kane . . . would you mind telling me about Waterloo? About what happened to you and Toby?"

His face seemed to stiffen, as if the tiny muscles around his eyes, his mouth, flinched and tightened. "Waterloo?"

"Not if it's too painful," Mattie said hastily. "In fact, forget I asked. It's not—"

"I don't mind telling you, Miss Chapple, but it's not pleasant listening." His dark brown eyes held hers. "Are you certain you wish to know?"

Mattie hesitated, and nodded silently. It was selfish of her, she knew, but she wanted to understand what had happened to Toby. She *needed* to understand.

"Very well." Mr. Kane shifted his weight in the armchair, settling, becoming more comfortable—but she had the impression that it was for show, that beneath the appearance of relaxation, he was tense. "We both fell in the first charge. My horse was shot from under me." He spoke baldly, without emotion, his gaze on the fire. "I didn't see Toby fall, but I assume his horse was hit, too."

Mattie nodded again.

"I was on the ground—my leg was trapped under my horse, caught in the stirrup—and Toby was trying to pull me free. He . . . a shell struck him. He died instantly."

Mattie bit her lip.

Mr. Kane was silent for a moment, staring at the fire, a frown furrowing his brow beneath the scars, then he turned his head and looked at her. "Toby died trying to save my life."

"From what I've heard of the battle, he would likely have died anyway," Mattie said quietly.

Mr. Kane lifted one shoulder in a shrug. "Perhaps. Perhaps not." He cleared his throat and resumed the tale: "After Toby was killed, I was attacked by a cuirassier, who cut me about the head with his sword." He gestured to the scars on his face, to his missing ear. "And after that I was bayoneted by an infantryman." His smile was wry. "I was still half under my horse, you see. Couldn't get my foot out of the stirrup."

Mattie nodded. Her throat was tight. She reached for her teacup and sipped, her eyes on his face.

"After the infantryman, came a lancer—" Mr. Kane held out his right hand, showing her the missing fingers, "—and after him, another infantryman." He grimaced. "I didn't have much fight left in me by then."

Mattie swallowed another mouthful of tea, almost choking as it caught in her throat.

"I spent the rest of the battle flat on my back," Mr. Kane said. He smiled, as if making a joke of it. "I heard a great deal of the action, but saw none of it."

"Did no one stop to help you?"

His smile became even wryer. "They stopped to plunder me."

"Plunder you!"

"My watch, my canteen, my money, my jacket." He shrugged. "Someone even pulled me out from under my horse and took my boots and trousers."

"Your trousers!"

He mistook her shock and flushed. "I beg your pardon,

Miss Chapple. I shouldn't have mentioned something so indelicate—"

She waved the apology aside. "How could anyone plunder a living man?"

Mr. Kane shrugged. "War isn't pretty. It brings out the worst in some men."

Mattie shook her head silently.

"Where was I? Oh, yes, someone pulled me out from under my horse." He grimaced. "I don't remember much after that. I drifted in and out of consciousness."

Mattie sat clutching the teacup, unable to drink, her eyes fixed on his face.

"I do remember that our cavalry charged over us at one point." He touched his chest. "That was painful. Broke a few ribs." He smiled again, lopsided and wry.

"But . . ." The word died on her tongue. She swallowed and tried again: "But someone rescued you?"

He nodded. "Yes. Eventually they did."

"How?"

"Once night fell and the battle was over, I called for help." He looked away from her, at the fire. "There were a lot of men calling out. I was one of the lucky ones. Some Scots Greys heard me."

Mattie shook her head. She looked down at the teacup clenched in her hands. She tried to imagine a battlefield at night, the sound of wounded men crying for rescue. "Did you think you were going to die?"

Mr. Kane was silent.

She lifted her head and looked at him. He was still staring at the fire. After a moment he glanced at her and smiled faintly. "I *knew* I was going to die."

She felt herself flinch.

"It didn't distress me, Miss Chapple. I assure you!" The sincerity in Mr. Kane's voice was unmistakable. He was telling the truth. "It . . . how can I explain it? I lay on that battlefield for hours. It gave me time to accept my death. To make my peace with it. Even when they loaded me into the hospital wagon, I knew I was going to die. I had so many injuries. The risk of infection . . ." He shrugged. "It wasn't until almost a week later that I realized I was going to survive. It was . . . surprising."

The muscles in Mattie's throat were so tightly locked that she couldn't speak.

"I have the constitution of an ox." He said it as a joke, smiling.

She returned the smile dutifully.

Mr. Kane's smile faded. "I told you it wasn't pleasant listening."

Mattie put down her teacup. She cleared her throat. "Thank you for telling me."

Silence fell between them. She should say something, put him at his ease, but her mind was blank. Mattie glanced desperately at the tea tray. "More plum cake?" she asked abruptly, holding out the plate to him.

"No, thank you."

She couldn't think of anything else to say. Images crowded in her mind: Mr. Kane trapped beneath his horse, Mr. Kane being bayoneted, Mr. Kane lying helpless while he was looted, while the British cavalry charged over him. But the strongest image, the one that swamped everything else, was the last one he'd given her: a battlefield at night, the darkness broken by the cries of wounded men. She took a piece of plum cake and bit into it. It was dry. The crumbs gathered chokingly in her throat.

Mattie gulped the last of her tea. She groped for a topic of conversation. "What will you do now that you've finished soldiering?" He was the youngest son of a viscount—that much she knew—but she had no idea what the state of his finances was.

"I plan to take up farming."

"Farming?" Mattie said, surprised, her gaze jumping to his face.

Mr. Kane nodded. "My maternal grandmother left me an estate in Cornwall. I'm heading down to see the bailiff next week." He glanced at the door and stood, making a small bow. "Mrs. Dunn."

Mattie looked around. Cecy Dunn hovered in the doorway to the library. "Am I disturbing you?"

"Not at all," Mattie said. "Do join us. I'll ring for more tea."

Mr. Kane pulled another armchair closer to the fire for Cecy and Griggs brought a fresh pot of tea. "Is my aunt sleeping?" Mattie asked as she poured.

Cecy nodded.

Mattie sat back in her chair. Tendrils of steam rose from her cup. The library was still gloomy, rain still streamed down outside, but the room seemed lighter somehow, as if Cecy's presence had made the dark horrors of Waterloo recede.

"Tell me . . . do you read sermons every evening, or is it just Wednesdays?"

Mattie exchanged a glance with Cecy. "Every evening."

"Hmm," Mr. Kane said, evidently unenthused by this news. He turned his teacup in its saucer. "Uh . . . I noticed that you were counting the *the*s last night, Mrs. Dunn."

Cecy's mouth fell open.

"You were asleep!" Mattie said, and then realized the accusation was grossly impolite. She bit the tip of her tongue.

Mr. Kane had the grace to look ashamed. "For a few moments, yes," he said. "You have an extremely pleasant reading voice, Miss Chapple."

Mattie's cheeks grew warm. Since living at Creed Hall, she'd fallen out of the habit of receiving compliments. She looked down at her teacup.

"I thought I'd participate in your game tonight, Mrs. Dunn. If you don't mind? So that I don't fall asleep again."

"Oh, do, Mr. Kane!" Cecy said eagerly. "I used to fall asleep, too, until Mattie thought of counting words. I've found it a most effective way of staying awake."

"It was your idea, Miss Chapple?"

Mattie glanced up. Mr. Kane was looking at her. She nodded.

"Clever," he said, raising his teacup to her.

Mattie felt herself flush again. *Fool, to be overcome by such a small compliment.*

"I usually decide on a word before Mattie starts reading," Cecy said. "We can choose one now, if you like."

"Please," Mr. Kane said, his gaze shifting to Cecy.

"*And* and *the* are always good. And *I,* with Fordyce. He uses it a lot." Cecy looked at Mattie for confirmation.

Mattie nodded.

"Which would you recommend?" Mr. Kane asked.

"*And,*" Mattie said. "The more often a word is used, the less chance you'll fall asleep, Mr. Kane."

"Very well; *and* it is." Mr. Kane grinned. The grin sat oddly on his scarred face. Those savage slashes carved across his brow and cheeks, that missing ear, seemed to call for a more brutal expression. "I look forward to this evening's sermon, Miss Chapple."

Mattie spent the afternoon in her bedchamber, writing. Outside, the rain came down unceasingly, but she scarcely noticed. Her quill scratched briskly across the paper. This was the last chapter, and she knew exactly how it was going to end: Chérie would fall in love with the ugly, pockmarked Colonel F. and marry him.

Her two sources lay open on the escritoire: *Fanny Hill,* and the diary of the young countess who'd lived so unhappily at Creed Hall half a century ago.

Mattie flicked through *Fanny Hill,* searching for a passage she could use. *My heated and alarm'd senses were in a tumult that robbed me of all liberty of thought; tears of pleasure gush'd from my eyes.*

Mattie frowned. It seemed a little excessive. She flicked further ahead. . . . *made every vein of my body circulate liquid fires: the emotion grew so violent that it almost intercepted my respiration.*

Mattie pulled a face. Liquid fire and tears of pleasure. It sounded rather unrealistic.

She laid aside *Fanny Hill*, picked up the diary, and turned the pages carefully. Within these calfskin covers, the young countess detailed her growing love for the servant who tended her horse—her groom. Her emotions shone through, even after fifty years.

Each day when I walk around to the stables, my chest tightens with such a mix of hope and dread that it becomes difficult to breathe.

Mattie swallowed. The physical sensations and emotions described by the countess seemed much more realistic. She flicked ahead several pages.

He touched me so tenderly, with such reverence, that it brought tears to my eyes. My trust in him, at that moment, was absolute.

No, she wanted something more physical . . .

Ah, this would do.

A wild eagerness grew inside me. When at last he made his entrance into my body, I shuddered with the pleasure of it. Our coupling was almost animal. I confess, I bit Will's shoulder to stop from crying out my pleasure. Afterwards, as we lay trembling and sated in each other's arms, I saw to my shame that my teeth had marked him.

Mattie copied the paragraph, substituting Colonel F.'s name for that of the countess's groom. She reread it, tapping the quill against her cheek, and then continued: *I had never experienced such throes of delight before, such abandonment of my senses, not even in the arms of my beloved—and sadly mourned—husband.*

She wrote until dusk fell, and then lit a tallow candle and continued. *Colonel F.'s face had become so dear to me that despite the dreadful scars that marked his face, I thought him handsome.*

Mattie's quill halted. She frowned. She crossed the last few words out and rewrote them: *. . . despite the dreadful pockmarks that scarred his face, I thought him handsome.* Good. She gave a sharp nod. He no longer sounded like Mr. Kane.

She continued. *I gazed upon his sleeping form and knew that I loved him.*

I would give Colonel F. everything: my trust, my love, my very soul if it were possible. And all he wanted from me was my body.

Mattie grinned as she reread the last two paragraphs. "Don't worry, Chérie. Tomorrow he asks you to marry him." She glanced at the clock. Half past five.

Hastily she gathered together the sheets of paper and opened the secret cupboard. Inside were four narrow little shelves. Mattie placed the diary on the top shelf, precisely as she'd found it on that fateful night eight months ago, when a windstorm had uprooted trees in the wood and banged the shutters against the windows, breaking panes of glass, and blown open the latch of the secret cupboard.

A pile of loose pages lay on the middle shelf: drafts of the confessions she'd sent to London. A much thicker pile lay on the next shelf down. Chérie's *Memoir*. In another day or two it would be ready to send.

Anticipation tightened in her chest, exactly as the young countess had described, stifling her breath. *Soon I'll be free.*

They were one less at dinner; Sir Arthur Strickland was still abed. After a silent and unappetizing meal, they relocated to the drawing room to listen to another sermon.

"Sermon Three," Miss Chapple read aloud from her position to one side of the fireplace. "On Female Reserve." She glanced up and for a brief moment her gaze met Edward's. Her expression was solemn, but a smile glimmered in her eyes.

Edward felt an unexpected urge to laugh. He clenched his teeth together.

Miss Chapple looked down at the open page. "Many of you, my honored hearers, have been addressed in the style of love and admiration."

One.

Edward glanced at Mrs. Dunn. She sat demurely on the sofa, her blonde hair gleaming in the dull candlelight, her expression attentive.

"I have taken the liberty to address you in that of zeal and—"

His attention snapped back to Miss Chapple. *Two.*

At last the sermon came to an end. Edward stifled a yawn and added his voice to Lady Marchbank's murmur of appreciation: "Excellent, Miss Chapple. Excellent."

Miss Chapple closed the book of sermons and came to sit on the sofa.

"You fell asleep again," she whispered.

"I deny that," Edward said, equally low-voiced. "There were ninety-three *and*s."

"Two hundred and sixteen," Mrs. Dunn whispered.

Edward opened his mouth to protest this number, and then closed it again.

A dimple quivered in Miss Chapple's cheek. Her lips pursed to hide a smile.

They sat for another half hour, while Mrs. Dunn embroidered and Miss Chapple knitted and Lady Marchbank discussed the Reverend Fordyce's work with Edward. Finally, the echoes of the longcase clock in the hall striking the hour penetrated the drawing room. "Nine o'clock," Lady Marchbank said, an expression of surprise crossing her narrow face. "I hadn't realized it was so late."

It felt like midnight to Edward.

Candles awaited them on a table in the entrance hall, one each, in silver holders. "I hope you had a pleasant evening, Mr. Kane," Miss Chapple said, while Lady Marchbank and Mrs. Dunn slowly mounted the stairs. Her voice was demure, polite, but amusement gleamed in her eyes above the tiny, flickering flame of her candle. She was laughing at him.

"I cannot recall that I have ever spent a more enjoyable evening," Edward said, trying to imbue his voice with a note of sincerity.

Miss Chapple grinned for a fleeting half-second, both cheeks dimpling.

Perhaps it was the candlelight casting a golden glow over her features, or perhaps it was the shadows crowding the hall, creating a sense of intimacy between them, but Edward felt a tiny stirring of desire. He wanted to reach out and brush Miss Chapple's cheek with his fingertips and see whether her skin was indeed as soft as it looked.

Edward blinked, astonished. "Er . . ." he said.

The dimples showed in her cheeks again, as if she suppressed another grin. "Good night, Mr. Kane."

He cleared his throat. "Good night, Miss Chapple."

Edward watched her climb the stairs. She was as tall as a man, wide-hipped, the drab, shapeless gray gown making her look almost stout, but—inexplicably—he'd felt a twinge of desire. The first such since Waterloo.

Edward frowned. He'd thought that part of him—lust, desire—had been excised on the battlefield, as his fingers and ear had been. He'd proven his impotence with mortifying thoroughness at Madame Solange's establishment in Brussels, not once, but twice. That his body should respond to Miss Chapple—however faintly—when even the most skilled and lovely of Madame Solange's girls had been unable to elicit any response at all, was more than odd; it was incomprehensible.

"Marry me."

I stared at the colonel, unable to believe my ears.

"Marry me," he said again, his pock-scarred face solemn in the candlelight.

My heart began to beat loudly in my breast and for a moment I almost swooned. The impossible was happening: my beloved colonel was asking for my hand in marriage.

Joy swelled inside me, bringing tears to my eyes. "Yes," I said, and then I fell into his eager embrace.

I gazed upon the colonel's dear, beloved face and swore a silent oath to . . .

Mattie tugged at her lower lip. To do what?

. . . to do everything within my power to make him happy.

She grimaced, and crossed the words out.

. . . to be the perfect wife.

"Ugh," Mattie said aloud, and crossed those words out too. She needed something romantic, something final, something—

She dipped the quill in ink and wrote . . . *to love him forever.*

There, that had a romantic, final ring to it. Mattie reread the sentence: *I gazed upon his dear, beloved face and swore a silent oath to love him forever.*

"Perfect!" she said aloud. And then she dipped the quill in ink again. *And so, dear reader, I come to the end of my memoir. The time has come to lay down my pen and bid you farewell for the final time.*

Chérie.

Mattie put the quill down with a sigh of relief. She shook out her cramped fingers. The clock on the mantelpiece told her it was a quarter past midnight. She walked across to the window, opened one shutter, and peered out. It was pitch black outside. The only thing she could see was her own reflection. Hard drops of rain pattered against the glass, making her look as if she was as pockmarked as Chérie's beloved colonel. The window frame rattled in the casement, letting in a chilly draft.

Mattie closed the shutter. She bundled up the pages she'd

written and hid them in the secret cupboard, then climbed into bed and pulled the covers up to her chin.

The sheets were cold. Mattie curled up on her side, shivering, hugging herself. Tomorrow she'd copy out the last chapter of Chérie's *Memoir* and take it in to Soddy Morton to be sent to London.

She closed her eyes and snuggled deeper beneath the covers. Soon she'd have enough money to start her new life.

CHAPTER 4

It was raining steadily in the morning. Edward ate breakfast alone in the gloomy breakfast parlor. Afterwards, he wandered the ground floor. Creed Hall was echoingly empty, as if it had been abandoned. The only footsteps were his own. Strickland's study was cold and dark, as were the drawing room and library. Small fires lay unlit in the grates.

Edward frowned as he looked around. The curtains were faded, the carpet threadbare, the chairs in need of reupholstering. Surely this shabbiness was more than a dislike of spending money? Was Arthur Strickland under the hatches?

He rang the bell to have the fire and candles lit in the library, and stood at the window looking out over the sodden landscape while these tasks were done. Then he fished Chérie's confession from his pocket and sat beside the fire. The pages were stiff and wrinkled and the writing less legible than it had been yesterday, as if the ink had faded as the paper dried.

He studied the handwriting. Was Chérie a woman—or a man pretending to be a woman? To his eyes, the handwriting was quite ordinary, neither overly bold and masculine, nor delicate and feminine. It lent no clue as to Chérie's gender.

Edward turned his attention to the content. The confession was six pages long, of which he could read only two: the first page and the third. He tried to peel the other pages apart and stopped when the paper tore.

So, he had two pages. *Better than nothing.*

He read the paragraphs carefully. The content was titillating, yet not crude, a romanticized description of a whore being bedded by a gallant.

Edward frowned down at the wrinkled pages. So . . . what did that tell him? That Chérie was a romantic? Which meant that she was most likely a woman?

Or not?

He read the pages again, and wished he had a copy of *Fanny Hill* to compare them to. Wasn't there a scene like this, where Fanny and one of her beaus sported in the water?

Edward glanced up at the library shelves and the sparse rows of leather-bound volumes. He didn't bother getting up to examine them. Of all the houses in England, Creed Hall was most definitely one in which he'd *not* find a copy of Cleland's infamous erotic novel.

He read the water scene again. The writing was rather good. Chérie—whoever he or she was—wasn't as given to hyperbole and euphemism as Cleland had been.

We sported in the water for some time, until Lord S.'s passion was manifestly aroused again. He pulled me close and devoted himself to a detailed examination of my naked charms. The pale roundness of my breasts, dewed with drops of water, in particular captured his interest, so much so that he felt himself compelled to sip from my skin, all the while uttering low murmurs of delight.

An image flowered in Edward's mind: sunlight sparkling on water, the soft weight of a woman's breasts cupped in his hands. He imagined bending his head and licking drops of water from warm, silken skin . . .

Astonishingly, he felt a stir of arousal.

Edward blinked, and lowered the page and considered the sensation for a moment. Yes, definitely arousal.

For the past few months he'd thought Waterloo had

castrated him—not physically, perhaps, but with as much finality as if a cuirassier's sword had made that fatal cut.

Now he wasn't so certain.

All the things he'd not allowed himself to think of flooded his mind. He could take a lover. More than that, he could take a *wife*. He could sire children, have a family.

Emotion surged painfully in his chest. His eyes stung, as if tears gathered there.

Edward blinked fiercely and cleared his throat. He forced his attention back to the confession.

Lord S.'s kisses grew more heated and his hands roamed greedily over my nakedness, until finally he could rein in his passion no more. He took me in the stream, as if he were Poseidon and I one of his nymphs. And the heat of our combined passion and the coolness of the water combined so delightfully that I was almost dizzy from the pleasure of it.

"Mr. Kane?"

Edward's attention snapped to the doorway. Miss Chapple stood there, the crown of her head nearly brushing the lintel.

His arousal fled. Edward hastily folded the confession and stuffed it into his pocket. "Uh . . . Miss Chapple." He stood and bowed. "Good morning."

"Good morning," she said, advancing into the room. Her smile was cheerful. "Terrible weather, isn't it?"

"Yes," Edward said. Chérie's confession felt as if it was burning a hole in his pocket. "Terrible. I, uh . . . had hoped to find a novel to read."

Her face screwed up in a brief grimace. "My uncle disapproves of novels. He won't allow them at Creed Hall."

"Shakespeare?" Edward asked, hopefully.

Miss Chapple shook her head. "Not even Shakespeare. There are, however, a number of religious works." Her voice was demure, but dimples showed in her cheeks. "I can recommend Sherlock's sermons."

"Cruel, Miss Chapple."

She smiled.

Edward's attention fixed on her mouth. It was surprisingly lush. He found himself wondering what she'd look like, disporting naked in a stream.

His mind fastened on this thought, and for a moment he actually saw it: a rippling stream with Miss Chapple standing naked in it, her smooth, pale skin glowing in the sunlight. It wouldn't be like Poseidon consorting with a nymph—as Chérie had described—but rather, Poseidon consorting with Venus, a tall and voluptuous goddess, with lush breasts and ripely curved hips.

His mouth went dry. The breath choked in his throat. Edward began to cough.

"Are you all right, Mr. Kane?"

"Yes," he said, once he'd got his breath back. "Something in my throat."

"Shall I ring for some tea?"

"Uh, yes."

They sat. Edward cast desperately about for a topic of conversation. He glanced around at the half-empty bookshelves, the faded curtains, the fraying carpet.

"The new curate will be dining with us this evening," Miss Chapple said, smoothing the ugly gray wool of her gown over her lap. "Mr. Humphries."

"Oh?" said Edward. And then, cautiously, "Will there still be a sermon afterwards?"

"Yes," Miss Chapple said. "And after that you shall have the pleasure of listening to the curate discuss it. His opinions are always . . . extensive."

"It sounds delightful," Edward said dryly.

Miss Chapple grinned.

Edward's attention fastened on her mouth again. His throat tightened and for a moment he couldn't breathe. Fortunately, the butler arrived with the tea tray.

Miss Chapple poured. "Shortbread?"

"Please."

The shortbread was pale and crumbly and, when he bit

into it, very dry. Crumbs caught in his throat. Edward laid the rest of the shortbread aside and swallowed a hasty mouthful of tea.

"I apologize for the shortbread," Miss Chapple said. He noticed that she hadn't taken a piece. "My uncle dislikes extravagance in the kitchen, so Cook cuts down on the butter, but the shortbread always suffers."

"No need to apologize, Miss Chapple." Edward brushed crumbs from his knee. "I hadn't realized your uncle's circumstances were so straitened." Too late he realized how rude the comment was. "I beg your pardon, Miss Chapple. What I meant to say was, uh . . ." *What?*

Miss Chapple seemed unoffended by his blunder. "My uncle's circumstances aren't straitened, Mr. Kane," she said, her voice matter-of-fact. "He merely likes economy. He prefers not to waste money on unnecessary luxuries."

Unnecessary luxuries? Such as sufficient butter in one's shortbread? The word to describe Arthur Strickland wasn't economical; it was *miserly*.

Edward opened his mouth to make that comment aloud, and then closed it. "Hmm," he said. He crossed his legs the other way. The faint crackle of paper in his pocket reminded him of the confession—and his promise to Sir Arthur.

Edward glanced at the water streaming down the windowpanes. He didn't relish the thought of riding into Soddy Morton in this weather. He sipped his tea—and froze, the cup held to his lips.

Hadn't the curate been one of the people on the list? A possible Chérie?

"What did you say the curate's name is?"

"Mr. Humphries."

Edward felt a twinge of excitement. Mr. Humphries *was* on the list. He glanced at the rain-blurred window again. Despite the foul weather, he might be able to cross someone off his list. "Will he come in this weather?"

"With any luck it will have cleared by evening," Miss

Chapple said. "But even if it hasn't, I expect he'll come. It's become his custom to dine with us on Fridays."

"The curate likes a free meal?"

"The curate likes Mrs. Dunn. He's courting her."

Edward blinked, and registered her tone. "You, er . . . disapprove?"

"Mr. Humphries is . . ." Miss Chapple hesitated. "I shall let you form your own opinion, Mr. Kane."

He lifted his eyebrows, amused by her careful neutrality. "I look forward to it."

Her lush mouth quirked, as if she suppressed a smile—and abruptly, Edward was reminded of the scene he'd just read in Chérie's confession.

He dragged his gaze from her, cleared his throat, and took a large swallow of tea. It wasn't that he was attracted to Miss Chapple; it was that—finally—after months of believing himself impotent, his body was returning to life. He could be sitting in the presence of *any* woman right now, and wonder what she'd taste like if he kissed her.

"How long has Mr. Humphries resided in Soddy Morton?" he asked.

"Two months. He has the curate's position my uncle hoped to gift to Toby." Miss Chapple put aside her teacup. "If you will excuse me, Mr. Kane, I have a letter to write."

Edward set down his own cup. He stood and bowed. As Miss Chapple disappeared through the doorway, he found himself wondering what her hair would be like if it was released from that tight knot at the back of her head. Sleek and straight, or curly?

Edward abruptly halted that train of thought.

His gaze turned to the window and the rain outside. He *would* ride into Soddy Morton this morning. The sooner he found Chérie, the sooner he could return to London—and find a nice, plump, clean whore, and prove to himself that he was as virile as he'd been before Waterloo.

Mattie spent some time rubbing the stub of a wax candle over brown paper, in the hope of rendering the paper more weatherproof. She wrapped Chérie's *Memoir* in the paper, tied it tightly with string, and sealed the knots with wax. When she tried to write the address, the ink slid off the waxed paper.

"Damnation," she muttered under her breath, and unwrapped the parcel, turned the paper over, and started again. This time she wrote the address *before* she applied the wax.

The package wrapped and sealed again, she prepared another sheet of paper, writing the address of her friend Anne Brocklesby before waxing it. She wrapped it around the parcel and tied it with string. After a moment's hesitation, she sealed those knots with wax, too. There. With luck the manuscript would reach its final destination unscathed.

Mattie looked out the window. She wanted to deliver the precious parcel to the postmaster herself, but rain still streamed down outside. She imagined her drenched gown, the heavy weight of wet wool, the smell, and pulled a face. No, she'd let Durce, the footman, with his oilskins and knee-high boots, carry the parcel into Soddy Morton.

Gathering the manuscript in her arms, Mattie went downstairs. Hope and anxiety twisted in her belly.

The fire was dead in the library and the candles had been snuffed. Mr. Kane was gone. Mattie rang the bell and waited, shivering slightly, in the dark, drafty room. After a minute she heard familiar footsteps, slow and measured. She bent her head and quickly kissed the parcel. "God speed," she whispered.

"You rang, miss?"

Mattie turned and smiled at the butler. "Yes." She held out the package. "Can you please see that this gets to Soddy Morton today? I'd like it to catch tomorrow's Mail."

Her uncle, had he seen the parcel, would have commented

on its size and weight and how much it would cost Anne to retrieve from the post office. Griggs merely said, "Very good, miss," and took it.

Mattie listened to the sound of his footsteps fade from hearing. Her future—her freedom from Creed Hall—lay within that waxed-paper package. "God speed," she whispered again.

She had a gown to finish sewing, gray worsted, to the same pattern as every other gown she possessed—loose-fitting and fastened down the side, so that she needed no maid to help her dress—but Mattie was too restless to sit still. She peeked into her aunt's parlor, on the chance of finding Cecy unoccupied, but her friend was reading aloud to Lady Marchbank.

Mattie backed away on tiptoe.

She changed her shoes for half boots, grabbed a shawl, went downstairs, and let herself out through the side door. Rain pelted down. Mattie drew the shawl over her head and dashed across to the stables.

There were stalls for dozens of horses, but fewer than a handful were occupied. Horses, in her uncle's opinion, were an unnecessary extravagance. The big gray Mr. Kane had hired was gone.

Mattie spent a few minutes rubbing the noses of the four horses that pulled Creed Hall's carriage to church every Sunday, made the acquaintance of the matched bays that had drawn Mr. Kane's curricle, and then climbed the ladder up to the loft. "Puss puss puss," she whispered, blinking in the half-dark.

She heard tiny rustlings—and then the squeak of kittens.

Mattie climbed the last few rungs and crawled on hands and knees into the hay. More peepings came, and a low *meow* from the mother. "I have a sausage," she said, reaching into her pocket. "See, Mama Cat? I saved it from breakfast."

The cat mewed again. The hay rustled more loudly, and then a warm, furry body rubbed against her.

"Hello, sweetheart." Mattie stroked the cat, then broke the sausage into pieces and laid it on the hay.

The mother cat ate hungrily, wolfing down the sausage, while the three kittens clambered over Mattie's skirts. Their furry little black-and-gray-striped bodies were almost invisible in the gloom.

Mattie lifted one kitten in her hand. She held it, soft and purring, against her cheek. "I shall take you with me, all of you, when I leave. I promise. No one will ever drown you."

The sound of booted feet echoed in the stables. The mother cat looked up from grooming herself, but the kittens paid no attention. Mattie crawled to the edge of the loft and peered down. An elderly man with a crooked back and bowlegged stride walked down the aisle below, broom in hand.

"Hello, Hoby," she called down.

He leaned the broom against the side of a stall and tugged his forelock. "Afternoon, miss. How's the kittens?"

"Very well," Mattie said. "How's your wife?"

"Oh, aye." Hoby put his gnarled hands on his hips. "She's right tetchy at the moment."

Mattie bit her lip to hide a smile. Mrs. Hoby was always tetchy. *Prettiest lass in the village,* she'd heard Hoby say on more than one occasion. *And with a tongue like a razor's edge. Lor', she were a catch all right.* "What is it this time?"

"Hens," Hoby said darkly.

Water ran in rivulets from the brim of Edward's hat and streamed off the shoulder capes of his coat. He dismounted in the yard and led Trojan into the stables, whistling under his breath. He'd managed to cross one person off the list of possible Chéries: the baker's wife. And he'd eaten two extremely tasty meat pies, followed by an even tastier apple turnover. And he had two thick slices of gingerbread wrapped in a clean handkerchief in his breast pocket, where the rain couldn't reach.

The groom, Hoby, was talking to someone in the hayloft.

Edward stopped whistling. He glanced up at the loft and saw the pale blur of a face.

Hoby hastened towards him. He had a rocking gait, like a sailor. "Sir?"

Edward's eyes slowly adjusted to the dim light. He blinked and squinted up at the loft. The pale blur resolved itself into a face he recognized.

"Miss Chapple?"

"Kittens," Hoby said cryptically, taking Trojan's reins.

"Kittens?"

He saw Miss Chapple's lips move, but the clatter of Trojan's hooves on the flagstones drowned out her words. "I beg your pardon?"

"Three kittens," she said, more loudly.

"Oh," Edward said. Water dripped steadily from his coat. He wanted to take off his wet clothes, sit in front of a warm fire, and eat his gingerbread. But something about Miss Chapple's face, peering down at him from the gloomy loft, caught his interest. "May I see them?"

He saw her shrug. "If you wish."

Edward took off his greatcoat, shook the water from it, and hung it from an empty harness hook. He removed his hat and stripped off his wet gloves, and hung them up, too. Then he climbed the ladder to the loft.

Hay rustled as Miss Chapple moved back. He heard faint peeping sounds.

Edward halted with his head and shoulders above the edge of the loft and peered around. *What am I doing here? I don't even like cats.* It was a fire and gingerbread he wanted, not a bunch of scrawny kittens in a dark, dusty loft. "How old are they?"

"Six weeks," Miss Chapple said. She held out one hand to him. Cupped in her palm was a kitten.

Edward clambered the rest of the way up the ladder and crawled onto the hay. "Six weeks? It's very small."

"Take it."

"Uh . . ." Edward hesitated and then obeyed. The kitten wasn't scrawny; it had a plump, round belly.

Tentatively, he stroked the little creature. Its fur was soft and warm. After a moment, a faint vibration rumbled against his palm. "It's purring," he said, astonished.

"It likes you."

Thoughts of a fire retreated. Edward settled down on the hay beside Miss Chapple, careful not to disturb the kitten. He discovered that the more he stroked it, the louder it purred. It was an oddly pleasant sensation—the warm, soft fur, the rumbling vibration, the tiny creature's trust that he wasn't going to harm it.

Above them, rain pattered on the slate roof. It was dark and shadowy and cozy up here, with the sound of the rain overhead and the rustling of the hay and the dry, dusty smell of late summer. He glanced at Miss Chapple. She lay on her stomach, playing with one of the kittens, a dimple on her cheek and a smile on her mouth.

He wondered if Chérie had written about a tumble in the hay. If she hadn't, it was an omission. There was something about a hayloft that made a man amorous.

Control yourself, Kane.

But his imagination took flight, telling him that Miss Chapple's mouth was made for kissing, that her breasts would be ripe in his hands, that her wide hips would cradle him while he made love to her.

Heat flushed his body. He felt a surge of arousal, stronger than it had been that morning in the library.

Edward looked abruptly away from Miss Chapple. He cleared his throat and forced his attention back to the kitten he was stroking. It began to chew on his thumb. The creature's teeth were astonishingly sharp, like little needles. "Ouch!"

Miss Chapple laughed.

Edward released the kitten. It scampered off to ambush one of its siblings.

He shifted his weight, leaning back on one elbow, aware of the gingerbread in his pocket. He no longer wanted to eat it by himself. "I purchased some slices of gingerbread, Miss Chapple, while I was in Soddy Morton. Would you like one?"

Her eyebrows rose. "From Oddfellow's?"

He nodded.

"Yes, please! Oddfellow makes the *best* gingerbread!"

Edward laughed—and discovered that she wasn't exaggerating. The thick slices were delicious—moist, sticky, rich, sweet, spicy—and quite possibly the best he'd ever tasted. Oddfellow, the baker, hadn't scrimped on butter or treacle or anything else.

They ate the slices sitting cross-legged in the hay, while the mother cat washed her kittens with ruthless thoroughness. Below them, in the stable, came the sound of a broom sweeping. Miss Chapple gave a sigh of contentment when the last crumb was gone. "Thank you," she said. "It's been a long time since I've had some of Oddfellow's gingerbread. It's every bit as delicious as I remembered."

"I'm surprised you don't buy some every day," Edward said, resolving to do just that while he was at Creed Hall.

"I have no money," Miss Chapple said simply.

"But surely your uncle gives you pin money?" Edward said, and then kicked himself mentally; it wasn't his place to ask such personal questions.

She shook her head. "Uncle Arthur provides for all my needs. Pin money is . . . unnecessary."

"Ah."

"Whenever Toby visited, he'd buy me gingerbread from Oddfellow's," Miss Chapple said, hugging her knees. "Once, I persuaded Uncle Arthur to let me send Toby some for his birthday. He was in Spain. He said that by the time it reached him, it had grown a handsome colony of mold!"

Edward grunted.

The sound of sweeping below stopped. "Miss Chapple?"

Miss Chapple crawled to the edge of the loft. "Yes, Hoby?"

"I'll be leaving shortly."

Miss Chapple glanced at Edward. "I think that's a hint," she whispered, amusement in her voice. "I think he thinks you might compromise me."

He wouldn't—but that didn't mean he wasn't thinking about it.

The scene unfurled in his mind: peeling off her clothes, exposing her breasts . . .

Edward clenched his jaw and shoved the image from his mind.

Miss Chapple's smile faded. "Don't be offended, Mr. Kane."

"I'm not," Edward said hastily. He tried to smile, to joke: "Of course he's worried; I look like a savage."

"Nonsense!"

Edward raised his hand to his left ear. Her eyes followed the movement. He knew what she saw: the stumps of his fingers, the ragged remains of his ear.

"You look like a soldier, not a savage."

Edward lowered his hand. He shrugged and changed the subject. "If Hoby is leaving, so should we."

Miss Chapple nodded, but she made no move to climb down the ladder. Her frown became slightly anxious. "Please, Mr. Kane . . . don't tell my uncle about the kittens. He has a profound dislike of cats! He'd drown them if he knew they were here."

"I won't tell him," Edward said. "I give you my word of honor."

Miss Chapple's expression relaxed. "Thank you." She stroked the kittens one last time, rubbed her knuckles over the mother cat's head, and then scrambled down the ladder.

Edward followed.

Miss Chapple briskly brushed hay from her gown.

"Mr. Kane," Hoby said, dipping his head. His manner was courteous, but also faintly aggressive.

Edward met the man's gaze, amused. So Hoby thought him a threat to Miss Chapple's virtue, did he?

Two days ago, the groom would have been wrong; he'd been no threat to any woman's virtue. But today, Hoby was right. Today his body was telling him that he was ready for sex again, that he *wanted* it.

"Afternoon, Miss Chapple." Edward dipped his head in farewell. He gathered his hat, gloves, and coat, and strode out into the rain-soaked stableyard, whistling a jaunty tune under his breath.

The sooner he got back to London, the better.

*C*HAPTER 5

*E*dward changed into dry clothes and gave his wet ones to Tigh. "Sorry about the mud."

"I seen worse."

Edward went downstairs again. In the shadowy corridor, the sound of a raised voice echoed. Lady Marchbank.

He trod cautiously towards the library and halted in the doorway.

"—will *not* have novels in this house!" Lady Marchbank said shrilly.

Miss Chapple and Mrs. Dunn sat side by side on a sofa upholstered in faded brown damask, looking for all the world like a pair of naughty schoolgirls. Lady Marchbank stood over them, shaking a slender volume bound in calfskin. "Whose is it?" she demanded. "Which one of you is reading this nonsense?"

Mrs. Dunn seemed to shrink slightly. She looked up at her employer and opened her mouth.

"It's mine, Aunt," Miss Chapple said.

Mrs. Dunn closed her mouth.

"I might have guessed!" Lady Marchbank said, and boxed Miss Chapple's ears soundly with the book.

Miss Chapple winced. Mrs. Dunn looked as if she wanted to cry.

Lady Marchbank opened the book to its title page. "*Sense and Sensibility,*" she read aloud, and shut the book again with a snap. "If you had any *sense,* girl, you wouldn't read such rubbish. Filling your head with lies and absurdities! No wonder you can't find a man to marry you!"

Miss Chapple looked down at her hands.

Lady Marchbank turned to the fireplace and cast the book into the grate. Mrs. Dunn's mouth opened in a gasp of horror. She rose from the sofa.

Miss Chapple caught her gown and pulled her back down.

Lady Marchbank picked up two more calf-bound volumes from the mantelpiece and threw them briskly into the fire. "Let that be a lesson to you," she told her niece.

"Yes, Aunt," Miss Chapple said in a colorless voice.

"I'm disappointed in you, Matilda. Extremely disappointed! Your uncle gives you a roof over your head and this is how you repay him!"

Miss Chapple bit her lip. Mrs. Dunn looked even closer to tears.

"Come, Mrs. Dunn." Lady Marchbank turned away from the sofa. "It's time I took my cordial."

Edward backed away from the doorway and down the corridor.

Lady Marchbank swept out of the library and headed for the staircase, as fast as an elderly lady using a walking stick could sweep. A very subdued Mrs. Dunn followed her. Neither lady noticed him standing in the shadowy corridor.

Once they were out of earshot, Edward returned to the doorway. Miss Chapple no longer sat on the sofa; she knelt beside the fire, trying to snatch the burning volumes from the flames.

"Careful!" Edward said. "You'll burn yourself."

Miss Chapple glanced at him. "I already have." She sat back on her heels and sucked a fingertip.

He trod across the threadbare carpet and came to stand beside her. The books were well alight, the pages burning with hungry crackling sounds. "*Sense and Sensibility?*"

"Yes," Miss Chapple said, and sighed.

"I thought it quite a sensible novel," Edward said, watching as one of the covers blackened and curled up at the corners. He held out his hand to her.

"You've read it?" Miss Chapple asked, as he helped her to her feet.

Edward nodded. "It wasn't yours, was it?"

She glanced at him sharply. "How much did you hear?"

"I arrived just before she boxed your ears."

Miss Chapple grimaced. "Not my finest moment."

Edward disagreed. What she'd done—taking the blame for her friend—was the mark of a fine character.

Miss Chapple sighed. "Poor Cecy. She saved for months to buy that copy. She hadn't even read the first chapter."

Edward felt a flash of anger towards Lady Marchbank. He swallowed it and said mildly: "I thought you said there were no novels in Creed Hall."

Miss Chapple glanced at him. "None that my aunt and uncle know about."

Edward raised his eyebrows in silent query.

"We had a number of Mrs. Radcliffe's novels, but the mice ate them all." She pulled a face expressive of dismay. "But the last time Toby was home he brought me *Pride and Prejudice,* which is excellent!"

"You still have it?"

Her eyes narrowed as she looked at him. "If you borrow it, you must *promise* to be careful. It's the only novel we have now."

Edward laid his hand on his heart. "I shall guard it with my life."

The dimples showed.

He followed Miss Chapple across the library. She stood on tiptoe, pulled out one of the *Histories of Herodotus,* in its original Greek, and produced from behind it three slender calf-bound volumes, like those now burning in the fireplace. "Well hidden," Edward said. "I'm astonished Lady Marchbank found *Sense and Sensibility*."

"Cecy hid it behind *The Decline and Fall of the Roman Empire,* because she's shorter." Miss Chapple glanced at the spines and put two of the volumes back. She held the third one out to him. "Have you not read this?"

Edward shook his head.

"It's quite the most amusing book I've ever read. Mr. Humphries is *so* like Mr. Collins."

Edward blinked, bemused. "I beg your pardon?"

"Mr. Humphries, our new curate, is like Mr. Collins." Miss Chapple tapped the cover of the book he held. "In here."

"He is?"

She nodded solemnly, but mischief sparkled in her eyes. "Cecy and I think so. Mr. Humphries isn't so *precipitate* as Mr. Collins, but in every other way—they could be twins!"

That gleam of laughter was contagious. Edward found himself smiling. "I look forward to making both gentlemen's acquaintance."

He read a chapter before dinner, in the privacy of his room, but Mr. Collins didn't make his entrance onto the page. Thus, it was Mr. Humphries, the curate at Soddy Morton, whose acquaintance Edward made first.

Mr. Humphries was a short, stout young man with a round and self-satisfied face. Edward knew within less than a minute of meeting him that the curate couldn't possibly be Chérie. He also—within that one minute—formed a strong dislike of Mr. Humphries. The man was pompous, not very bright, and basking in an inflated sense of his own worth.

The curate recoiled slightly at his first glimpse of Edward's face. He blinked several times, an exaggerated opening and closing of his eyes, like a *coquette* batting her eyelids. "My, my," he murmured, after Sir Arthur had made the introductions. "My, my. A soldier, one assumes?"

"Yes," Edward said curtly.

"Not one of our heroes from Waterloo?"

No. Not a hero. "I was at Waterloo," Edward said, even more curtly. "But I fell early in the piece."

Someone less self-absorbed than Mr. Humphries would have listened to his tone and turned the subject, but the curate had espied a possibility to expound. He tutted loudly. "Wellington made a dreadful mess of that battle. Really, the man should have been stripped of his command long ago."

Edward bridled. He opened his mouth, caught Miss Chapple's anxious gaze, and shut his mouth again. *Not worth it,* he told himself. *Let it go.* A man as portentous and self-important as Humphries wouldn't listen anyway.

And so he gritted his teeth and smiled tightly, while anger built inside him. What did this soft, overweight curate know about Waterloo and the decisions Wellington had been forced to make in the turmoil of battle, and how *dare* he think he could have done better?

After five endless minutes, dinner was announced. Edward was relieved. His jaw had begun to ache.

Mr. Humphries obtained Mrs. Dunn's arm with alacrity, so Edward found himself escorting Miss Chapple from the parlor. "I'm sorry," she whispered, as they exited the room.

"Not at all," Edward said, though anger still burned in his chest.

Miss Chapple glanced at him, then rose on tiptoe. "He's a pompous idiot," she breathed in his ear.

Edward bit back a sudden laugh. His anger vanished. "Yes," he said. "He is."

"Thank you for being so forbearing."

He nodded as they entered the dining room. The smell of last night's boiled cabbage still lingered in the room.

Dinner was as silent as it had been the previous two nights. The only sounds were the clink of cutlery and the loud chewing of Lady Marchbank. The curate spent much of the meal gazing admiringly at Mrs. Dunn, who ate with her eyes fixed firmly on her plate.

Miss Chapple watched Mr. Humphries watch Mrs. Dunn, a faint frown furrowing her brow. Edward agreed silently with her; the curate was *not* a good match for Mrs. Dunn. Or any woman—unless she was desperate.

Edward speared some overcooked beans with his fork. Was Mrs. Dunn desperate?

He glanced across the table at her, seeing the shining blonde hair, the porcelain fragility of her features. Mrs. Dunn was an uncommonly attractive young woman. Surely she could do better than an overweight fool of a curate?

But her choices in Soddy Morton are limited, Edward reminded himself while he chewed the beans. They squeaked against his teeth.

Mrs. Dunn was a widow, obviously impoverished or she wouldn't have taken this position. If she wanted to escape life as a paid companion, she must marry.

Edward glanced from Mr. Humphries to Lady Marchbank and back again. Which was worse?

He grimaced—both options seemed equally bad—and focused his attention on a piece of boiled pork.

The dinner dragged to its conclusion, the ladies withdrew, and Edward braced himself to endure both oversweet port *and* Mr. Humphries' further commentary on Wellington's errors.

He kept Miss Chapple's words in the forefront of his

mind—*pompous idiot*—and managed not to snarl at the curate when the man picked up his criticism of Wellington where he'd left off.

Arthur Strickland sat at the head of the table, nodding his head. "My son would still be alive if Wellington had known what he was doing," he said once, when the curate paused to draw breath.

I doubt it, Edward thought. But he saw that Strickland believed it. Humphries believed it, too. "Yes, yes," the curate said fussily. "Without doubt, my dear sir. Without doubt."

Edward gritted his teeth. He was still in possession of his temper when Strickland pushed back his chair and announced it was time to go into the drawing room—but only just. As they filed out of the dining room, he realized that he was actually eager for the evening's sermon to start. *I've been in this house too long.*

His gaze went to Miss Chapple as he entered the drawing room. She was watching him, a slightly anxious expression on her face. Her eyebrows rose in a silent question.

Edward rolled his eyes.

A dimple appeared briefly, and was quickly subdued.

Edward bit back a grin, and immediately felt better. He sat and tried to decide what to count tonight. *The,* or *and?* He settled on *the.*

The reading was from Fordyce's sermons again. Edward sat back in his chair, listening to Miss Chapple's warm contralto, sipping his tea, counting the *the*s.

Ten minutes slid past, and then another ten.

Mrs. Dunn wasn't counting words this evening; she sat stiffly, her hands clasped in her lap and her gaze fixed on Miss Chapple.

"Nothing can be more certain than that your sex is, on every account, entitled to the shelter of ours," Miss Chapple read.

Mr. Humphries nodded as he listened to these words, his eyes on Mrs. Dunn.

"Your softness, weakness, timidity, and tender reliance on man; your helpless condition in yourselves, and his superior strength for labor . . ." Miss Chapple read the words without expression, either in her voice or on her face.

Mr. Humphries nodded sagely, secure in his conviction of his own superiority.

Edward almost snorted. Miss Chapple was easily superior to the curate in character, intellect, *and* physical strength.

He allowed his gaze to rest on her for a moment. Her hair was tightly pulled back, her gown shapeless, but he no longer thought her as plain as he had that first night. In the last day he'd learned to see past the drab exterior. The dimples were hidden now, as was the smile and the mischief gleaming in the gray eyes, but he knew they were there, and that made her attractive.

Edward blinked. Attractive?

He scanned her, no longer listening to the sermon.

Miss Chapple wasn't pretty like Mrs. Dunn. Other than her mouth, her features were unexceptional. Her figure, though, was another matter. She was tall, wide-hipped, deep-breasted. Goddess-like in her dimensions. Edward's thoughts slid sideways. Venus would be just as lushly built . . .

He jerked his thoughts back to the drawing room, to the book of sermons in Miss Chapple's hands, to Mrs. Dunn sitting stiffly on the sofa while Mr. Humphries observed her from across the room. He straightened in the chair and concentrated on counting the *the*s again.

Mattie knocked softly on the door to Cecy's bedchamber. After a moment, she heard a quiet, "Come in."

Mattie slipped inside. The room was dark. She shielded her candle with one hand and whispered, "Did I wake you?"

Bedclothes rustled as Cecy sat up. "No."

Mattie tiptoed across the floor and climbed up on the end of the bed. "His attentions were quite marked," she said, reaching over to place her candle on the bedside table. "He never took his eyes off you."

Cecy sighed. "I know."

Mattie hugged her knees. "If he should ask you to marry him . . ."

Cecy didn't reply for a long moment. She pleated the bed sheet between her fingers, unpleated it, and then pleated it again. At last she looked up and met Mattie's eyes. "If he asks me . . . I shall accept."

"Cecy, no! You *can't*!"

Cecy looked away. "What else would you have me do?"

"Say no!"

Cecy sighed again. "I'm not likely to get a better offer."

"But if you marry Mr. Humphries you'll have to spend the *rest of your life* with him. And even worse . . ." Mattie lowered her voice into a whisper, "you'll have to share his bed."

Cecy swallowed. "I want children," she said staunchly.

"Yes . . . but with him?"

Cecy looked down at her clenched hands. "I'm penniless, and I'm twenty-five. Where else am I going to find a husband? If I was in London or Bath, or . . . or York, or somewhere larger, it might be different. I might meet a gentleman who didn't mind my lack of fortune. Who . . . who liked me for who I am. But here?" She shook her head.

Mattie opened her mouth to disagree, and then closed it. Cecy was right.

"The only respectable bachelor in Soddy Morton is Mr. Humphries, and if I don't have him, there are others who will."

"He may be respectable . . . but is he someone you can respect?"

She read the answer on Cecy's face. No.

"This may be my only chance, Mattie. If he offers for me, I'll have to accept. You must see that!"

Mattie shook her head. "But you don't even like him."

"He has a good income." Cecy flushed faintly. "I know it sounds mercenary, Mattie, but money is important."

"But—"

"Mr. Humphries will be able to provide for his wife and children. They'll never want for food or clothes or a roof over their heads."

Mattie frowned. "Shouldn't there be more to marriage than that?"

"I married for love," Cecy said flatly. "And when Frederick died, I couldn't even afford to bury him decently." Sudden tears filled her eyes. She blinked them back and said fiercely, "If I marry again, it will be to a man who can afford his own funeral!"

Mattie found herself unable to say anything.

Cecy hunted under her pillow for a handkerchief and blew her nose. "I'm sorry. I know what you must think of me, but Mattie . . . I'm not like you. I don't have family who'll take me in. When Frederick died, I was alone, without any money and with no one to turn to. It was terrifying. And I will do *anything* to not be in that situation again."

Mattie looked down at the counterpane. She picked at a loose thread.

"If I marry Mr. Humphries, I'll have a home of my own," Cecy said. "I'll never have to worry about my future again. For that, I'd marry him."

Mattie looked up and met her friend's eyes.

"I'm sorry, Mattie. I know you're disappointed in me."

Mattie shook her head.

Cecy smiled crookedly. "If Mr. Humphries is Mr. Collins, then I'm Charlotte Lucas."

Mattie stopped picking at the loose thread. "Cecy . . . I wasn't going to tell you until everything was certain, but . . . I have a plan."

"What kind of plan?"

"To leave Creed Hall. To buy a boarding house."

Cecy's mouth opened in a silent gasp.

"I want you to come with me."

"But . . . how? A boarding house? You have no money!"

"Not yet. But I hope to within the month. And once I have it, I'm going to leave." Mattie leaned forward. "Come with me, Cecy! Our own boarding house! We can run it together!"

Cecy blinked. "Where?" Her voice was bemused.

"By the sea," Mattie said. "Somewhere fairly big. Where people won't notice us." *And where there'll be plenty of suitors for you. And maybe even one for a hulking great creature like me.* But even if she never found a husband, it wouldn't matter, because she'd have a home of her own.

Cecy's brow creased in a frown. "Mattie . . . where are you getting the money from?"

"I can't tell you. Not yet."

"But . . ." Cecy bit her lip and then leaned forward. "Oh, please, tell me!"

Mattie shook her head. She looked down and found the thread again and pulled at it. "I'm not precisely *lying* to my uncle and aunt, but I'm keeping a secret from them. I guess you could say I'm deceiving them." She glanced up. "It's not a nice feeling. I don't want you to be doing it, too."

Cecy sat back, frowning. "Mattie . . . what you're doing, it's not illegal, is it?"

Mattie shook her head. "No, but it's not entirely respectable. You may not approve."

Cecy's brow wrinkled in perplexity. "But what—"

"Please don't ask me."

Cecy sighed. "Very well." She stared at Mattie. The tears were gone from her eyes. In their place was a bright, intent curiosity.

"If my plan works, will you come with me, Cecy? You might meet another man. Someone better than Mr. Humphries."

For a long moment Cecy sat in the huddle of her bedclothes, staring at Mattie, and then she nodded, a decisive movement. "Yes. I'll come with you."

"Promise me you won't give Mr. Humphries an answer until I hear about the money. Promise!"

"I promise," Cecy said. "If he asks me, I'll ask for a little time. But Mattie . . . if your plan falls through, I will have to marry him."

"It won't fall through," Mattie said confidently. *And even if it does, I won't let you marry him.* Cecy deserved better than a pompous idiot of a man. She had a sudden thought. "What about Mr. Kane?"

"Mr. Kane?" Cecy blinked. "What about him?"

"He's a bachelor," Mattie pointed out. "And he's a nice man." She remembered his gentleness with the kittens, surprising in a man so large. *He's even more of a giant than I am.* "I like him."

"Mr. Kane's not looking for a wife."

It was Mattie's turn to blink. "How do you know?"

Cecy shrugged. "He doesn't look at us that way."

"What way?"

"Like we're goods on display in a store." Cecy yawned, covering her mouth with one hand. "And anyway, if he was looking for a wife, he'd probably prefer you."

Mattie felt herself flush. "Why?"

"You're more his size. He must weigh three times what I do. If he rolled over on me, I probably wouldn't survive." Cecy patted the mattress, her meaning clear.

Mattie's cheeks became red-hot. She cleared her throat, scrambled off the bed, and reached for her candle. "Sleep well."

"Sleep?" Cecy said. "After you've dangled your plan in front of my nose and not told me the details? I'll be awake all night!"

Mattie let herself out of the bedchamber. She trod quietly back down the dark corridor, thinking of Mr. Kane. His appearance was intimidating—his hulking build, the brutal scars—but despite his size, she knew he'd be gentle in the marriage bed. He was like the countess's groom: a rough exterior, but a kind heart. A good husband for Cecy. For any woman.

Mattie let herself into her bedchamber. Her reflection in the tall, warped mirror in the corner caught her eye. She grimaced and turned away. The mirror made the contrast between herself and Cecy abundantly clear. *No man would look twice at me when he could look at Cecy.*

Mattie climbed into bed and blew out her candle.

*C*HAPTER 6

*T*he morning was gray and chilly, but it wasn't raining. Edward rode to Soddy Morton across the increasingly swamplike mire of the fallow fields, and interviewed two more people on the list of possible Chéries: the beadle's wife, and a retired schoolmaster. The beadle's wife was a plump, cheerful woman with no understanding of grammar whatsoever, so he crossed her off the list; Chérie had an excellent command of the King's English.

The retired schoolmaster had a thorough understanding of grammar and a prim, pursed-mouthed face. The primness could be a cover, but the lines were so deeply etched into the man's face that Edward doubted it. He crossed him off the list, too.

The schoolmaster, Mr. Crippington, wanted to see the letter, but Edward evaded him. "It's of a personal nature."

Mr. Crippington frowned. "But shouldn't Joe Potts be doing this? He's responsible for the post in Soddy Morton."

"He's too busy for a task like this," Edward said. "Oh, is that the time? I really must be going, Mr. Crippington."

He escaped the man's gray cottage, put his hat back on his head, and wondered, for the umpteenth time, how he'd allowed himself to become involved in this fool's errand. "You're a cod's head, Ned!" he told himself.

He fortified himself for his next interview with a large steak pie, half a roasted fowl, and a tankard of ale at the inn, and then set out to find Widow Weeks, who, it transpired, was half-blind and dictated her letters to her housekeeper. The next person on the list—a farmer by the name of Plinhoe— wasn't at home. "Market day in Gripton," Mr. Plinhoe's wife informed him.

Edward gave up for the day. He stopped in at the village bakery on his way back and emerged from that fragrant establishment bearing several slices of gingerbread for himself and Miss Chapple.

Fortuitously, Miss Chapple was in the stableyard when he reached Creed Hall, a thick cloak over her shoulders, a bonnet on her head, and sturdy half boots on her feet. From the unmuddied state of her boots he deduced that she was departing, not returning.

"Walking down to the village?" Edward asked, swinging down from Trojan's back.

She shook her head. "I'm going around the park."

A gust of wind rippled the muddy puddles.

"In this weather?"

"I walk every day," Miss Chapple said. "Unless it's raining."

Edward handed Trojan off to the elderly groom and glanced up at Creed Hall's grim façade. It looked half-blinded, with so many windows bricked up. He shivered, reluctant to enter that bleak, cold building. "May I join you?"

"Are you well enough to be walking?"

"I'm not an invalid."

"Yes, but—"

"I'll be fine," Edward said firmly. "As long as there are no steep hills."

82

The park was larger than Edward had thought, five square miles of sodden, leafless woodland. The wind was raw, mud sucked at his boots, and water splashed up from the puddles, but Edward found that he was enjoying himself. It was a pleasant experience to walk with Miss Chapple. He was able to stretch his legs and breathe deeply.

They maintained a brisk pace. He saw Miss Chapple glance sideways at him while they climbed one muddy incline. "How do you feel, Mr. Kane?"

"Fine," he said, ignoring the faint ache in his thigh bone.

"Do you intend to stay long? There are other walks."

"I don't know how long I'll be here," Edward said, relieved when they reached the top of the rise. He was almost out of breath and the scar tissue over his ribs had begun to twinge. If Miss Chapple walked this route every day, at this pace, then she was a remarkably fit young lady. She didn't look athletic, she looked well-padded, but clearly that was deceptive. "Perhaps another day or so." He shrugged. "Perhaps a week." *I hope not.* "I've undertaken to perform a . . . uh, a small task for your uncle."

"A week?" She frowned. "But weren't you planning to go down to your property in Cornwall? Surely my uncle doesn't expect you to put off your own plans?"

I doubt he's given any thought to my plans. Sir Arthur appeared to have a decided streak of selfishness. If he ever placed other people's comfort above his own, Edward had yet to see evidence of it.

"What is the task, Mr. Kane? Perhaps I can help?"

"Thank you," Edward said. "But no." Chérie's confession was *not* something Miss Chapple should see.

"But—"

"The task is . . . somewhat difficult to explain," Edward said.

She turned her gaze to him. "What do you mean, Mr. Kane?"

"Um . . ." Edward found himself unable to prevaricate

beneath that steady gray gaze. "Your uncle has asked me to return a letter to its sender in the village."

Miss Chapple blinked. "A letter? But surely that's easily done?"

"The sender is unknown."

"Oh," she said. "But even so, that's something I can do for you! You needn't stay. You can go down to Cornwall."

"No," Edward said firmly, remembering several of the more explicit sentences.

"But—"

"It isn't something for a lady to be involved in, Miss Chapple."

Not something for a lady to be involved in. Mattie knew instantly what he meant: Chérie's confession.

Horror gripped her. She stumbled and almost fell. Mr. Kane took her arm for an instant, steadying her. "Are you all right, Miss Chapple?"

"Perfectly," Mattie said. But she wasn't. Her throat was almost too tight for breath, almost too tight for speech.

Uncle Arthur had seen Chérie's latest confession. He knew someone in the village had written it. And worst of all, he had set Mr. Kane the task of finding her!

She gripped her trembling fingers tightly together and forced herself to inhale. *Don't panic!*

They reached the lake. The water was a dull gray-brown. Mattie forced herself to speak calmly as they stopped in front of the folly. "In the summer it's quite pretty here."

"Hmm," Mr. Kane said, his tone unconvinced.

Mattie glanced sideways at him. *He won't be able to find me out.* There was nothing in the confession that could identify her. However many days he stayed at Creed Hall, her secret was safe.

She began to regain her self-control. "It does look very unattractive right now, I grant you, Mr. Kane. But in the summer I often come here to sit in the folly and sew."

Mr. Kane turned to look at the folly. The faux Greek temple was rather shabby, its pillars streaked with mold, its marble steps half-hidden beneath deep drifts of rotting leaves, but it was still recognizable from the countess's diary—perfectly round, with a pantiled roof and colonnade. Here, the young countess and her groom had spent many happy hours. *And here, Lord S. beds Chérie in the latest confession.*

Would Mr. Kane recognize it?

"This property used to belong to the fifth Earl of Malmstoke," Mattie said hastily, turning back to the lake. "His wife is believed to have drowned here. Suicide."

Mr. Kane spun on his heel and regarded the lake, his eyebrows rising. "Suicide?"

Mattie nodded and began to walk away from the folly. "Her husband was an extremely unpleasant man, so I believe."

"Oh?" Mr. Kane matched her stride.

"He liked to inflict pain."

"Ah." Mr. Kane grimaced. "The poor woman."

"Yes." Mattie glanced at the lake. "Her body was never found."

They walked for several minutes along the curving shore, until the dark roof of Creed Hall came into sight, rising above the treetops. Mattie halted and stared across the lake at it. If Uncle Arthur discovered she was Chérie . . .

"It's hard to believe the remains of a countess lie beneath these waters," Mr. Kane said.

"I don't think so," Mattie said, unthinkingly.

He turned to look at her. "You don't?"

Mattie blushed, annoyed with herself. "I think she ran away."

His eyebrows rose as he surveyed her. "You do?"

She nodded. *I know she did. She fled with her lover, the groom.*

"Hmm." Mr. Kane turned back to look at the lake. "A nicer version of the tale, I grant you."

"Yes."

"And on that note . . ." He pulled something from one pocket. "Would you like a slice of gingerbread?"

"Gingerbread?" Mattie blinked, and stared at him. At this moment Mr. Kane was quite surprisingly attractive. It was the color of his eyes—that warm dark brown—or perhaps the smile lines creasing his face beneath the disfiguring scars.

She swallowed. "Thank you."

They strolled in companionable silence along the lakeside path, eating gingerbread. Mattie was acutely aware of Mr. Kane's closeness. Their shoulders almost brushed as they walked. *I like him.*

She gave herself a mental shake. If Mr. Kane was hunting Chérie, he was no friend of hers.

"Better than Gunter's," Mr. Kane said.

"One day I hope to visit Gunter's," Mattie said. "Toby always said they made the best ices he'd ever tasted."

Mr. Kane paused in mid-bite, his surprise clear to see. "You've never been to London?"

"My parents died just before I was to make my début."

"But surely . . . once you were out of mourning?"

"Uncle Arthur felt that a début was an unnecessary expense." Mattie smiled brightly at him. "He was quite correct; it's extremely unlikely that I should have taken."

Mr. Kane frowned. "Yes, but—"

"I have no dowry to speak of," Mattie said matter-of-factly. "And I'm far too tall. If there's one thing I've learned, Mr. Kane, it's that men prefer not to dance with females who tower over them!" It was far better to stay at home than to be a wallflower, sitting out almost every dance—she'd learned *that* from the few assemblies Toby had taken her to in Gripton.

Mr. Kane's frown deepened. "I would dance with you."

"Yes," Mattie said. "But you're uncommonly large." *Like me.* "We are both of us giants!"

Mr. Kane smiled at this sally, but it was a mechanical movement; his eyes were unamused. "London is a mere seventy miles from here, Miss Chapple. A day's journey. Surely your uncle would allow you to visit—"

"For what reason, Mr. Kane? Merely to taste the ices at Gunter's? My uncle would consider that a great waste of money—and he would be correct!" Mattie turned the subject: "Tell me about your property in Cornwall. Have you visited it before?"

Talking about Cornwall gave Edward the same itchy feeling of frustration that he'd experienced while waiting for his leg to heal. He didn't want to *talk* about Blythe Manor, he wanted to *be* there. The stableyard came into sight, and the grim, gray bulk of Creed Hall. *One more day,* he promised himself. *One more day and I'll be gone from here.*

He turned his head at the clop of hooves. His mouth fell open as a man rode into the stableyard, a valise strapped behind his saddle cantle.

"Gary! What the devil—!" He recollected Miss Chapple's presence. "What on earth are you doing here?" He strode forward, heedless of the puddles.

"Bringing your clothes, as requested," Sir Gareth Locke said, sliding down from the saddle. He managed it creditably, despite the lack of his left arm.

"I didn't expect *you* to bring them!" Edward gripped his friend's hand, hard. "You didn't ride all the way?"

Gareth shook his head. "Came by carriage. I rode up from the village because the bridge is out." His gaze went past Edward's shoulder. "I have the . . . uh, papers you wanted."

Edward remembered Miss Chapple. He turned and made the introductions.

Miss Chapple held out her hand. She seemed not at all disconcerted by Gareth's missing arm. "Sir Gareth, I'm so pleased to meet you!" Her smile was welcoming and friendly. "Toby spoke often of you."

Miss Chapple was an inch taller than Gareth and looked as if she outweighed him by quite a few pounds; Gareth's frame was lean, his face thin and lined with pain—but he smiled as he shook Miss Chapple's hand.

Seeing Gareth like this—with only one arm—was jarring. For a moment, Edward felt a dizzying sense of dissonance, of wrongness. Gareth should have two arms, not one.

Edward shook his head to get rid of the feeling.

"Do come inside, Sir Gareth. My uncle will be delighted to meet you." Miss Chapple turned to the elderly groom, now hurrying from the stables. "Hoby, see to Sir Gareth's horse, please, and have the valise sent up to Mr. Kane's room."

Miss Chapple led them indoors through a side door. In the gloomy corridor they encountered a maidservant. Edward leaned close to Gareth. "If they invite you to stay, make your excuses," he whispered, while Miss Chapple issued instructions to the maid. "The inn will be a thousand times more comfortable—and the food immeasurably better!"

Amusement flickered across Gareth's face. "It can't be *that* bad here."

Edward grimaced. "You'd better believe it."

The maid hastily lit the fire and half a dozen candles in the chilly library. A few minutes later, a tea tray was brought in. The thump of Strickland's cane echoed down the corridor while Miss Chapple poured the tea.

Miss Chapple made the introductions. Strickland shook Gareth's hand and then gestured to the man's missing left arm. "Waterloo, I understand. Bad luck."

"There were men worse injured than I," Gareth said. He paused, and then said, "My condolences on the death of your son, sir."

Strickland's mouth tightened. He gave a curt nod. "Thank you."

In the silence that followed, Miss Chapple offered shortbread and plum cake. Edward declined; Gareth took a piece of each.

"What brings you to Soddy Morton?" Strickland asked.

"Soddy Morton?" Gareth glanced at Edward. "No particular reason, sir. Just passing through."

Strickland grunted. "Not a good time of year to be traveling." He embarked on a complaining monolog about the washed-out bridge. Edward sipped his tea and watched Gareth bite into the shortbread.

Gareth chewed once, twice, and then glanced at Edward.

Edward smiled. *Told you so.*

Gareth chewed again, doggedly.

"Might be another week before the bridge is fixed," Strickland said, a sharp note of petulance in his voice. "A week! I don't know what this parish is coming to."

Gareth finally swallowed. He washed the mouthful down with a large gulp of tea and laid the rest of the shortbread on his plate.

"I've been saying for years that it needed to be replaced," Strickland said testily. "But no one paid the slightest attention to me! Why, it was plainly obvious—"

The entrance of Lady Marchbank and Mrs. Dunn into the library halted his complaint. The introductions were made again, more tea was poured, and Strickland continued his criticism of the parish's roads.

Edward idly watched the others. Lady Marchbank nodded in agreement to everything her brother said, her head going up and down like a marionette's. Miss Chapple didn't appear to be listening to her uncle. She was watching Gareth. A slight frown sat on her brow. He thought she was seeing the thinness of Gareth's face, the lines of pain.

He caught Mrs. Dunn glancing at Gareth, too. Her gaze wandered over him. She paused at the missing arm. She didn't recoil or show revulsion. Her mouth tucked in slightly at the corners. He wasn't certain how to interpret that. Pity?

Edward grimaced. No man wished to be the object of pity.

"—you must stay at Creed Hall, Sir Gareth."

Edward's attention jerked back to his host.

"Here, you'll know the sheets have been properly aired!"

But the bedchamber will be colder than a witch's teat. Edward caught Gareth's eye and shook his head fractionally.

Gareth took the hint. "Thank you, but the inn is perfectly adequate for my needs."

Strickland looked at Gareth's left arm. "Hardly suitable for a man in your condition."

Gareth's mouth tightened. "I shall stay at the inn."

A short silence fell. "Looks like snow, don't you think?" Edward said, at the same time that Miss Chapple and Mrs. Dunn also spoke.

The moment of awkwardness passed. The discussion turned to the weather. Five minutes later, Gareth stood to take his leave. "You'll dine with us tonight, of course," Strickland said.

Edward caught his friend's eye again. He shook his head minutely.

Gareth accepted the invitation.

Edward accompanied Gareth out to the stableyard. "Extremely foolish," he said, as they strolled between the puddles.

"What is?"

"Accepting an invitation to dine here."

Gareth snorted. "I've eaten bad food before."

"It's not just the food," Edward said. "It's what comes afterwards."

Gareth narrowed his eyes at him. "What?"

"You'll see. A word of advice: counting helps."

Gareth's expression became baffled. "What?"

Edward spied the groom. "Hoby! Sir Gareth would like his horse."

The groom touched the brim of his battered cloth cap and disappeared into the gloom of the stables.

Gareth dug in his coat pocket. "The *Confessions*," he said, handing Edward a packet. "All of them."

"*All* of them?" Edward said, startled. The first installment of Chérie's *Confessions* had been released—and immediately sold out—several months ago. "Where on earth did you find them?"

"Bought them off Roxborough. He had the whole collection. Cost me a small fortune." Gareth fixed him with a piercing stare. "What the devil do you want them for?"

Edward turned the package over in his hand. "Chérie's in the village."

Gareth's mouth fell open. "Here? In Soddy Morton?"

Edward nodded.

Gareth blinked. "Well," he said. "I never."

"I've promised Strickland I'll find her." Edward's fingers itched to open the package. Resolutely, he thrust it in his pocket. "I'm hoping the confessions will give me a clue to her identity."

"Well, I never," Gareth said again.

Gareth returned to Creed Hall just before six. He had shaved and changed his clothes. Edward waited impatiently for the clock to strike the hour. He was eager for the evening to begin, eager to see Gareth's reactions to the treats in store for him.

First came the pronouncement that dinner would be a silent meal. "For the sake of our digestion," Strickland said solemnly.

"Er . . . of course," Gareth said.

Edward hid a grin.

Second was the food itself. Boiled veal, boiled cod, boiled cabbage. Even the mushrooms appeared to have been boiled.

Gareth ate deftly with one hand, choosing those dishes

that were easily managed with just a fork. Edward watched as his friend speared a boiled kidney on the fork tines, as he chewed—hesitated—and then resolutely chewed again. Finally he swallowed and reached for his glass of wine.

The wine was thin and watered-down.

Gareth almost choked. He placed the glass back down, his lips moving in a barely suppressed grimace. He glanced across the table at Edward.

Edward smiled blandly. *I warned you.* He returned his attention to his food, chuckling inside.

But when he next looked up from his plate, his amusement was quenched. Gareth was gazing at Mrs. Dunn.

Edward watched while Gareth cataloged Mrs. Dunn's features, apparently liking what he saw. His heart sank. Gareth had always had a liking for petite blondes and Mrs. Dunn was a particularly fine specimen—but a lightskirt was what Gareth needed in the wake of Miss Swinthorp's desertion, not a penniless widow who'd leap at the chance of a wealthy husband.

He speared a piece of boiled cod and frowned across the table at an oblivious Mrs. Dunn. *Don't you dare take advantage of him.*

After dinner, came the port. Gareth manfully drank the oversweet wine. Catching Edward's eye, he grimaced expressively. Edward smirked—*I told you so*—but his heart wasn't in it. He observed carefully as they entered the drawing room. Gareth's gaze went straight to Mrs. Dunn.

Mrs. Dunn looked up. She, too, seemed to be searching for one face in particular: Gareth's. When their eyes met, she colored faintly and dropped her gaze to her needlework.

Hell and damnation.

"My niece reads to us each evening," Strickland told Gareth.

"How delightful," Gareth said, wrenching his gaze from Mrs. Dunn.

They sat, accepted cups of tea, and settled back to listen.

"The reading is from Fordyce," Miss Chapple told Gareth. She looked down at the open page. "Sermon Five. On Female Virtue, Friendship, and Conversation."

Edward intercepted an appalled glance from Gareth. He sipped his tea. *I did warn you.*

This evening he didn't try to count words; he let his thoughts drift. Miss Chapple's voice was melodious. It was like listening to music—the cadence of the words, the rise and fall of her voice, the mellow tone.

His thoughts looped slowly, from the dank woods and gray lake, to gingerbread, to Gareth's unexpected arrival, to the full set of Chérie's *Confessions* Gareth had brought.

He'd read the first two confessions before dinner, trying to ignore Tigh's tuneless whistling while the bâtman laid out his evening clothes. The confessions had been less explicit than the later ones, but still quite candid. The paragraphs had brought vivid memories to life: the warm softness of a female body in his bed, teasing fingers trailing over his skin, the urgency of escalating arousal, the exquisite moment of physical release.

Thinking about it made a tendril of desire unfurl inside him. Heat shivered over Edward's skin. He jerked his thoughts away from the confessions. It was a relief that his body was capable of arousal again, but now was not the time or place. He focused his attention on Miss Chapple, but her voice was warm and smooth and silken. It made his thoughts slide sideways again, to Chérie's *Confessions,* to the heat and pleasure of sex.

Edward frowned. He shook himself mentally. *For heaven's sake, Ned. Control yourself!* For the rest of the sermon, he concentrated on counting the *the*s.

Edward fell asleep in his frigid bedchamber and awoke lying on the battlefield at Waterloo. For a moment he blinked, dizzy, while the sky swung above his head and the roar of cannons filled his ears. "Get up, Ned!" someone shouted.

Edward tried to focus his eyes. He saw Toby's face above him, urgent. "Get up!"

Edward squeezed his eyes shut. *Wake up!* he told himself. *Wake the hell up!*

Shells whistled overhead, a horse screamed—and then abruptly he was awake.

Edward lay beneath the covers, gasping. His heart thundered against his ribs, trying to batter its way out of his chest. After a moment he pushed up on one elbow and rubbed his face, feeling the prickle of stubble beneath his hand and the ridges of the scars.

He blew out a breath. It was getting easier to tear himself free from that particular dream. He'd managed not to witness the moment of Toby's death, had managed not to feel Toby's blood spray across his face.

He could taste the memory of blood on his tongue, though. Could smell it. And Toby's voice still rang in his ears. *Get up, Ned!*

Edward pushed aside the bedclothes and climbed out of bed. The room was dark but for a tiny glow from the coals in the fireplace. The floor was icily cold.

Fumbling, he found a candle and lit it. The room sprang into view. The solid reality of it—faded curtains, dying fire—pushed the dream even further away. The taste and scent of blood faded.

His heartbeat slowed, his breathing steadied, but he knew that a return to sleep was impossible.

Edward fished the first volume of *Pride and Prejudice* out from under his mattress and climbed back into bed. He flicked to the tenth chapter and settled down to read, but the words failed to hold his attention. The book was well-written and amusing, but his thoughts kept straying to the other tales hidden beneath the mattress.

After rereading the same page three times, Edward gave up. He hid *Pride and Prejudice* again and took out Chérie's *Confessions*. He put aside the two he'd read that afternoon and settled down to read the next in the sequence. It was dated September, 1815.

In response to your request, dear reader, for another confession from my pen, here is a tale from when I was but new in this most ancient of professions. I had recently come under the protection of a most worthy lady, Mrs. B., who kept an elegant and discreet house in L. Street.

Upon this particular occasion, Mrs. B. introduced me to a bashful young gentleman who was far more of a novice than I. Indeed, dear reader, it was to be my task to initiate him into that most pleasurable and tender of mysteries! In short, I was to be the recipient of his virginity.

Edward read the tale with amusement. The confession was more explicit in its detail than the first two, but as far as he could tell, it held no clues as to Chérie's true identity. Just to be certain, he read it twice.

Next, he read the fourth confession, the tale of a brawny sailor whose "noble proportions" once he'd removed his clothes had made Chérie's eyes almost start from her head. Edward snorted a laugh at this description. He read on: *Indeed, dear reader, I was so alarmed by his dimensions that I shrank back and declared myself unable to accommodate his needs.*

The sailor, however, was undeterred. After a page of coaxing, he succeeded in removing Chérie's clothes and the tale proceeded to its predictable conclusion, where the sailor's "excessive vigor" took Chérie to such heights of pleasure that she momentarily lost consciousness.

Edward snorted again. He laid the confession aside and sat thinking for several minutes, while the candle flickered in the draft. It seemed to him that each of the first four confessions had been more explicit than the last, as if Chérie had been gaining confidence in her writing.

Was it fact, or fiction? The physical descriptions rang true—the heat and the urgency—but the characters were mere ciphers: the bashful young gentleman, the brawny sailor.

For the life of him, he couldn't tell whether Chérie was a man pretending to be a woman, like the author of *Fanny Hill*, or a woman. He wished he had a copy of *Fanny Hill* to compare with the confessions. It might give him a clue as to Chérie's true gender.

Edward yawned. He hid the confessions under the mattress, blew out the candle, and climbed back into bed. Waterloo was utterly gone from his mind. The only subject on his thoughts while he drifted to sleep was how soon he could return to London and acquire a *chère-amie* of his own.

*C*HAPTER 7

*S*unday was notable for two reasons. Firstly, it rained all day, a cold, driving rain that was almost sleet. Secondly, the members of the household attended three Bible readings in the small, dark chapel attached to Creed Hall. Edward went to the first one and listened to Arthur Strickland read from the Corinthians for an hour in a thin, dry voice and then lead the household in prayers.

"Usually we attend services in the village," Miss Chapple told him afterwards. "But the weather, the broken bridge . . ." She shivered and pulled her shawl more tightly about her.

Edward didn't attend the next two Bible readings. He agreed with Tigh. "I ain't a godless man," the bâtman said. "But thrice? Nobody needs that much preachin'."

Edward stayed in his room, dragging the armchair as close to the fire as he could, and read *Pride and Prejudice*. He was aware of Chérie's confessions lying hidden beneath his mattress. Resolutely, he ignored the temptation to read them instead, bending his concentration to Elizabeth Bennett and her family. It was Sunday, and Chérie's confessions could remain where they were for the day.

The footman, Durce, collected the mail each morning from Soddy Morton and placed it on the refectory table in the entrance hall. On Monday morning, one of the letters was addressed to Mattie. The handwriting was familiar: her friend Anne Brocklesby in London.

Mattie's pulse quickened. At the top the postmaster had scrawled *1/4*, postage eight pennies dearer than usual, which meant there were two sheets of paper inside. Anne's letter— and one from her publisher?

"Matilda!"

Mattie's heart lurched in her chest. She turned swiftly, clutching the letter.

Her uncle stood in the doorway of his study, leaning on his cane. "A word with you, please, Matilda."

"Yes, Uncle."

Mattie followed him into his study. The letter seemed to burn in her hand.

"Sit, sit!" her uncle said testily, waving at a chair.

Mattie did, laying the letter on her lap as if it was nothing important. She endured her uncle's frowning stare, trying not to shift nervously. Was guilt stamped on her face? *Please, don't ever let him find out.* She owed Uncle Arthur for the gown she was wearing, for the shoes on her feet, for the breakfast she'd eaten—and not just for today but for every day during the past ten years. Repaying him by causing him distress would be unforgivable.

"I have been giving serious thought to your future," her uncle said. "With Tobias dead . . ." He cleared his throat and continued. "As you know, I've decided to gift my entire estate to the Missionary Society. Creed Hall is to become a school."

"Yes, Uncle." Uncle Arthur had announced his intention shortly after news of Toby's death had reached them. The

Tobias Strickland School for Missionaries' Children—a memorial to his son.

"You may, of course, assist at the school in some capacity—but when we spoke about this, I had the impression that the prospect didn't appeal to you." His thin lips pursed in disapproval and—which was worse—disappointment.

Mattie flushed and lowered her eyes. It wasn't the thought of teaching she disliked; it was the thought of spending the rest of her life at Creed Hall.

"If you have no wish to assist with the school, then the only other solution I see for your future is marriage."

Mattie's head jerked up. For a moment she stared at him, speechless, then she found her voice: "I'm to have a Season, Uncle?"

Her uncle frowned. "At your age? Of course not!"

Mattie bit her lip and looked down at the letter on her lap.

"I have been in correspondence with an acquaintance of mine. A most worthy gentleman. He is seeking a wife. I have suggested to him that you might be suitable. Fortunately, he is prepared to overlook your age and lack of fortune and appearance on account of . . . er."

Mattie looked up. "On account of what, Uncle?"

Uncle Arthur cleared his throat. "Mr. Quartley has lost two wives in childbirth. He has only daughters. He wants an heir."

Mattie blinked. "And he thinks I can provide him with one?"

Her uncle's pallid cheeks colored faintly. His gaze slid away from hers. "You have childbearing hips," he muttered.

Mattie opened her mouth, and then closed it again. Childbearing hips. Uncle Arthur had written to Mr. Quartley about her *hips*.

Uncle Arthur continued briskly: "I have just received a letter from Mr. Quartley." He tapped a piece of paper lying on his desk. "He is arriving tomorrow and will stay for several days."

"Tomorrow?" Mattie said, startled.

"I expect you to do everything in your power to make him look favorably upon you." Her uncle's expression was stern.

"How . . . how old is Mr. Quartley?"

"That is irrelevant," her uncle said, shuffling paper on his desk.

Not to me. "How old is he, Uncle?"

"He is sixty."

Sixty! Mattie tried not to let her uncle see how appalled she was. "Um . . . how old are his daughters?"

"I believe that the youngest are still in the nursery," her uncle said evasively.

"And the eldest?"

"His eldest daughter was born the same year as Tobias."

Her mouth opened in a gasp. *Mr. Quartley has daughters who are older than me?*

Her uncle's eyebrows drew sharply together. "Must I remind you again, Matilda, that you are in no position to be particular?"

"No, Uncle," Mattie said hurriedly, standing. "I know." She tried to smile. "Thank you. I am most grateful." It was a lie; it wasn't gratitude she felt, but horror. *Sixty! More than twice my age!*

Uncle Arthur looked at the unopened letter in her hands. "And please ask your friend to confine her letters to one page in the future. One shilling and fourpence that cost me!"

Mattie bowed her head. "Yes, Uncle. I apologize."

Her uncle sniffed. "You may go now."

Mattie hurried upstairs. In the privacy of her bedchamber, she tore open Anne's letter. Just as she'd thought, a letter from her publisher was tucked inside. Mattie closed her eyes for a moment, holding the letter to her breast—*Please let him want the memoir!*—and then she broke the seal with trembling fingers.

She read swiftly, and with growing hope. Mr. Brunton liked Chérie's *Memoir*. He wished to publish it. He named a sum that made the breath catch in her throat. *Two hundred pounds!* It was a fortune. Enough to buy a small boarding house.

Mattie closed her eyes, feeling light-headed. No more charity. She could be independent.

She opened her eyes and reread that marvelous sentence: Two hundred pounds.

Of course, two hundred pounds wouldn't last forever. If she wished to keep food on her plate, she'd need to pen more confessions. But the boarding house would be hers.

Mattie blew out a breath. She resumed reading. *My partner and I are of the opinion, however, that the memoir requires an additional chapter before it can be published. At present, it traces Chérie's journey from young widow to courtesan to wife. One important milestone is lacking. The most important milestone, perhaps! We strongly feel that your loyal readers would wish to experience the very beginning of Chérie's journey, namely the surrender of her virgin flower to her ill-fated husband.*

Upon receipt of this chapter, payment will be deposited in your name and the memoir will be most expeditiously published.

I remain, yours, etc.,

Samuel Brunton, Esq.

Mattie stared at the letter. One more chapter. "I can do that," she said.

Casting the letter aside, she scrambled off the bed and crossed to the hidden cupboard.

The countess's diary began several months after her wedding night. Her growing intimacy with the groom was described in its pages, from their first kiss to when they had run away together. Mattie turned to the entry detailing their first sexual encounter. She read, frowning. The countess dwelt mainly on the gentleness and tenderness of the groom, and her astonishment at the physical sensations she experienced. *Nothing could have been more different from that dreadful night when my husband wrested my virginity from me! I had not dreamed that such wondrous pleasure was possible.*

Mattie sighed. There was nothing helpful in those passages.

"The surrender of her virgin flower," she muttered as she thumbed through the copy of *Fanny Hill*.

She found the passage detailing Fanny's loss of virginity and skimmed it quickly. *Extreme pain . . . reek of virgin blood.* Mattie pulled a face. How true to life was that?

She flicked ahead further, to where the young whores swapped accounts of the loss of their maidenheads. *I lay utterly passive,* the first one said, *till the piercing pain rous'd and made me cry out. But the pleasure rising as the pain subsided, I was soon reconciled to fresh trials, and before morning, nothing on earth could be dearer to me than this rifler of my virgin deserts.*

Mattie snorted. She turned ahead to the next description and read quickly. *A sense of pain that pierced me to my vitals . . . streams of blood.*

"Streams of blood!" she said aloud. "Streams!"

Mattie closed the book with a snap and resisted the urge to throw it at the wall. "Claptrap!" How could anyone *believe* such nonsense?

It had been written by a man, she reminded herself. For men. Which would account for its absurdity.

Well, *she* wouldn't write something so patently ridiculous! Chérie's virginity scene would be tender, titillating, and realistic.

The only problem was, she didn't know what realistic was. Exactly how much blood and pain did the loss of one's virginity entail?

Frowning, Mattie replaced the diary and two volumes of *Fanny Hill* in their hiding place. How could she find out?

She closed the secret cupboard and went in search of Cecy.

Cecy wasn't in Lady Marchbank's parlor, or the downstairs parlor, or the library—but in the doorway of the latter room Mattie met Edward Kane.

"Miss Chapple," he said cheerfully, bending his head slightly to avoid touching the lintel. "Good morning."

Absurdly, her pulse fluttered at the sight of him. It was his height and his solidness, the smile in his eyes.

"I've been looking for you," he said.

Mattie blinked. "For me?" Sudden fear struck her, tightening her throat. *He knows!*

Mr. Kane nodded. "I'm riding into Soddy Morton to attend to . . . uh, that business of your uncle's. I wondered if there were any commissions I might perform for you while I'm there?"

Mattie found herself able to breathe again. "Thank you," she said. "But there's nothing I require."

"Nothing from the baker's?" Mr. Kane asked, his tone faintly teasing.

He loomed in the doorway, huge, scarred, draped in shadows. He should have been frightening; instead, he was dangerously attractive. That smile hovering on his mouth, that silent laughter in his eyes . . .

Mattie felt herself blush. She felt flustered, as if she were seventeen, not twenty-seven. "No, thank you," she said hurriedly.

"As you wish," Mr. Kane said. He dipped his head to her and turned away. She heard his footsteps echo in the corridor.

Foolish girl! Mattie scolded herself. *To be overset by a smile!* Mr. Kane's kindness towards her didn't mean anything. Unlike Mr. Quartley, he wasn't looking for a wife.

She found Cecy in the morning room, which should have been flooded with sunlight but was shrouded in gloom on this gray, wintry day. "My aunt is napping?"

"Yes." Cecy glanced up from her embroidery. "Have you been out walking? I couldn't find you."

"No, I was in my uncle's study." Mattie sat alongside her friend. "Cecy . . ." How to broach the subject of losing one's virginity? Not for the first time she wished she could tell Cecy the truth. *Not yet,* she told herself. *Not until I have the money.* "My uncle is encouraging me to marry."

"Marry!" Interest lit Cecy's face. "Who?"

"An acquaintance of his."

"Oh? That's good."

Mattie grimaced.

Cecy's eyebrows rose. "It's not good?"

"He's sixty."

"Oh."

"I was wondering . . ." Mattie cleared her throat. "The first time one performs one's marital duty . . . how painful is it?"

Cecy's mouth opened and then closed. After a moment she said, "It is rather painful."

"Did you faint?"

Cecy blinked. "Faint? Of course not!" She laid down her embroidery. "It's not *that* painful. It's like . . . like stubbing one's toe."

"Oh," Mattie said, thinking of *Fanny Hill's* fainting heroines. "Um . . . is there any blood?"

Cecy's brow creased. "I don't remember. A little bit, perhaps."

"Not streams of blood?"

Cecy laughed. "No! Of course not! Whoever told you that?"

"I . . . um, can't recall."

Cecy leaned forward. "Don't worry about it," she said earnestly. "The first time is painful and . . . and awkward and a shock in its newness, but after that . . ." She shrugged. "It's uncomfortable and messy, but one gets used to it. It never takes very long. A few minutes at most."

"Oh."

Cecy picked up her embroidery again. She set a stitch. "If this man should offer for you," she said diffidently. "Will you marry him?"

"I haven't even met him!"

"Yes, but . . ." Cecy looked up. "A husband, Mattie. Children. It's what every woman wants."

Mattie looked down at her lap. She smoothed the gray fabric of her gown over her knees. *Then I must be an unnatural woman.* "All I want is a home of my own. Which I hope to have shortly." She looked up. "And I hope you will join me. Just think, Cecy! In Scarborough or Brighton you would meet many eligible bachelors. You wouldn't have to settle for Mr. Humphries."

Cecy sighed. Her gaze fell to the embroidery, but she didn't ply the needle. "He doesn't compare well to other men, does he?"

"Mr. Humphries?" Mattie shook her head. "Mr. Kane is a thousand times more attractive, for all he is so scarred!"

"And Sir Gareth Locke."

"Sir Gareth?"

Color crept across Cecy's cheeks.

Mattie stared at her friend. "You like Sir Gareth?"

Cecy picked up her needle again. "I don't know him well enough to make that judgment."

"But . . . ?" Mattie prompted.

Cecy's blush deepened. "He has a nice face."

Mattie considered this for a moment, and then nodded. Gareth Locke did have a pleasant face—marked with pain, but attractive nonetheless.

But his friend, Edward Kane, was far more attractive, despite the red scars that slashed across his cheeks and brow. She liked the square solidity of his jaw, the humor in his eyes.

What would it be like to be married to Edward Kane?

Mattie pushed the thought away. She cleared her throat. "Did you get the impression that Sir Gareth is looking for a wife?"

Cecy refused to meet her eyes. "Perhaps," she said, and then she bent all her attention to her embroidery.

Back in her bedchamber, Mattie sat down at her writing desk. On it were fresh sheets of paper, a newly trimmed quill, and an inkwell. She stared at the paper, turning over in her head what she would write. No streams of blood, she decided firmly. And no fainting.

She picked up the quill and dipped it in ink. *Dear reader, I begin my memoir with that momentous event in a woman's life: the plucking of her virgin flower. This occurred on my wedding night, when I was a shy and blushing maiden, not yet eighteen years of age. The mixture of anticipation and apprehension within my bosom you can well imagine, for I was quite innocent and had no idea what to expect.*

Mattie rubbed her brow. Now what?

Pain and awkwardness, according to Cecy.

She glanced out the window. Edward Kane was riding across the fields to Soddy Morton.

In the act of intercourse, how much of a woman's pleasure depended upon the man she lay with? Mattie tapped the quill against her chin, pondering this question, while her eyes followed Mr. Kane.

According to Cecy, intercourse was an uncomfortable and messy experience; according to the countess, it could be wondrously pleasurable. And yet both had loved the men they'd lain with.

Mattie frowned. What could she conclude from that?

That the groom knew what he was doing, and Cecy's husband didn't.

Mattie followed Mr. Kane's progress across the fields. He was a giant of a man, broad-shouldered and barrel-chested, battered and scarred, but something about him—the gentleness with which he'd handled the kittens, the laughter in his eyes—made her fancy that he'd be like the countess's groom. A good lover.

Mattie tore her eyes from Mr. Kane's distant figure and turned her attention firmly back to Chérie's wedding night.

Edward found Gareth in the private parlor of Soddy Morton's inn, midway through a late and leisurely breakfast. He looked at the food spread out on the table, at the tankard of ale by his friend's elbow, and experienced a moment of pure envy.

Gareth grinned. "Sit," he said around a mouthful of sirloin. "Eat."

Edward needed no second urging. He pulled up a chair.

"So what's this about Chérie?" Gareth asked, as the servant went off to procure a second tankard of ale.

"I promised Strickland I'd look for her."

"Why?"

Edward grimaced. "So he can run her out of the village." He reached for a plate and began to pile food on it.

The servant returned with the tankard of ale. Edward took a deep swallow. *Bliss.* He began to attack his food. Between bites of sirloin he told Gareth how he'd come to offer his aid to Strickland.

Gareth shook his head. "You're far too soft-hearted." He pushed his plate away and leaned back in his chair. "Toby would've been the first to toast Chérie."

"I know, damn it."

"Then why on earth are you—"

"Because I gave my word of honor!"

Gareth shook his head, grinning. "You're a fool, Ned."

Edward didn't disagree.

He spent several frustrating hours in Soddy Morton, running to ground the last four letter writers on his list. First was Farmer Plinhoe, a stolid, worthy man who was—in Edward's opinion—no more capable of writing Chérie's confessions than he was of dancing on the moon. Next, he crossed the apothecary's wife off the list, a hubble-bubble female with more hair than wit, followed half an hour later by Miss Spencer, the butcher's daughter, who was eight years old. Which left one name on his list: Mrs. Thomas.

Mrs. Thomas's cottage wasn't a particularly attractive specimen. Nor was Mrs. Thomas. She was a slatternly woman, running to fat, with a heavy, jowled face. It wouldn't have surprised Edward if she had once been a whore, but Chérie she most definitely was not. Mrs. Thomas was vulgar and not particularly intelligent, and Chérie—whatever else she was—was neither of those things.

Scowling, Edward rode back to Soddy Morton. "Who the blazes is Chérie?" he demanded of Gareth, striding into the private parlor at the inn and casting his hat upon the table.

Gareth glanced up from the newspaper he was reading. He shrugged. "I don't know," he said. "I don't particularly care, either."

Edward grunted. He stripped off his gloves and threw them down alongside his hat. He settled himself in an armchair beside the blazing fire. Unlike the chairs at Creed Hall, the armchair was sturdy. It didn't groan beneath his weight. "I'm going to die in Soddy Morton," he said glumly.

Gareth laughed.

"If you were staying at the Hall, you wouldn't laugh." Edward slumped deeper in the armchair. "God-awful food. Freezing rooms."

"Don't forget the sermons."

Edward closed his eyes and basked in the warmth of the fire. "Don't get me started on the sermons." Although Miss Chapple's voice was very pleasant to listen to.

"No wonder Toby hardly ever went home."

Edward grunted—and thought about Chérie. Where had he gone wrong? He'd been so certain Chérie was one of the people on the list . . . and yet she wasn't. *I made a mistake somewhere.* But where?

He opened his eyes and pushed to his feet. The letter had been found in Soddy Morton; therefore, Chérie lived here. He would find her. Somehow.

"Where are you going?"

"Creed Hall." Where the fires were too small and the food as bad as any he'd ever eaten on campaign. "But I'll come down here and dine with you tonight."

"I'll be up at the Hall."

"What?"

Gareth shrugged. "Strickland invited me to dine at Creed Hall for as long as I'm in Soddy Morton."

"And you accepted? Are you insane?"

"Apparently."

Edward observed his friend for a moment, then turned away. "Pretty little thing, Mrs. Dunn," he said casually while he pulled on his gloves.

"Is she?" Gareth said, returning to his newspaper. "I hadn't noticed."

"Looks a lot like Miss Swinthorp, I thought."

Gareth lowered the newspaper. "She's nothing like Miss Swinthorp!"

"Pretty. Blonde. Petite."

"Anyone would look petite alongside Miss Chapple. She's a colossus."

Edward bridled. "She's not a colossus. She's statuesque!"

Gareth's eyebrows rose. "Touchy."

Edward felt himself flush. He crammed his hat on his head and strode to the door.

"That wasn't a slur, by the way. On your Miss Chapple."

"She's not my Miss Chapple," Edward said. And he shut the door behind him with rather too much force.

Back at Creed Hall, in the gloom and the chill of the entrance hall, Arthur Strickland waylaid him. "Have you found anything yet?" the old man asked.

"Not yet, sir," Edward said. "But I will soon." *Because I'm damned if I'm going to stay in this wretched place for much longer.*

He looked in the library. Miss Chapple wasn't there. Nor was she in the drawing room or the parlor.

He climbed the stairs, and met her on the first landing. She wore stout half boots, a bonnet, and a thick cloak.

"Going for a walk?"

She nodded.

"May I accompany you?"

Miss Chapple led him on a different route this time, looping around the gray lake from the south. They fell into an easy way of conversing, as if they'd known one another for years. Her frank, open manner, her laugh, her sense of humor, reminded him of Toby. She was an unusual woman, quite unlike the simpering females one met in London's ballrooms.

But then, simpering wouldn't sit well on a female who was six feet tall.

"How are you progressing with *Pride and Prejudice*?" Miss Chapple asked.

"Slowly," Edward replied. "I've been reading something else. Er . . . business matters."

"Oh?" Her nose wrinkled. "How dull for you."

He had an abrupt recollection of the confessions he'd last read: the bashful young gentleman, the brawny sailor. *No. Not dull.*

Edward cleared his throat. Memory of the confessions made him uncomfortably aware of Miss Chapple's physical charms. They were quite abundant: the deep bosom, the ripe hips. She had a robust, voluptuous figure. "I shall read a few chapters of *Pride and Prejudice* tonight," he promised.

They maintained a brisk pace, covering the two miles to the lake in half an hour. "How's your leg?" Miss Chapple asked, when they halted at the lakeshore.

"Fine, thank you." The pewter-colored water rippled sluggishly before a raw breeze. How the devil was he to find Chérie? The answer came as he gazed across the dismal lake. He turned to her. "How well do you know the villagers, Miss Chapple?"

"Oh, I know everyone! Why?"

Against this bleak backdrop, her cheeks flushed with exertion and her gray eyes sparkling, Miss Chapple was almost beautiful. The straight nose, the high brow, the lush mouth . . . Edward shifted his weight. "As you know, I'm attending to a piece of business for your uncle. Looking for someone."

The smile faded from Miss Chapple's face.

"I was wondering . . . is there anyone you can think of in the village who has come into money recently?"

Miss Chapple blinked. "Money?"

"Yes," Edward said, feeling foolish. "Someone who has money that can't reasonably be accounted for."

Her eyes were fixed on his face.

"The person I'm looking for is engaged in an activity that . . . that would earn them money."

"What kind of activity, Mr. Kane?"

"I'd rather not say."

Her gaze dropped. "Forgive me, Mr. Kane. I didn't mean to pry."

"No, no," Edward said hastily. "There's nothing to forgive. It's merely that . . ." *Merely what?* Damn it, why had he promised Strickland he'd find Chérie? He sighed. "I should never have agreed to do this for your uncle. Call me a fool, Miss Chapple. Gareth does!"

She glanced up at him. A smile glimmered in her eyes. "I would never be so rude."

They resumed strolling along the muddy path. Edward looked sideways at her, seeing nut-brown hair half-hidden beneath an ugly bonnet, and smooth, creamy skin, and cheeks flushed pink in the chill air.

"You should wear red. Once you're out of mourning." And then he bit his tongue. Where had those words come from?

Miss Chapple glanced down at her gown. "Gray is a practical color. It wears well."

"You mean . . . ?"

"I mean that I always wear gray, Mr. Kane. Whether I'm in mourning or not."

"All the time?" Edward said in disbelief.

She nodded, and then laughed at his expression. "I've shocked you!"

"But . . . a red scarf," he said. "Red gloves! Red ribbons on your bonnet."

"And how, pray, would I buy such things?"

He recalled her words from yesterday: *I have no money*. "I shall buy some red ribbons when I'm next in the village."

The amusement vanished from Miss Chapple's face. "Oh, please don't!"

Edward frowned. "Why not?"

"Because my uncle *particularly* dislikes baubles and ribbons and such. He thinks they're a sign of vanity."

"Vanity?"

She nodded. "So, please, Mr. Kane, *don't* buy ribbons for me!"

But cherry-red ribbons would look good on her. Either trimming that plain bonnet, or even better, wound through her hair. The color would enhance the rosy flush of her cheeks and the rich brown of her hair.

Your uncle is a miserable clutch-fist. But Edward didn't say the words aloud. Instead, he said: "Very well. No ribbons."

Miss Chapple smiled her relief. "Thank you."

Edward didn't reply. He frowned across the lake. The steeply pitched rooftop of Creed Hall was visible through the trees. *Someone needs to rescue her*.

*C*HAPTER 8

"*Y*ou didn't answer my question, Miss Chapple," Mr. Kane said, as they started back around the lake.

"Which question was that?"

"Have any of the villagers come into money within the last few months?"

"Oh . . ." Mattie bit her lip and pondered how to answer this. She glanced at Mr. Kane, seeing the square jaw, the laughter lines creasing the corners of the eyes, the cruel scars that scored his skin.

He had a nice face. The sort of face one could trust. She wished she could confide her secret in him.

Don't! an urgent voice whispered in her head. *He'll tell Uncle Arthur.*

She imagined confessing her secret, imagined watching the smile drain from Mr. Kane's face, imagined him stepping back, his expression changing from friendliness to contempt.

What she was doing was so far beyond the pale that there was no one word for it. It was sordid, shameless, unforgivable. People would look at her with all the condemnation they'd reserve for a woman who truly *was* a courtesan; worse, perhaps, because she'd dared to write about such things and sell them for public consumption.

The urge to tell Mr. Kane shriveled in her breast. "Come into money?" Mattie said, prevaricating.

"Yes."

Which was worse? To send Mr. Kane on a wild goose chase, or to set him on the trail of an innocent villager?

Both were contemptible.

Mattie cast about for a third option. There wasn't one—except the confession of her secret. "I can't think of anyone who's come into money, but . . . but . . . Miss Eccles might know."

"Miss Eccles?"

"She's a retired governess." Guilt twisted in Mattie's breast as she uttered the words. She *liked* Edward Kane, and yet she was deceiving him. "She lives on the other side of the village. She knows everyone and everything."

His eyes lit with interest. "That sounds promising."

Mattie nodded, feeling slightly ill.

"Miss Eccles lives alone?"

Mattie nodded again.

"Er . . . perhaps you could accompany me to visit her?"

She lifted her eyebrows in a silent question.

"My face alarms ladies. I look rather villainous." Mr. Kane smiled, making the comment partly—but not wholly—a joke.

"Hardly villainous!"

He shrugged. "You think Miss Eccles will happily confide Soddy Morton's secrets to me?"

Mattie bit her lip. With his towering build and that scarred face . . . To an elderly lady, he probably would look quite terrifying. "It would be my pleasure to accompany you, Mr. Kane."

"Thank you."

Mattie felt herself blush. Something about his smile made the day seem brighter, as if the sun had come out from behind the clouds. She looked down and scuffed the ground with her toe.

"Tomorrow morning?" Mr. Kane asked.

"Certainly," Mattie said, and wondered if there was some way she could delay visiting Miss Eccles for a couple of days.

But delaying the interview with Miss Eccles would entail yet more deception.

They resumed walking. Mattie trod miserably through the mud alongside Mr. Kane. It wasn't meant to be like this: lie upon lie upon lie.

The path dipped into a dank hollow, then climbed a steep rise. Mr. Kane began to limp slightly. Mattie slowed her pace.

Mr. Kane glanced at her, smiling. "Tired?"

"Your leg," she said. "You're limping."

"No, I'm not." The faint drag in his stride disappeared. He picked up their pace again—but after a few yards, he slowed. "Perhaps a little," he admitted.

Mr. Kane's limp vanished once the path leveled, but even so, Mattie kept their pace slow. They strolled back towards Creed Hall. The woods were dark and bare and almost funereal. Guilt built inside her with each step that she took, until it clogged her chest and throat. It was unconscionable that Mr. Kane be tied to Soddy Morton, wasting his time in a fruitless search, unconscionable that she be deceiving him.

They reached the stableyard. Mattie halted. "Mr. Kane, leave Soddy Morton!" The words burst from her. "Let me conduct your search!"

Mr. Kane blinked. "I beg your pardon?"

"I know you've promised my uncle to find someone, but there's no reason for you to stay here," Mattie said urgently. "*I* can look for you. I know the villagers! It will be much easier for me!"

"No," Mr. Kane said firmly. "It's not the sort of thing a lady should be involved in."

He didn't want her to have anything to do with Chérie. The irony of it almost made Mattie cry. "But you can't wish to stay here, Mr. Kane. Creed Hall is . . . it's . . . You can't *like* being here!"

"I have given my word to see this matter to the end, Miss

Chapple. And I always keep my word." The sternness left his face. He smiled. "Is my company so disagreeable that you wish to see me gone?"

"No, of course not!" To her annoyance, Mattie felt heat rise in her cheeks. "It's merely . . . I don't like to see you trapped here when there are any number of things you'd rather be doing!"

"Trapped?" The smile faded. "Is that how *you* feel?"

Mattie bit the tip of her tongue. She looked down at the ground. "I am very grateful for my uncle's hospitality."

"Yes," Mr. Kane said. "Of course you are. Forgive me for asking. Shall we go inside?"

Mattie worked on the memoir until dinner, laboring over Chérie's emotions upon her first sight of a naked man. *My beloved Joseph stripped off his clothes. I gazed upon him with awe. He looked like the statue of a Greek god, perfect in his proportions, manly yet beautiful.*

"No," she said aloud, and scratched out the last two sentences. She tried again: *I gazed upon him in a mixture of trepidation and awe, and shrank back as he approached me.*

"Don't be afraid," he whispered, stroking his hand down my cheek. "I won't hurt you."

Reassured, I relaxed into his embrace.

Then what? Mattie frowned and glanced at the clock. Hurriedly she hid the pages and went downstairs for dinner. Several hours later, when she returned to her bedchamber, she picked up where she'd left off.

Tenderly, he divested me of my clothing. I blushed and shrank shyly from his heated gaze. Emotions rose in my breast. Fear was foremost, but close on its heels was an eager impatience to become an initiate of the mysteries of womanhood. My heart beat within my chest like the wings of a caged songbird. I was in the grip of such a painful mix of terror and anticipation that I felt myself close to swooning.

Joseph led me to the bed and bade me lie down and set himself most enthusiastically to the task of plucking my virgin flower.

Mattie frowned at the last sentence for a long time, and then crossed out *enthusiastically* and replaced it with *tenderly*.

He soothed my fears with soft kisses and then . . .

And then what?

Awkwardness. Mess. Pain. Blood.

Mattie stared at the page until the ink had dried on the nib of her quill. No inspiration came.

She reached for a fresh sheet of paper, dipped the quill in the inkwell again, and started on the next scene.

I was a woman now, initiated into that most wonderful mystery of womanhood. I gazed at Joseph, slumbering alongside me, and knew myself to be the happiest of mortals.

But alas, dear reader, little did I know that in less than a month my beloved Joseph would be torn most cruelly and fatally from me, the victim of a tragic accident, and that I should be forced to walk quite a different path from that which lay shining before me in that happy moment.

Mattie wrote swiftly, detailing Chérie's descent from blissful bride to inconsolable widow. In a few words, she ruthlessly dispatched of any relatives who might have been able to help the young relict and reduced Chérie to homelessness.

As I stood weeping, with nowhere to go but the poorhouse, I became aware that I was being addressed by a stranger, a tall and handsome young woman who was most elegantly dressed in the latest style. "Pray tell me, why do you cry so?" she enquired.

Upon hearing my sorry tale, she exclaimed that she had the solution to my problems. At first I refused most vehemently. What she proposed was in every way repugnant to me! But gradually her persuasive words overcame my scruples. Her evident prosperity, her claims of the superiority of the house to which she was attached, her eloquent portrayal of my plight, convinced me that I had but one course ahead of me.

Miss Abbott (for that was the name she went by) praised my decision effusively. My physical charms and youth, she predicted, would soon see me most satisfactorily established.

And thus it was, dear reader, that I, penniless and alone in the world, with my beloved Joseph not yet cold in his grave, embarked upon that oldest of professions.

I put aside both my true name and my virtue and became Chérie.

Mattie reread what she'd written. Yes, that would do.

She shivered. Her fingers were almost numb with cold. The clock on the mantelpiece told her it was past midnight. She hid the pages in the secret cupboard and climbed into bed. Wind rattled the window in its casement. An icy draft crept through the shutters, stirring the stink of her tallow candle. Mattie shivered again. In a few short hours she would accompany Mr. Kane to visit Miss Eccles.

"Please let it rain," she whispered as she blew out the candle. "Please, *please* let it rain."

It didn't rain, and the visit to Miss Eccles was every bit as dreadful as Mattie had anticipated. The elderly spinster was delighted to receive visitors. Mattie sat, sunk in miserable guilt, while Miss Eccles conversed with Mr. Kane, her thin cheeks becoming flushed with animation and her faded eyes sparkling as she discussed her favorite subject: Soddy Morton and its inhabitants.

Mr. Kane introduced the topic of unexpected windfalls.

Miss Eccles knew of a number of people who'd come into money; she proceeded to list them.

"None from Soddy Morton?" Mr. Kane said with a smile. "An unlucky village!"

Miss Eccles clucked her tongue at this. "Not at all, Mr.

Kane! Not at all! Why, Mrs. Starling came into money recently, and so did . . ."

Mattie stopped listening. She stared down at her hands, clenched on her lap. *I am a despicable person.*

She walked back to Creed Hall with Mr. Kane across the fallow fields. The sky seemed to press down on them, heavy clouds riding just above the bare treetops. Mattie's thoughts turned in a tight, unhappy loop as she trudged through the mud. Her eyes were gritty with tiredness.

"Are you quite all right, Miss Chapple?" Mr. Kane asked when they reached the final field.

The question startled Mattie out of her reverie. She glanced at him. "Perfectly. Why?"

"You were frowning."

"Oh. Was I?" She tried to laugh. "I can't think why!"

Guilt, a silent voice told her. And although she tried to prevent it, she felt the frown settle on her brow again, pinching between her eyebrows.

"What is it, Miss Chapple?"

Mr. Kane's voice was so kind, the smile in his eyes so friendly, his expression so sympathetic, that for a moment Mattie hovered on the brink of confiding in him—and then common sense reasserted itself. "Oh, nothing!" she said, casting about for a reason. "We're expecting another guest tonight and . . . and I'm not looking forward to it."

"May I ask why not?"

She pulled a face. "He's coming to look me over. Like a cow being chosen for breeding."

Mr. Kane halted, his eyebrows rising. "A cow?"

Heat flooded Mattie's cheeks. She looked down at the ground, mortified. "I beg your pardon! I shouldn't have spoken so . . . so crudely."

"A cow?" Mr. Kane repeated.

"I beg your pardon. I should never have said such a thing." She'd spoken as if he was Toby, when he was practically a stranger.

"Please don't apologize. Your frankness is . . . refreshing."

She glanced at him. There was no censure on his scarred face, just amusement.

Her heart skipped a beat and then sped up. Mattie looked away from him. "It's Toby's fault." She tried to make her voice light, joking. "He told me so much about you—about you and Sir Gareth both—that I feel as if I know you far better than I actually do!"

"Everyone should have someone they can talk to without having to guard their tongue," Mr. Kane said.

She glanced at him, meeting his eyes. Time seemed to stand still for a moment, as if the earth had stopped spinning on its axis and the world held its breath.

Mattie ducked her head and began to walk again, squelching through the muddy field towards Creed Hall.

Mr. Kane fell into step beside her. "Is this gentleman really coming to . . . er, look you over?"

"Yes."

Mr. Kane walked in silence beside her for several seconds, and then ventured: "He may be more amiable than you anticipate."

"He's sixty," Mattie said bluntly. "He has children older than I."

"Ah."

She glanced at him. *Tell me I'll be lucky if he offers for me.*

Mr. Kane didn't. He frowned and said nothing.

As if from nowhere, rage surged inside her. "Mr. Quartley wants an heir, and my uncle thinks I may be able to provide him with one because of my childbearing hips." *I am not a piece of livestock, Uncle, I am a person. There is more to me than the width of my hips!* Mattie laughed, an angry sound. "What he seems to have forgotten is that Stricklands don't breed

120

well. My Aunt Marchbank never fell pregnant and my mother succeeded only once, and that after ten years of marriage."

Mr. Kane glanced at her, but said nothing.

Mattie's anger died away. In its place was mortification. "I apologize," she said again, ashamed. She should never have said such things to a man who she barely knew.

"Not at all, Miss Chapple. I meant what I said: everyone should have someone they can talk to without guarding their tongue."

Her throat tightened. For a horrible moment she thought she was going to burst into tears in front of him. How could someone she'd known only a few days seem so much like her friend?

The elderly groom, Hoby, was shoveling up a fresh pile of horse droppings in the stableyard. "Who's arrived, Hoby?" Miss Chapple asked. "Not Mr. Quartley already?"

"Don't know 'is name," Hoby said, leaning on the shovel. "The chap with one arm."

"Sir Gareth Locke," Miss Chapple said. "He was a friend of Toby's."

"Thought 'e likely was," Hoby said, and returned to his shoveling.

They scraped their boots and entered Creed Hall through a side door. Edward followed Miss Chapple down the gloomy corridor. The sound of voices came faintly to his ears: Gareth's, and a light female voice.

"Oh, good," Miss Chapple said, pulling off her gloves. "Cecy's with him."

Gareth and Mrs. Dunn were in the library. Edward halted in the doorway for a moment to watch. Mrs. Dunn sat with her back to them, but Gareth's face was clearly visible. His expression—intent, focused—gave Edward a twinge of foreboding.

Gareth glanced up and saw them. He stood. "Miss Chapple."

Miss Chapple advanced into the library, taking off her bonnet. "Sir Gareth. How lovely to have you visit us! Mrs. Dunn has been looking after you, I see."

Gareth smiled at Mrs. Dunn. "She has."

Edward's foreboding intensified.

Miss Chapple rang for a fresh pot of tea. Edward, even though he'd drunk more than enough tea at Miss Eccles's, accepted a cup. He sat across from Mrs. Dunn and watched her narrowly while he sipped.

There was nothing flirtatious about Mrs. Dunn's manner. She was everything that was demure and modest—and yet Edward's uneasiness grew with every laughing comment Gareth made to her, each blushing sideways glance she sent him.

To Mrs. Dunn, Gareth must seem like a gift from the gods: well-heeled, lonely, and clearly entranced by her looks. *Don't you dare try to ensnare him,* he warned her silently.

"Shall we see you tonight at dinner, Sir Gareth?" Miss Chapple asked.

Gareth's gaze returned to Mrs. Dunn. "You shall."

Edward had had enough. "Let's go for a ride," he said to Gareth. "Before it rains again. I'll show you the lake."

"Oh, yes!" Mrs. Dunn said. "You should, Sir Gareth. Who knows how long the rain will hold off?" She stood and smoothed her gown. "If you will excuse me, I must wake Lady Marchbank from her nap."

Gareth watched her leave the library, then turned to Edward with a sigh. With the smile gone from his face, the lines of recent pain and illness were easily seen. "A lake, you say?"

Mattie should have spent the rest of the day sewing her new gray gown; instead, she went back to work on Chérie's wedding night. Cecy's words—*awkward, uncomfortable, messy*—kept repeating in her head, stifling her imagination. Where, amid awkwardness and discomfort and mess, was there room for pleasure?

At four o'clock, the clatter of carriage wheels told her Mr. Quartley had arrived. Peering out the window, she saw a yellow-wheeled post-chaise. The postboys must have detoured through Gripton to bypass the washed-out bridge. If Mr. Quartley was as economical as her uncle, he wouldn't be pleased by the extra expense.

Mattie closed the shutters and lit a candle. She bent her concentration even more fiercely to the problem of Chérie's wedding night, while the mutton reek of melting tallow filled her bedchamber. *The novelty of the moment was mixed with awkwardness, and when Joseph breached that innermost sanctum of my body, I experienced pleasure and pain in equal measure.*

No. There was absolutely nothing titillating about so plain a description. Mattie crossed out the sentence and tried again. *Joseph took me to transports of pleasure, made more piquant by the seasoning of pain.*

No, that was even worse. It sounded like a recipe.

Mattie screwed up the page and started again. *In my innocence, I knew not what to expect when Joseph plucked my virgin flower. Both the agony and the attendant rapture were beyond my expectation. It felt as if I were being crucified and raised to Heaven at the same moment—*

No. That was more ridiculous even than *Fanny Hill*. Mattie rubbed her eyes. "Think!" she said aloud.

But no inspiration came. Finally, Mattie threw down the quill, burned the pages she'd written in the fireplace, and dressed for dinner. She surveyed herself in the spotted mirror. A cow for breeding.

She grimaced at her reflection, blew out the candle, and went downstairs.

Edward made Mr. Quartley's acquaintance in the parlor. Quartley was a short, stout squab of a man, with a florid face, meaty jowls, and a broad, snubbed nose. *He looks like a pig,* was Edward's first, involuntary thought. *Fattened up and ready for the spit.* He glanced at Miss Chapple.

Miss Chapple betrayed no emotion as she watched Mr. Quartley advance into the room. She curtsied and greeted him politely, her manner as dull and drab as her gray gown.

Quartley glanced at Miss Chapple's face dismissively, but took a more thorough survey of her figure. His eyes rested on her hips and then rose to her breasts, where they lingered long enough for Edward to feel a surge of outrage.

Arthur Strickland didn't notice. He completed the introductions, naming Gareth and Edward. "Friends of my late son."

Mr. Quartley bowed, a movement accompanied by the creak of a whalebone corset. "Pleased to make your acquaintance."

Edward smiled tightly.

They moved through into the dining room. For the third time, Edward heard Strickland explain the tenet of silence: "To aid our digestion."

It was all so awful—the food, the silence—that for a moment Edward was almost overcome by laughter. He clenched his jaw to hold it back. The clink of cutlery echoed in the room as the other diners began to eat. Edward forced himself to concentrate on his food. He speared a piece of boiled mutton on his fork and looked across the table.

Mr. Quartley was examining Miss Chapple. *To see whether she's a cow worth breeding from.* The urge to laugh vanished. There was absolutely nothing amusing about the thought of Quartley marrying Miss Chapple.

After the ladies had withdrawn, the port was brought out. During the time it took to drink one glass, Strickland and Quartley discussed the poor state of the nation's coaching inns, the laziness of postilions, and the general insolence of ostlers. On each of these subjects, they were in complete accord. Gareth glanced at Edward and rolled his eyes.

Finally, it was time to remove to the drawing room. Strickland led the way, thumping his cane. Quartley followed, wheezing slightly as he walked.

"My niece reads to us each evening," Strickland said, ushering his most recent guest into the drawing room.

"How delightful," Quartley said, his eyes finding Miss Chapple. Once again, he ignored her face. His gaze fastened on her breasts.

Edward suppressed a snarl.

They settled themselves with cups of tea. Miss Chapple rose and opened Fordyce's *Sermons.* "Sermon Six," she said. "On Female Virtue, with Domestic and Elegant Accomplishments."

Edward let his thoughts drift while he listened to her voice. He went over the three names he had from Miss Eccles. With luck he could visit them all tomorrow.

And then I can get the hell out of here.

He'd bundle Gareth into his curricle and take them both back to London. Creed Hall and Soddy Morton and husband-hunting widows would soon be forgotten.

"How often do we see them disfigured by affectation and caprice?" Miss Chapple read aloud. "How often disgraced and ruined by imprudence? What shameful inattention to the culture of their minds, in numberless instances."

Quartley sat in his chair, with his hands clasped over his belly, his eyes on Miss Chapple.

Edward followed his gaze, trying to see Miss Chapple as Quartley might. Her youthfulness, her evident good health, her bountiful figure, must make her extremely tempting. She looked fruitful. The sort of woman who would easily produce a healthy heir.

An image flashed into his head: Quartley untrussed from his corset, naked, straining over Miss Chapple as he attempted to impregnate her.

The image was so nauseating that bile actually rose in Edward's throat. He hastily gulped the last of his tea and placed his cup down. It tipped over in its saucer with a loud clatter. Miss Chapple paused in her reading.

"I beg your pardon," Edward said, righting the cup.

Her eyes smiled at him for a brief second, before she resumed reading. ". . . frequently occasioned by vacancy of thought, and want of occupation which expose the mind to every snare."

Edward fixed his gaze on the fireplace and kept it there. If Quartley was staring at Miss Chapple's breasts, he didn't want to know.

After an interminable hour, the sermon came to its end. Gareth left, and Edward made a grateful escape from the drawing room, climbing the stairs to his bedchamber. The room was frigid.

"I had 'em put a warm brick in yer bed," Tigh said, as he collected Edward's discarded clothes.

"And one for yourself, I hope."

Tigh grunted. "You can believe it."

Edward washed his face and brushed his teeth. Shivering, he climbed into bed. There was indeed a warm brick tucked beneath the covers.

With Tigh gone, he set himself the agreeable task of reading the remaining confessions Gareth had brought from London. The first, a tale of Chérie's involvement with a dashing young Grenadier of "splendid proportions," should have held him rapt, but when the Grenadier stripped off Chérie's clothes and ardently fondled her breasts, all Edward could think of was Mr. Quartley's scrutiny of Miss Chapple.

He shook his head to dispel the image and read further, to where Chérie and her lover sported in bed, but in his mind's eye Mr. Quartley replaced the young Grenadier, corpulent and wheezing, and Chérie became Miss Chapple, not enjoying her swain's attentions, but enduring them.

His hands clenched, crumpling the confession. If Quartley married Miss Chapple, if he bedded her . . .

It would be legal, but it would also be little better than rape. *She deserves so much better.*

My beloved Joseph was gentle, but his possession of my body wasn't without pain. I cried out as he plucked my virgin flower, and blood flowed onto the sheets, but with the pain came a quickening of pleasure. My body began to glory in his possession of me.

Mattie stared down at what she'd written. It sounded extremely unrealistic. How could there be pain and blood *and* pleasure?

She kneaded her forehead. A headache was building in her temples.

Finally, she gave up, hid the draft in the secret cupboard, and went to bed.

CHAPTER 9

In the morning, a light drizzle was falling. Edward rode into Soddy Morton and visited a farmer two miles east of the village, who, according to Miss Eccles, had recently been flush in the pocket. But neither the farmer nor his wife could read or write.

The drizzle became rain. Edward looked at the addresses he had—one three miles west of the village, one two miles south—and decided to call it a day.

Back at the Hall he changed into dry clothes and went downstairs, four slices of gingerbread wrapped in a handkerchief in one pocket. As he passed Strickland's study, he heard the murmur of male voices behind the closed door. Were Strickland and Quartley discussing Miss Chapple's suitability as a bride?

Edward grimaced.

He looked in the library, the drawing room, and the parlor. Miss Chapple was nowhere to be found. As he passed Strickland's study again, the door opened.

"Have you seen my niece?" Sir Arthur demanded.

"No, sir," Edward said. "Perhaps she went for a walk?"

"It's raining."

Edward shrugged. "Perhaps she's in her room."

"She's not!" the old man snapped.

Edward didn't offer another suggestion. He stood politely while Strickland scowled at him.

"Stupid girl," the old man muttered. "Disappearing now of all times!" He shut the door with something approaching a slam.

If Quartley is about to offer for her, she's picked the perfect time to disappear.

Edward headed for the stableyard. Hoby was in the stables, rubbing down Trojan.

"Miss Chapple in the hayloft?" Edward asked.

The elderly groom looked up from his task and nodded.

Edward climbed the ladder to the loft, and there, in the cozy dimness, he found Miss Chapple lying on her stomach on the hay. "The irresistible lure of kittens?" he said, as he stood with his elbows resting on the top rung.

"Yes," Miss Chapple said, and then she added with frank honesty: "And a desire to avoid Mr. Quartley."

Edward crawled up into the loft, breathing in the dusty, familiar scent. "Your uncle's looking for you."

"Do you know why?"

"Quartley, at a guess."

Miss Chapple pulled a face and returned her attention to the kittens.

Edward decided to be as frank as Miss Chapple. "Will you refuse his offer?"

"Yes," she said. And then, after a pause, "If he should offer."

Edward recalled the way Quartley had gazed at her breasts. "He'll offer."

Miss Chapple sighed.

One of the kittens began climbing up Edward's arm, its claws digging into the green superfine. He carefully detached the tiny creature and stroked it.

Miss Chapple cupped her chin in her hand and frowned at the other two kittens, rolling together in the hay. "If you were me, would you marry Mr. Quartley?"

"No."

She turned her head and transferred the frown to him. "Why not? He has money."

"He's too old. Too . . ." The only word he could think of was *grotesque*. He groped for another description. "Too portly."

"Portly." Miss Chapple snapped a stalk of hay in half. "Yes, he is that." Then she grinned at him. "Portly Quartley."

Edward was surprised into a laugh.

Miss Chapple's grin faded. She sighed. "I suppose I'd better go." She crawled over to the ladder.

"Oh," Edward said. "I forgot. I have this for you." He pulled the gingerbread from his pocket and held it out to her.

A smile lit Miss Chapple's face. "Gingerbread?"

Edward stared at her. In the dusky light, she looked like Venus. It was the abundant curves of her body, the lush and smiling mouth, the half-seen dimples.

The muscles in his throat and groin tightened. He wanted to reach for her, to kiss her, to tumble her in the hay.

Edward nodded.

Miss Chapple hesitated. She glanced in the direction of the Hall. "I think . . . if you don't mind, I'll deal with my uncle and Mr. Quartley first."

"Of course," Edward said. "I'll put it behind Herodotus for you."

"Thank you." She disappeared from sight.

Edward stayed where he was, a kitten cupped in one hand. Above his head, rain pattered on the roof tiles.

Venus. Ripe and beautiful.

"I'm going mad," he told the kitten. Then common sense reasserted itself. It wasn't madness, merely the natural urges of his body, dormant for so many months and now flaring to life again. A physical hunger for sex, combined with a shared moment of laughter and friendship, and a trick of the light. That was all it had been. Nothing more.

Mattie tapped on the door to her uncle's study. "Mr. Kane said that you wished to see me, Uncle Arthur?"

Her uncle looked up from the letter he was writing. "Where have you been?"

"In the stables, sir."

Her uncle sniffed. "The stable is no place for a lady. Come in, come in! Shut the door." He placed his quill in its holder and gestured to a chair. "Sit."

Mattie sat and folded her hands on her lap. She sent up a silent prayer. *Please let Quartley have decided I'm not suitable.*

"You will be pleased to know that Mr. Quartley has found you acceptable," her uncle said. "I have given him my permission to marry you."

Mattie's heart sank. "Thank you, Uncle, but . . ." She took a deep breath and squared her shoulders. "But I don't wish to marry him."

Her uncle's sparse eyebrows snapped together. "I beg your pardon?"

"I don't wish to marry Mr. Quartley."

"What?" Disbelief and indignation warred on her uncle's face. Indignation won. "You refuse him?"

"Yes, Uncle."

Uncle Arthur inhaled a hissing breath. The air around him seemed to bristle. He made a choking sound, as if rage had strangled his voice.

"I'm sorry, Uncle."

The apology didn't placate her uncle; if anything, it enraged him. Color flushed his pallid face. "After all the effort I've gone to? After Mr. Quartley has traveled all this way to see you?"

"I'm sor—"

"After everything I've done for you, you repay me with this . . . this *insolence*! This stupidity!"

Mattie bowed her head and stared down at her clasped hands. She was aware just how much she owed her uncle.

"Look at you! You'll never get a better offer!"

I know. Mattie looked up. "I'm sorry, Uncle. But I can't marry him."

"Not can't; *won't*." Fury vibrated in his voice.

"I'm sorry, Uncle," she said again.

"Sorry!" Uncle Arthur cried. "Get out!" He threw his quill at her. It missed. "Get out, you ungrateful creature! Get out!"

Mattie retreated upstairs to her bedroom. Her uncle's words rang in her ears. *Look at you! You'll never get a better offer!*

"I don't want a better offer," she said in a low, fierce voice as she laid her writing materials out on the little escritoire. "I don't want a husband. I just want to be *free*."

She sat down to finish the memoir, but it was impossible to concentrate. Her thoughts were too agitated. The words Uncle Arthur had thrown at her echoed in her head. *After all that I've done for you!*

Mattie closed her eyes. She bowed her head into her hands. *He's right. I am an ungrateful creature.* She might hate Creed Hall, might long to be free of it, but it was a thousand times better than a poorhouse. She owed Uncle Arthur for every bite of food she'd eaten in the past ten years, every stitch of clothing she'd worn. She owed him for the tallow candles she wrote by, for the ink, the quill, the paper, everything. It was a massive debt. One she'd never be able to repay.

Mattie opened her eyes and stared down at the blank piece of paper. Stupid. Insolent. Ungrateful. Yes, she was all those things.

Mattie sighed. She picked up the quill, dipped it in ink, and bent her thoughts to her most pressing problem: Chérie's wedding night.

In the afternoon, the clatter of carriage wheels heralded the arrival of a post-chaise. Ten minutes later the carriage left, presumably taking Mr. Quartley with it. Not long afterward, someone knocked softly on Mattie's door.

Mattie hastily covered her writing. "Yes?"

The door opened a crack. "It's me," Cecy said, peeping inside. "May I come in?"

"Of course."

Cecy closed the door quietly. She came and sat on the end of the bed. Her expression was sober. "I heard about Mr. Quartley. Are you all right?"

"I'm fine."

"Your uncle's very angry." Cecy pulled a face. "Did he shout at you?"

Mattie nodded. *Ungrateful, insolent, stupid.* "Cecy . . . do you believe it's better to be married to a man one dislikes than to be a spinster?"

Cecy frowned. "No," she said, after a moment. "I believe it's better to be married to a man one dislikes than to be a *penniless* spinster." Her gaze was steady. "But you won't be penniless, will you, Mattie?"

"No," Mattie said. *I hope not.*

Cecy smiled. "Then it doesn't matter, does it?" She stood. "I'd better get back to your aunt."

"What about Sir Gareth?" Mattie asked.

Cecy flushed. She looked down at her cuffs and straightened one of them. "What about him?"

"He seems to like you."

Cecy's blush deepened. She devoted all her attention to straightening her other cuff.

"Does he know he has Mr. Humphries for a rival?" Mattie said, unable to resist a little gentle teasing. "And Mr. Kane?"

Cecy looked up. "Mr. Kane doesn't like me."

"What? Of course he does!"

Cecy shook her head. "The way he looks at me . . . I think he disapproves of me."

"Nonsense!" Mattie said. "Why ever should he?"

"Perhaps he thinks I'm not good enough for Sir Gareth."

"Any man would be lucky to marry you," Mattie said emphatically. "You would be the perfect wife!"

Cecy sighed. "I should try to be." Her expression grew wistful. "I like Sir Gareth."

My beloved Joseph laid siege to my body, and when he at last broke through the barrier of my maidenhood I cried out at the pain of that invasion. But battered and bleeding though I was, I gloried in his possession of me.

Mattie grimaced and crossed out what she'd written. She dipped the quill in ink and tried again: *My beloved Joseph laid siege to my body, and like Joshua at Jericho, he carried all before him. My innocence was torn most absolutely from me, just as Jericho's walls fell most absolutely.*

No, that was even worse.

Mattie sighed. She rubbed her face and looked out the window again. The distant roofs of the village reminded her of the gingerbread Mr. Kane had brought back for her.

Mattie placed the quill in the holder and went downstairs. The library was dark and empty. In the distance she heard the thump of her uncle's cane.

She crossed to Herodotus's *Histories* and pulled out the first volume.

The thumping became louder. Mattie thrust the book back into place and turned to face the doorway.

Her uncle stamped into the library, a scowl on his face.

Mattie was conscious of a craven desire to stay hidden in the shadows. Instead, she drew in a breath and stepped forward. "Good afternoon, Uncle."

Her uncle's head lifted. His scowl deepened. "You."

Mattie dipped a curtsy. "Yes, Uncle. I . . . I'll just leave you in peace." She started towards the door.

"Peace!" Uncle Arthur said. "Peace! As if one can have a moment's peace when one encounters such insolence and ingratitude in one's household!"

Edward strode across the stableyard, scraped the worst of the mud from his boots, and entered Creed Hall through a side door. He paused to let his eyes adjust to the gloom. Strickland's voice came loudly from the library, punctuated by thumps from his cane. "You will never get a better offer! Never!" The old man's voice echoed down the corridor. "Look at you!"

Edward frowned. He walked quietly towards the library.

"You have nothing to recommend you." *Thump.* "Nothing at all!"

Edward halted to one side of the doorway. Strickland wasn't visible from this angle, but he could see Miss Chapple. She stood with her hands clasped and her head bowed, weathering the diatribe.

"Your age, your lack of fortune, your appearance, must all count against you!"

Anger kindled in Edward's chest. How dared Strickland say such things?

"Get out of here!" Strickland said, waving his cane at her. "Out of my sight!"

Edward backed away from the doorway. Seconds later, Miss Chapple emerged. She didn't see him, but hurried down the corridor in the direction of the entrance hall and staircase.

After a moment Edward followed, slowly stripping off his gloves. He climbed the stairs and hesitated at the top. Part of him wanted to find Miss Chapple.

It's none of your business, he told himself. *If she needs a friend, she'll turn to Mrs. Dunn.*

That evening, her uncle requested the sermon on female meekness. Mattie read it, aware of him glowering at her across the drawing room. His comments afterwards were particularly pointed.

It was a relief when the clock struck nine and she could finally go upstairs to her bedchamber. Mattie sat down at the escritoire and uncapped the inkwell. Tonight, she'd finish the wedding night scene. She *had* to.

But when she stared at the paper, all she could think of were the words her uncle had thrown at her in the library. Tears pricked her eyes. Mattie blinked them back fiercely. It was foolish to be so overset. Her uncle had only spoken the truth, only said aloud things that she thought every time she looked in the mirror.

Mattie blew her nose firmly and picked up the quill again.

Joseph applied himself most vigorously to the task of plundering my maidenhead. In my innocence I didn't know what to expect and as he forced his entrance into my body a cry of pain fell from my lips.

Mattie grimaced and crossed out the word *forced*. It sounded too brutal. She tried again.

As the barrier broke—

No, that sounded like something to do with construction.

As my maidenhead tore asunder—

No, that was too violent. Mattie flung down the quill in despair. She bowed her head into her hands and squeezed her eyes against more tears. "I can do this," she told herself aloud. The rest of the chapter was written; all she needed was this one scene. Blood and lost innocence, pain and awkwardness—fused with passion and pleasure.

Mattie blew out a breath and opened her eyes and stared down at the page. *What am I to do?*

No inspiration struck.

She remembered the gingerbread hidden in the library. For a moment she tasted it on her tongue—sweet, spicy, rich. Her stomach growled.

Mattie pushed back her chair, picked up the sputtering tallow candle, and let herself quietly out of her bedchamber. The corridor was dark, silent apart from the whisper of drafts.

She tiptoed down the creaking stairs. The longcase clock in the entrance hall struck the hour loudly as she passed. Mattie nearly dropped the candle. The flame jerked, almost snuffing out. The notes boomed in the entrance hall while her heart galloped in her chest and the candle struggled to stay alight.

When the last echo had faded, she set off down the corridor. The library was as black and cold as a tomb. The musty smell of old books was strong. Mattie groped behind Herodotus until her fingers found an object wrapped in a linen handkerchief. She lifted it down and folded back one corner. Several slices of gingerbread nestled inside, dark and dense. The scent wafted up.

Mattie took the handkerchief across to the sofa and curled up on the lumpy, under-stuffed seat, tucking her feet beneath her. She took out a slice and bit into it. It was perfection: moist, sweet, spicy. She closed her eyes and chewed slowly, savoring the taste.

She gave a sigh of pleasure, opened her eyes, and took another bite. She was chewing when a shadowy figure filled the doorway, holding a candle.

Mattie inhaled sharply, choked on a crumb, and began to cough.

"I beg your pardon, Miss Chapple," the person said, stepping into the library. "I didn't mean to startle you. I've come for the third volume of *Pride and Prejudice*."

Mattie hastily uncurled her legs and sat up properly. "Are you enjoying it?" she asked when she'd recovered her breath.

"Very much." Mr. Kane's face was heavily shadowed, the scars almost invisible. His teeth caught the candlelight as he smiled. "You were correct; it's a most entertaining read."

Mattie held out the gingerbread nestled in the handkerchief. "Would you like some?"

"Thank you." Mr. Kane took a slice and sat across from her in a leather armchair that creaked beneath his weight. He'd untied his neckcloth, but like her, was still fully clothed. Mattie averted her gaze from the sight of his bare throat. It seemed unnervingly intimate to glimpse his skin. "What do you think of Mr. Collins?"

Mr. Kane grinned around a piece of gingerbread. "Clearly based on Mr. Humphries," he said, once he'd finished chewing.

"Isn't he absurd? So self-important. So foolish!"

They dissected Mr. Collins's character, then moved on to his patroness, Lady Catherine de Bourgh. When the last of the gingerbread was eaten, Mr. Kane sighed, a satisfied sound. He leaned back in the armchair and stretched his legs out. "I shall buy some more tomorrow."

Mattie curled her legs under her again. It was cozy in the candlelight, informal and friendly. "Aren't you afraid you'll lose your taste for it if you have it every day?"

Mr. Kane shook his head. "I shan't be here much longer."

Mattie looked down at her lap. She brushed away a crumb. *I don't want you to go. You make Creed Hall so much more bearable.*

"Miss Chapple . . ."

She glanced at him.

"I . . . er, I couldn't help overhearing this afternoon. The things your uncle said to you."

Shame heated Mattie's cheeks.

"I beg your pardon," Mr. Kane said. "It wasn't my intention to eavesdrop. But, Miss Chapple—I must tell you that your uncle is quite wrong!"

"On the contrary, my uncle is perfectly correct. I have nothing to recommend me." Mattie forced her lips into a smile and said flippantly, "Other than my childbearing hips, of course."

"Nonsense!" Mr. Kane said. "You have a great deal to recommend you!"

Mattie's throat tightened. Tears stung behind her eyes. She blinked them back and took refuge in irony. "Such as my advanced age," she said dryly. "And my appearance and my—"

"Fustian! You are not at all old! And as for your appearance, I think that you look very well. There's no reason why you shouldn't contract an advantageous marriage."

Mattie shook her head. "When I was nineteen, it was made perfectly clear to me that my chances of marrying well are so slight as to be nonexistent."

"Who told you that?" Mr. Kane demanded.

"My uncle," she said. "When he told me that a Season would be a waste of time and money. And he was quite correct. Men like Mr. Quartley are the best I can hope for."

"Quartley?" He made a sound of disgust. "You can do better than him!"

"In Soddy Morton?" Mattie shook her head. "I am a giantess, Mr. Kane. And quite plain. I've been on the shelf for years. In fact, if I'm completely truthful, I've never been off it."

He pushed to his feet, an angry movement. "You are not a giantess! Nor are you plain!"

"Beauty is in the eye of the beholder," Mattie reminded him. "And most people would concur with my uncle."

"Well *my* eye says that you look very well!"

The words hung in the air for a long moment, echoing in the shadowy library. She thought that Mr. Kane colored faintly.

Mattie looked away from him. The handkerchief lay alongside her on the sofa. She picked it up and folded it. "Pray don't be angry on my account, Mr. Kane. I have plans for my future that involve neither a husband nor Creed Hall."

"Plans?"

She glanced up at him. "Yes, plans."

His eyes narrowed. "What kind of plans?"

"I shall run a boarding house with a friend."

"A boarding house!" His voice was as appalled as his face. "Miss Chapple, that's hardly—"

"It's better than Creed Hall," Mattie said, lifting her chin. "And better than portly Quartley."

Mr. Kane closed his mouth. After a moment he said, "Yes, I quite see that it is. But . . . a boarding house!"

"Boarding houses must be run by someone."

"Not young ladies!"

"Of course not," Mattie said, a tart note creeping into her voice. "Young ladies should marry and beget children, shouldn't they? Well, we both know that's not going to happen in my case!"

Mr. Kane's eyebrows lowered in a scowl. "You would be the perfect wife for the right man."

Mattie's annoyance with him evaporated. In its place was a flare of awareness of Mr. Kane. She looked down at the folded handkerchief in her lap and doubled it over again, making it even smaller. "I have always known I should be a spinster, Mr. Kane." She glanced up at him and forced a smile. "Don't picture me unhappy. In fact, I can't tell you how much I'm looking forward to the boarding house!"

Mr. Kane didn't return the smile. In the candlelight he was a towering figure. The shadowy, half-seen scars made him look quite savage.

Mattie's breath caught in her throat—not with fear, but with an emotion she thought might be lust. He was so intensely *male*.

Images flashed into her head—scenes the countess had described in her diary. If she stood and unbuttoned Mr. Kane's waistcoat and then pulled his shirt free of his breeches, if she slid her hand up to feel his chest . . . how hot would his skin be, how hard the muscles?

Mattie stood hastily. "Thank you for the gingerbread, Mr. Kane. It was perfectly delicious!" She headed for the door.

"I must disapprove of your intention to run a boarding house," Mr. Kane said to her back. "And I'm certain Toby would, too, were he alive."

Mattie froze. Had there been an underlying threat in those words? She turned back to face him. "You won't tell my uncle, will you?"

"No," Mr. Kane said. "But there must be an alternative, surely? Perhaps something that I can assist you with?"

A notion leapt into her mind. A shocking, scandalous notion that came straight from the pages of the countess's diary.

"No, thank you." *The only thing you can assist me with right now is writing Chérie's wedding night.*

"Miss Chapple, I know it's not my place, but . . . if I can be of service to you in any way, then I beg that you let me know." Mr. Kane's eyebrows twitched down into a frown and he qualified that statement: "In any way that does not result in you running a boarding house."

She stared at him. *Yes, there is a service you can perform for me. You can instruct me in a certain subject. Teach me what I need to know.*

Mattie bit down hard on her lower lip. She felt possessed of a recklessness and a heady sense of devil-may-care, like the time Toby had sneaked her a glass of brandy at Christmas. She knew she should say goodnight, knew she should hurry upstairs to her bedchamber and shut the door firmly behind her; but she didn't. She stayed where she was.

Carpe diem. Toby's favorite saying.

She stared at Mr. Kane for so long that at last his eyebrows lifted. "Miss Chapple?"

Seize the day, a voice whispered in her head.

"Mr. Kane, I have no intention of marrying, but . . ." Cowardice dried the words on her tongue.

He smiled at her encouragingly. "But what?"

Mattie felt as if she was teetering on the edge of a precipice. Should she retreat to safety? Or step forward to discover whether she would fall or fly?

Carpe diem.

Mattie inhaled deeply and grabbed hold of her courage.

"But I should like to know what it's like," she said in a rush. "To have physical congress with a man."

The smile vanished from Mr. Kane's face. Blank astonishment replaced it.

Blood rushed to Mattie's cheeks until it felt as if they were scorching. She was falling, not flying. Plummeting towards humiliation.

Mr. Kane cleared his throat. "I beg your pardon?"

Mattie clasped her hands tightly together. *Carpe diem,* she told herself. *Carpe diem.* "Toby always used to say . . . seize the day." Her voice was slightly breathless. "So I am. Seizing the day. Would you . . . I mean, if it's not too distasteful for you . . . would you consider, uh . . ." The phrase that came to mind was *pluck my virgin flower,* which she hastily rejected. "Would you have intercourse with me?"

*C*HAPTER 10

*E*dward blinked. *She wants me to bed her?*

Arousal flared inside him as his imagination took flight. He saw that tall, voluptuous body naked in his bed. He saw himself exploring those ripe breasts, imagined the weight of them in his hands, the silken smoothness of the skin.

He stared at Miss Chapple, transfixed with lust.

Her blush grew more fiery. "If it would be too distasteful—"

"Distasteful? On the contrary, it would be . . ." He couldn't think of any word to describe how utterly pleasurable it would be. How utterly reprehensible.

As if she had heard his thoughts, Miss Chapple said, "I realize that my request is quite improper, Mr. Kane."

It was more than improper; it was so far beyond proper that—

"But I shall never marry, and I should like to know what it's all about."

He knew exactly what she meant by *it*. Sex.

"So, will you? Please?"

Edward swallowed, torn between propriety and lust. He knew what he *should* do—and he knew what he *wanted* to do.

"I know it's possible for a man to lie with a woman without

making her pregnant, if he can just . . . just restrain himself until he's, um . . . not within her any longer."

Edward watched her lips move, and imagined kissing them. The lust in his body burned even hotter.

"Can you do that?"

Edward nodded, and then realized what he'd just done. He shook his head.

Her eyebrows quirked. "You can, or you can't?"

Edward opened his mouth to speak, but found his throat too dry for words. He cleared it and tried again. "I can," he said. "But I can't take advantage of you." He tried to speak firmly, but even to his own ears, he sounded unconvincing.

"You wouldn't be taking advantage of me, Mr. Kane. *I* should be taking advantage of *you*." One corner of her mouth lifted up in a wry smile; bringing a dimple to life.

Edward's gaze fastened on the dimple, and he knew that he was lost. *I can't. It's wrong.* But every fiber in his body clamored that it was right, that it was something he needed desperately, something he *had* to do. "Your uncle . . ."

"Will never know. And you'll be gone shortly. In all likelihood, we shall never meet again."

Edward stared at her. How could he walk away from Venus without tasting her delights? He wasn't that strong. No man was that strong.

He moved without conscious thought, stepping closer to her. His hand lifted and touched her cheek. Her skin was as soft as he'd imagined, as smooth.

Miss Chapple's eyes widened. She seemed to freeze, to hold her breath.

"I . . ." The words dried on his tongue.

"You what?"

He stroked her cheek—and felt an answering fire erupt in his belly. The muscles in his groin clenched, telling him that his body wanted this, *needed* this.

"I'll do it," Edward said. Dimly, in the back of his head, his conscience cried out. This was wrong. Dishonorable.

Wicked. But the voice of his conscience was drowned out by more urgent things: the roaring heat in his blood, the surging arousal that had taken control of him. He said it again, "I'll do it. With pleasure."

Mattie undressed in her bedchamber. Her heart beat high in her throat while she stripped out of her clothes. She was afraid—terrified—and yet excited at the same time. In a few minutes, Mr. Kane would present himself at her door and the question burning inside her would be answered. She would *know* what it was like to be bedded by a man.

She washed hastily, using the icy water in the ewer, and then dressed in her nightgown, a shapeless garment of thick gray flannel. A glance at the mirror told her just how ugly it was, how ugly *she* was.

Mattie turned away from the mirror and shoved the thought aside. If she thought about how she looked, she wouldn't be able to do this. "Carpe diem," she said aloud.

She pulled the pins out of her hair and hesitated over whether to plait it or not. What would Chérie do?

Leave it loose.

Mattie brushed her hair until it crackled, not looking in the mirror. She had just placed the brush back on her dresser when she heard a faint *tap tap* on the door.

Her pulse gave a spiky leap. Dread and anticipation clenched in her chest. She inhaled a shaky breath. "Come in."

The dread squeezed even more tightly when Mr. Kane entered the bedchamber, when he closed the door and turned to face her. He didn't advance into the room; he stood with his back to the door, looking at her.

Her dread was absurd. She'd *invited* him here.

Mattie inhaled another breath. She tried to find her

courage, her confidence. *Carpe diem,* she told herself, but the words had lost their power. "I . . . I'm sorry, it smells of mutton in here. Uncle Arthur prefers me to use tallow candles in my room. It's cheaper." She bit her lip. *Don't babble.*

"It doesn't matter," Mr. Kane said. He wore a dressing gown of red brocade, cut with military severity, and a pair of leather slippers.

Mattie crossed her arms over her chest, aware of how unflattering her baggy nightgown was. The movement drew Mr. Kane's gaze to her breasts. She saw him swallow. His eyes lifted to her face. He stared at her for a long moment, as if memorizing her features. "Your hair. It curls."

"Yes."

"It suits you."

"Thank you."

An awkward silence fell. Mr. Kane didn't move from the door. He glanced at the bed, and abruptly away. She saw the muscles in his throat move as he swallowed again. "I . . . uh, are you certain about this?"

"Yes." She needed to know. For herself. For her book.

Mr. Kane took one step and halted. The muscles in his throat moved again. He was nervous. The realization made some of her own nervousness ease slightly. *I can trust him.* "How do we do it?"

"Do it?" A smile almost crossed his face—a tiny flicker of the muscles at the corners of his mouth, at the corners of his eyes. "There's only one way."

Mattie felt herself blush. "I thought there were many ways."

"Many variations. But in the end, it all comes down to one thing."

She knew what that was: *Putting himself inside me.*

Fear ambushed her. The muscles in her belly clenched. Her gaze jerked away from his. She studied the collar of his dressing gown. "How . . . how do we start?"

"Slowly."

Mr. Kane took two steps towards her. She could reach out and touch him if she wished. Absurdly, her instinct was to draw back. Mattie held herself rigid, forcing herself to stay where she was. *You asked for this. Don't be a coward.*

What must he think of her? A spinster, inviting him into her bedchamber, asking him to bed her.

Mattie couldn't raise her gaze to his, couldn't look at his face.

Mr. Kane reached out and touched her cheek, as he'd done in the library. The breath froze in her lungs.

"We'll start very slowly," he said, lightly stroking her cheek.

Mattie's skin tightened and seemed to burn where he touched. She tried to concentrate on breathing. It was surprisingly difficult. His fingers slid over her cheek, a feather-light caress. "You have lovely dimples." He touched the middle of her cheek, a light tap, as if marking a precise location.

The compliment brought a flood of heat to her face. "Thank you." It was a whisper, barely audible.

His fingers left her cheek and slid into her hair. Mattie stood utterly still as he stroked the long, loose curls.

"Your hair is beautiful. So soft."

"Thank you," Mattie said again. She still couldn't raise her gaze to look at him.

"Matilda—"

"Mattie." The only people who called her Matilda were her uncle and aunt.

"Very well . . . Mattie." Mr. Kane stepped closer, until their bodies were almost touching. His fingers were still laced into her hair. "Tonight, you must call me Edward."

She risked a tiny glance at him. His face was alarmingly close. Close enough to clearly see the red scars that scored his cheeks and brow. Close enough to see the rich brown of his irises. Close enough to kiss.

He caught her gaze and held it. "Say it," he said softly.

Mattie moistened her lips. "Edward," she whispered, and then blushed even more fiercely.

He smiled at her. "That wasn't so hard, was it?"

No harder than standing still while he stroked her hair. His fingers skimmed past her cheek, her shoulder, again and again, a slow rhythm.

The heat of her blush didn't fade. It stayed, burning beneath her skin. She was intensely conscious of him. Her dark, cold bedchamber had become a warm and private cocoon. The only two people in the world were Mr. Kane and herself.

She and Edward.

His fingers left her hair, slid along her jaw, tilted her chin. "If you want to stop at any time, just say so."

Mattie nodded, unable to speak. Her gaze was caught fast in his.

Edward waited for a moment, as if expecting her to draw back, and then bowed his head and lightly touched his mouth to hers.

Mattie's heart began to beat hard and staccato in her ears. *He's kissing me!* She squeezed her eyes shut.

Edward slowly traced her lips with kisses that were feather-light. Time slowed down and sped up at the same time. Each tiny kiss took an eternity to come, was over in an instant, and yet the impression lingered, leaving her lips warm and tingling.

When he'd traced her mouth, Edward didn't raise his head. Mattie held her breath, hoping he'd do it again. He didn't; instead his tongue lightly touched her lower lip.

Mattie inhaled sharply as an unfamiliar sensation lanced through her: a quicksilver flare of pleasure that originated deep in her belly. Her eyelids lifted. For a moment she stared at Edward, at his face looming so close, shadowed in the candlelight.

He touched her lip again with his tongue. Mattie trembled and squeezed her eyes tightly shut again.

"Open your mouth," Edward whispered.

Mattie hesitated for a half-second, and then parted her lips.

Edward explored her lower lip with his tongue, with gentle nips of his teeth. Each touch brought another quicksilver flare of pleasure. Heat washed through her, mounting until she felt almost feverish. She swayed towards him and clutched his dressing gown.

Edward pulled her even closer, his hands on her hips. Mattie's eyes opened briefly in shock. She felt the solid warmth of his body, the hardness of his chest and thighs, the firm grip of his hands at her waist. Her body gave an instinctive pulse of pleasure that she felt to her fingers and toes.

Edward deepened the kiss, entering her mouth. He tasted of gingerbread. He tasted of man.

Mattie tried to kiss him back, tried to mimic his movements, tried to taste him as he was tasting her. Need grew inside her, a twisting, urgent sensation. She lost all sense of time. Perhaps they kissed for five minutes, perhaps fifteen, perhaps fifty. Her whole being was focused on Edward, on his clever, teasing mouth.

When Edward finally broke the kiss they were both breathing raggedly. He didn't release her. Mattie blinked her eyes open and stared at him, seeing the darkness of his eyes, the flush that colored his face.

"You have a mouth made for kissing, Mattie." Edward's voice was hoarse, low.

So do you.

Edward released her. He took her hand and led her to the bed. Mattie understood precisely how Chérie should feel on her wedding night. Eager, afraid.

Edward drew her to sit on the edge of the bed. He kicked off his leather slippers. The sight of his bare feet, his bare toes, was surprisingly intimate. Mattie's throat tightened until it was almost impossible to breathe.

I'll be seeing more than that of him soon . . . and with that thought came an intense surge of *want*. She wanted to see him, wanted to touch him, wanted to know what a naked man looked like—and she wanted it more fiercely than she'd wanted anything in her life. And not just any man; him. She wanted Edward Kane, with his scarred face and missing fingers and smiling eyes.

"Shall I blow out the candle?" Edward asked.

Mattie shook her head. She swallowed, found her voice, and spoke: "I want to see you."

The comment seemed to hold him motionless for a moment. After a pause, he said, "You do?"

She nodded.

A smile lit his face. "Good. Because I want to see you too."

Mattie was abruptly aware of her size, her wide hips and large breasts, her giant-like proportions—

"When I look at you, I think of Venus."

Her thoughts stuttered to a halt. Mattie blinked and stared at him. "Venus?"

Edward nodded. "Statuesque." He reached out and undid the topmost button of her nightgown, high at her throat. "Voluptuous." The second button. "Beautiful." The third button. "Exactly how a goddess should look."

Her face was hot with embarrassment—from the compliments, from the fact that her chest was bared almost to her cleavage. Edward touched his knuckles lightly to the upper slope of one breast, still covered by thick flannel, a fleeting and barely-felt caress. She heard him swallow. "This nightgown *definitely* needs to come off."

Mattie found her voice quickly: "You first."

"Me?" He hesitated for a moment, as if he wished to refuse, and then said, "Very well."

Edward stood and took a step back. He felt in his pocket, withdrew a folded handkerchief, and placed it on the little bedside table. Then his hands went to the belt of his dressing gown. He hesitated. "I have scars."

"I know." Her gaze flicked to his left ear.

Edward caught the glance. One hand lifted, touched what remained of his ear, as if trying to hide it—a gesture she thought he wasn't even aware he'd made.

"Edward, I like how you look." That strong, square face, that strong, broad body. He was Goliath, looming in her bedchamber. The sheer size of him, the savage scars, should have been intimidating—but she knew there were laughter lines hiding beneath the sword slashes on his face, knew how gentle his big, battered hands were, knew how innately kind he was.

"You do?" His hand lowered from his ear.

Mattie nodded.

She hadn't realized that he'd tensed until she saw his shoulders relax. He began to untie the knot, and hesitated. "Uh . . . Mattie, when a man is, uh . . . aroused, his body changes. His, uh . . . his organ becomes quite large."

"I know." Reading *Fanny Hill* had enlightened her about that.

Still Edward hesitated. "Don't be alarmed."

"I won't."

Edward didn't look entirely convinced, but he shrugged out of the dressing gown, letting it drop to the floor.

Mattie's eyes widened in astonishment. The male body was less similar to the female than she'd realized. It wasn't just his organ—as he'd called it—it was the crisp curls of hair on his chest, the broad ribcage, the slabs of muscle on his abdomen and thighs, the sheer strength of his body.

After one startled glance at that disconcertingly large organ, she skirted around it, examining the rest of his body.

His forearms were almost as badly scarred as his hands and face, a dozen or so cuts scoring his skin. A much broader scar slashed jaggedly down the left side of his ribcage.

Edward caught the direction of her gaze. "Bayonet," he said, running his fingers down the ridge of scar tissue. "Almost skewered me."

"Does it hurt?"

He lifted his shoulders in a shrug and then said, "No."

She believed the shrug, not the word: it did still hurt him sometimes. "Which leg was broken?"

He pointed—and again she avoided looking at his organ. There were no obvious scars on his left leg, but there was one at his right hip. She pointed. "What's that?"

Edward glanced at it. "Shell fragment. But that wasn't Waterloo."

"What was?"

"Waterloo? Everything else you can see. And some broken bones." He touched his chest. "Cracked a few ribs when the cavalry rode over me."

Mattie stared at him. The heat and excitement had subsided to the pit of her belly. Uppermost was a choking tightness in her throat and a stinging in her eyes. She looked down at her lap, blinking back tears.

"Don't be afraid," Edward said hastily. "I know it must seem a little . . . uh, daunting, but, uh . . . there are men who're bigger than me, truly."

His words drew her attention to his groin. "I'm not afraid," Mattie started to say, but the words dried in her throat. She stared at his organ. It jutted aggressively from his body. *Perhaps I am a little afraid.*

Edward stepped close, until she almost felt the heat of his body. "It's nothing to be scared of."

Mattie released a shaky breath. She couldn't stop staring at his organ. It looked so strange and primitive, so alarmingly large. Fierce, almost brutal.

It will never fit inside me.

Edward reached out and took one of her hands. He placed her palm beneath his organ.

They both jerked slightly, as if her touch had burned. The breath caught sharply in Mattie's throat. She lifted her head and stared up at him.

Time seemed to stop. Edward's dark, hot eyes held her gaze. The heavy heat of his organ pressed against her palm.

"I think you should take your nightgown off now," Edward said, his voice a hoarse whisper.

Mattie couldn't find the breath to speak, could only nod.

Edward released her hand. He stepped back.

Mattie rose from the bed. She pulled the nightgown over her head before cowardice could ambush her. Embarrassment scorched her cheeks. She dropped the nightgown and held herself rigid, willing herself not to shrink from his gaze.

Edward made a strangled noise in his throat. "Venus," he said, while his eyes devoured her, tracing a path from her breasts to her waist, to her hips, to the dark triangle of hair at the junction of her thighs. Her skin seemed to tighten and tingle, to flush, where his gaze lingered. Finally he met her eyes again. He wanted her; she saw it clearly on his face. "Mattie . . . you're more beautiful than I imagined."

Her cheeks burned even more hotly. She looked down at the floor.

Edward took her hands, holding them clasped in his. "You still want this?"

Mattie nodded. She stared down at his toes. Strong toes, with tiny, crisp curls of hair on them.

She wanted to touch them, to learn what his skin felt like.

Edward released her hands. He stepped even closer. His hands slid around her hips, cupped her buttocks, pressed her to him.

Mattie's mouth opened in a gasp. She felt him. All of him. The burning skin. The tickling hair. The hard, scorching heat of his organ.

Every muscle in her body clenched for an instant—in shock, in pleasure, in anticipation. She couldn't breathe, couldn't move, could only stand trembling, almost drowning in the sensations.

Edward dipped his head and pressed a kiss to her temple.

Mattie dragged a shaky breath into her lungs, intensely aware of the pressure of his organ against her belly. *I want more.*

"Kiss me," Edward murmured against her brow.

She tilted her face up to him.

They kissed until Mattie was dizzy with heat. When

Edward finally raised his head, the sound of their breathing was loud in the bedchamber. He held her tightly against him, as if trying to imprint her upon his skin. "Ready?" he asked, his voice hoarse.

Mattie nodded, past speech.

They lay down on the counterpane, side by side. Mattie found a wanton boldness she didn't know she possessed and reached out to touch him, running her hands over his chest, tracing the bayonet scar, circling his nipples with her fingertips. His scent filled her nostrils, clean and unmistakably male. Edward caught her hands before she found the courage to touch his organ again. "My turn." He pressed her onto her back.

He was thorough in his exploration—and he didn't just use his hands. He explored her breasts with his mouth, tasting her with his tongue, nipping gently.

Mattie caught herself moaning, and sank her teeth into her lower lip to subdue the sound. She hadn't realized her skin was so exquisitely sensitive, hadn't realized such burning pleasure was possible.

Edward's mouth moved lower. He kissed her belly while his hands roamed across her hips, skimmed down her thighs, parted her legs.

Dimly, Mattie was aware that she should be halting him— this was it, the broaching of her virtue—but all she wanted was for him to continue. If Edward stopped, she'd die of the fierce, wild, pulsing *want* that consumed her.

Edward's mouth returned to her breasts, but his left hand stayed between her legs, cupping her mound, moving in a rhythmic, rocking motion that caused her to arch up against him. Another moan escaped her.

Mattie felt a puff of hot breath against her nipple as Edward laughed. "Like it?"

She couldn't answer, could only moan again and arch against his hand. A tiny corner of her brain told her she should be embarrassed; the rest of her was lost in pleasure beyond anything she'd ever known.

The movement of his hand continued until the pleasure inside her rose to a peak that was almost painful. She squeezed her eyes tightly shut—and then the pleasure broke, cascading through her body until she even felt it in the tips of her toes.

Mattie slowly opened her eyes. She lay on the counterpane, dazed, struggling to catch her breath. Her toes still tingled.

Edward uttered a satisfied murmur. His hand delved intimately between her legs. Suddenly, two of his fingers were inside her.

Mattie stiffened.

"Does that hurt?" Edward asked.

It took her several seconds to find her voice. "No."

His fingers slid from her. Edward nudged her legs further apart with his knee and moved until he was braced over her. "Mattie . . ." His voice was rough with need. "I can't wait any longer. I'm sorry."

She shook her head and reached up to touch his face, tracing the curving line of one scar, from brow to cheek to jawbone. His skin was hot to the touch, flushed, and his eyes were so dark they looked black in the candlelight.

Mattie slid her hand behind his neck and drew his head down and kissed him.

Edward kissed her back, more urgently than he had before. She felt the fierceness of his need, the trembling of his body, the tension. He dragged his mouth from hers. "It might hurt."

"I don't mind." She wanted more of him, wanted all of him, wanted him inside her—and she didn't care whether it hurt or not.

She felt his fingers between her legs again, opening her, and then his organ nudged inside her.

I'm no longer a virgin. Mattie held her breath, trying to notice every sensation, to capture the moment in her memory. There was pain—a sharp, tearing little pain—but she was less aware of that than of the sense of invasion, of something large inside her that shouldn't be there. She felt a surge of panic and stiffened.

Edward froze. "Does it hurt too much?" His voice was tight, breathless.

It feels like I'm bursting.

But even as she thought it, her body began to adjust to the invader, relaxing a fraction. "No," Mattie whispered. "It's just . . . strange."

He grunted and held motionless for a moment longer, resting his forehead against her shoulder, as if trying to gather his control—and then he pushed slowly into her. "Still all right?"

Mattie nodded. "Yes."

Edward released his breath, a sound that was part sigh, part groan. She heard pleasure in it.

He stayed absolutely still for several seconds. She was aware of the burning heat of his skin, the racing of his heart, the trembling tension in his body. Then he lifted his head. He stared into her eyes. "I won't be able to last long."

She shook her head mutely, lifting her hand to touch his face again.

Edward slid one arm around her hips, lifting her, pressing her against him. "Venus," he whispered against her mouth, and then he began to move, a rocking, rhythmic motion, driving himself into her, withdrawing, driving in again.

Mattie's body responded instinctively, lifting to meet him. Pleasure clenched inside her. She moaned against his mouth.

Time blurred. She lost all sense of who she was. She was primitive, animal, spiraling towards a cascade again, splintering into pleasure, bucking against him . . .

Edward withdrew abruptly, thrusting himself away from her, turning his back to her. His large body shuddered convulsively. She heard him groan, a sound like pain.

Mattie's brain belatedly began working again. He'd done what she'd asked him to do: removed his organ before he could impregnate her.

She lay, struggling to catch her breath, her head turned towards him, watching Edward's ribcage expand with each rasping inhalation he took. Did he feel the same bone-deep, languid pleasure she did?

Edward blew out a deep, shuddering breath and rolled to face her. They stared at each other for a long, silent moment.

It would be easy to love him. She hovered on the brink of it—a trembling, swelling emotion in her heart.

"Are you all right?" He reached out to lightly brush his knuckles over her cheek.

Emotion clenched in Mattie's throat. *Edward Kane, I could love you.* She swallowed and nodded. "Did it hurt you?" she asked, remembering his strained groan. "To stop like that?"

He hesitated, and then said, "No."

"It did!" The languid pleasure evaporated. Mattie pushed up to sit. "Edward, why didn't you tell me it would hurt you? I wouldn't have asked if I'd known!"

Edward sat up too. He captured one of her hands. "It didn't hurt."

"But—"

"It doesn't hurt to stop, Mattie. It's just . . . not easy."

Mattie frowned, studying his face. The candlelight cast a shadow over it. She couldn't see his eyes clearly. "It feels better to, um . . . to finish inside a woman?"

"Oh, yes," Edward said. "Infinitely better."

She remembered the spiraling pleasure, the cascade. Had withdrawing before he was finished meant that he'd not experienced that? Guilt gathered in her chest. "I'm sorry, Edward. I didn't realize that it—"

"Don't apologize. It was still good." His grip tightened on her hand. "In fact, it was excellent." He hesitated, and then said, with the air of making a confession: "This is the first time I've lain with a woman since Waterloo."

"Because of your injuries?" More guilt swamped her. "I didn't think!"

"Why should you?" Edward sounded amused. "I'm not an invalid, Mattie."

"But your leg, your ribs—"

"Are healed now."

"You limp. And this still hurts you." She pulled her hand free of his grip, touched the bayonet scar, remembering how he'd shrugged when she'd asked if it hurt.

Edward recaptured her hand. "It pulls a little sometimes. But not now."

"But what we just did—"

He laughed softly and shook his head. "Mattie, trust me, when a man is making love to a woman, he doesn't feel pain. He feels . . ." He paused, not as if searching for a word, but rather as if savoring a memory. "He feels only pleasure. Pleasure so intense it's almost impossible to think."

Her skin was cooling rapidly. Mattie shivered.

Edward gathered her in his arms. "Cold?"

Not now that he held her. Mattie shook her head, inhaling the scent of his skin. He smelled so different from her, so *male*. The smell gave her a feeling of contentment, low in her belly.

"Was it what you expected?"

"Much, *much* better," she whispered against his shoulder.

"Yes," Edward said. "I thought it was, too." One hand stroked down her back, coming to rest on the curve of her hip. "You have the body of Venus, with hips to cradle a man." He gave a sigh and released her. "I should go."

Don't. Please. Stay with me. Mattie bit back the words. She nodded, mute.

Edward climbed off the bed. He handed Mattie her night-gown. "Get into bed before you freeze."

Mattie pulled on the nightgown. Her skin shrank from the touch of the cold flannel. Edward shrugged into his dressing gown and picked up his handkerchief from the floor. It was no longer neatly folded. His seed lay within it. He thrust the crumpled handkerchief into his pocket. "Sleep well, Mattie."

Don't go. Stay with me. She swallowed the words. "You, too."

He grinned, a sudden flash of white teeth. "I shall. Believe me." He bent, kissed her cheek, whispered "Good night," against her skin, and was gone.

158

The bedchamber was echoingly empty without him. Mattie lay down on the counterpane and stared up at the shadowy ceiling. Her body felt different, stretched and replete in a way it had never been before.

And bereft, too. Alone.

She missed Edward. His warmth, his scent. She wanted to curl into the heat of his body and sleep with him.

Her throat tightened. Tears gathered in her eyes. She blinked them back. *Don't be a fool. Don't imagine yourself in love with him.* What they'd done had nothing to do with love.

Mattie went over it all in her head again, making certain she remembered everything—kissing Edward, watching him undress, touching his organ, the shocking, wild pleasure he'd given her with his hand. Most vivid of all was the sensation of Edward inside her, the tiny flare of panic and then her body's instinctive acceptance of his invasion.

She sat up abruptly and checked the counterpane for blood. There was none. All she found was a tiny smear on her inner thigh. That smear and the slight ache where he'd breached her body were the only signs that her virginity was gone.

"So much for rivers of blood," Mattie said aloud. She climbed off the bed, wrapped a thick shawl around her shoulders, and sat down to write Chérie's wedding night.

CHAPTER 11

The morning was well advanced when Edward finally woke. He stretched beneath the covers, feeling rested and invigorated—and more than that, feeling *alive*. The funereal gloom of his bedchamber—the dark paneling, the dark bed curtains—failed to diminish his sense of well-being. He lay for several minutes, savoring the sense of contentment, before ringing for Tigh. For the first time since Waterloo the sight of his right hand—the stumps of his missing fingers—didn't bring a jolt of disbelief or grief.

Edward whistled beneath his breath while he shaved. His scarred face in the mirror, the clumsiness of his butchered hands, failed to dampen his mood. It was as if he'd been wearing someone else's skin—ill-fitting and uncomfortable—for the past five months. Today he fitted into himself again, *was* himself.

He stopped whistling when he caught Tigh's puzzled, sideways glance. Could the bâtman tell he'd had sex last night?

I am a man, not a eunuch. Edward buried a grin in his towel, drying his face.

He kept his expression carefully bland while he dressed. It was hard not to whistle; he had to bite the tip of his tongue several times to stop himself. "I'll eat breakfast down in the village," he told Tigh, as the bâtman helped him into his riding coat. The dark blue superfine was snug across his shoulders.

Tigh grunted. "Lucky."

Edward tucked an extra handkerchief in his pocket for gingerbread, pulled on his gloves, and headed for the stables, swinging his riding crop against his thigh. Contentment hummed beneath his breastbone. The guilt of Toby's death was still there—as it always must be—but somehow, overnight, he'd found Edward Kane again. A little battered by Waterloo, but still the man he'd once been. Recognizable. Familiar. Someone he could live with.

Mattie copied the precious first chapter in her best copperplate. It was past noon by the time she finished. She folded it inside a letter to Anne Brocklesby, sealed it with wax, and walked into Soddy Morton to post it. She lifted her face to the gray sky and felt relief bubble inside her. *Soon I'll be free of Creed Hall.* She felt like spreading her arms and pirouetting in the middle of the boggy field.

"Another letter to Lunnon, Miss Chapple?" the innkeeper asked when she entered the taproom, her half boots heavy with mud.

"Yes." Mattie's buoyant mood faltered for a moment. What had happened last night between her and Edward was private and precious, something to be kept just between the two of them, not to be shared with thousands of readers.

She took a deep breath—*Forgive me, Edward*—and handed the letter to Mr. Potts.

Edward visited the second person Miss Eccles had mentioned—a gentleman by the name of Scudley. Signs of Mr. Scudley's new wealth were evident; the paint on the drawing room walls was so fresh Edward could almost smell it.

Scudley's manner was welcoming, but Edward had been an officer long enough to see beneath the façade; the man was nervous and edgy.

"Pleasant room," Edward said as he took the chair Mr. Scudley indicated. "Newly decorated? What color is the paint?"

"Er . . . Turkish red." The man's eyes were fixed on his face, wide and slightly dilated, fearful.

There was only one thing Scudley could be afraid of. *He's Chérie.*

Edward was conscious of a pang of disappointment. He'd wanted Chérie to be someone more interesting than a plump little man dressed in a tight spotted waistcoat and yellow pantaloons and with perspiration shiny on his face.

Scudley cleared his throat. "How can I help you, Mr. Kane?"

Edward pulled Chérie's letter from his pocket. It was almost in shreds. "I believe you wrote this."

Mr. Scudley glanced at it. His nervousness evaporated. "That's not my hand." He jumped to his feet and scurried over to the writing desk. "See?"

Edward didn't need to look at the document Scudley held out; the man's posture, his eyes, his manner, told him all he needed to know. Whatever Scudley was afraid of, it wasn't being unmasked as Chérie. "I apologize for wasting your time."

Edward rode back to Soddy Morton, whistling under his breath. The fact that Scudley wasn't Chérie didn't dampen his mood, nor did the raw wind and the heavy pewter-colored clouds that promised snow. Even the sight of the Hall, glimpsed across the valley, bleak and gray, failed to depress his spirits. His body was alive again, *he* was alive. The world was a different place from the one he'd been living in for the past five months. The colors were brighter, the air sweeter.

Memory swept over him—not blood and smoke this time, but the scent of sex, the heat, the delicious friction of being inside a woman. Edward inhaled deeply, feeling his ribcage expand, feeling the sense of well-being swell inside him. Underlying the well-being was a deep gratitude to Miss Chapple. *Mattie,* he reminded himself. Because of Mattie, he was himself again.

He knew he ought to feel guilty about what he'd done last night—knew he *would* feel guilty once the relief subsided— but for now relief was paramount, and with it, well-being and contentment and gratitude and something close to joy. *I'm not a eunuch.*

Edward stopped at the bakery for gingerbread, examined the sky, and prudently returned to Creed Hall. The last person on Miss Eccles's list could wait until after the coming storm.

In the stables, he swung down from Trojan's back and handed him over to Hoby. "Have you seen Miss Chapple?" he asked, aware of the gingerbread nestling in his pocket.

Hoby glanced up at the hayloft.

Edward nodded and strode towards the ladder, but as he climbed the whistle died on his tongue. How did one greet a respectable spinster whose virtue one had taken?

He climbed the rest of the rungs slowly. *Should I apologize? Thank her? Pretend that nothing happened?*

She lay on the hay, watching kittens play. Miss Chapple. Mattie. A Venus he'd seen naked, had kissed, had coupled with.

Edward gripped the topmost rung as memory swept over him again. The muscles in his groin tightened.

She didn't look like a Venus now. The voluptuous body was

hidden beneath a shapeless sack of a gown and the lush hair was pulled back into a tight knot at the back of her head.

What the devil am I going to say to her?

No inspiration came. Edward hesitated, aware of a craven urge to creep back down the ladder, to postpone this moment until he'd decided how to greet her.

Miss Chapple turned her head. For a moment they stared at each other in silence, and then she said, "Edward," and sat up. The awkwardness in the way she spoke the two syllables, the tension in the way she sat, told him she didn't know what to say any more than he did.

Edward climbed the last few rungs and crawled up into the hay. "Miss Chapple. Mattie. Good afternoon. I, uh . . ."

I, what?

I can't thank you enough for last night. You've given me back myself. Edward rejected those words. "I, uh . . ."

What?

What had last night been for Mattie? A moment to be treasured? A terrible mistake?

The silence became awkward. Discomfort spurred Edward into speech: "I must apologize, Miss Chapple. Last night was . . . I should never have . . . it was very wrong of me—"

Mattie's face tightened as if he'd slapped her.

Edward bit back the rest of the words crowding on his tongue. Dismay swept through him. He'd said the wrong thing.

"The fault was mine," Mattie said in a stiff voice.

"No, no," Edward said hastily. "That's not what I meant! What I meant was . . ."

What? What did he mean?

He shifted his weight uncomfortably. *I should never have come up here.*

Mattie looked down at the hay. "I am very grateful for your kindness," she said in that same, stiff voice.

"Uh . . ." Edward said, and cast desperately about for an appropriate answer. There didn't appear to be one. *So tell*

164

her the truth. "It wasn't kindness. I wanted you." He wanted her now, in the dusty, shadowy hayloft. He wanted to taste her mouth again, wanted to peel off her clothes and explore the ripeness of her body, wanted to bury himself in her. "I, uh . . . as I told you last night, I haven't been with a woman for a long time." And then he realized how that sounded: as if any woman would do. "You're very beautiful."

Mattie looked at him. She made a small, derisive puff of sound. The gloom didn't hide the tightness of her mouth, the disbelief.

"It's the truth." Edward reached across and touched her cheek lightly. Her skin was as soft as he remembered. "You're a beautiful woman."

Mattie turned her head away. She squeezed her eyes shut for a moment. He thought she was trying not to cry.

Edward eased closer to her on the hay. "Mattie . . ." He stroked her cheek again, and then dipped his head and kissed where his fingers had touched, inhaling her scent. "Believe me."

"I know what I look like," she said, pulling away from him. "I can see it in my mirror."

"Beauty is in the eye of the beholder. You told me that last night. Remember?" And Mattie, naked, was one of the most beautiful sights he'd ever seen in his life. He captured her chin, turned her face to him, and kissed her softly. "Thank you for last night," he whispered against her mouth.

Her lips stayed closed for a moment, and then trembled and opened to him. She was as sweet as he remembered, as intoxicating.

Edward gathered her closer. His awareness of his surroundings faded. The hayloft, the kittens, the horses in the stalls below, all ceased to exist. His world narrowed to Mattie's mouth, to the utter pleasure of kissing her.

A clatter in the stables below, a muffled curse, brought him to his senses. Edward lifted his head and dragged air into his lungs. He was drowning in heat, in lust. He was aware of the soft fullness of Mattie's breasts pressed against his chest, aware of the throbbing, urgent heat in his groin. He wanted—quite desperately—to bed her again.

Edward pushed away from her. "I beg your pardon," he said, struggling to find his breath, aware of Hoby moving in the stables below them. "I didn't mean to do that."

Mattie shook her head mutely. She looked as flushed and dazed as he felt.

"I . . . uh . . ." He'd been trying to make a point, hadn't he? "I'm sorry, I've forgotten what I was saying."

"I haven't." Mattie reached out and touched the back of his hand lightly. "Thank you, Edward."

He captured her fingers. "You're welcome."

He knew he should go, but he daren't while his breeches were stretched so tightly across his groin. He lay down at arm's distance from her, holding her hand. After a moment, Mattie turned her hand in his and traced the stumps of his missing fingers, a light, stroking touch, as if she was trying to fix the shape in her memory.

"Does your hand hurt?" she asked.

"Only when I knock it."

Mattie nodded. She didn't withdraw her hand; instead, she stretched out beside him on the hay. For long minutes they lay side by side, holding hands, listening to Hoby sweeping out the stalls. Finally, Edward released her and sat up. "I'd better go."

And then he remembered why he'd climbed up to the hayloft in the first place. "Here," he said, fishing in his pocket for the slices of gingerbread. "I brought this back from the village."

Mattie sat up. "Thank you." She unfolded the handkerchief. The gingerbread was almost black against the white linen. "Would you like some?"

What I'd like is to have sex with you again. Edward shook his head and kissed her lightly on the cheek, inhaling her scent for a brief second, and climbed down from the hayloft.

Mattie didn't eat the gingerbread. She wrapped it again in the handkerchief, bade the kittens farewell, and went back to her bedchamber, where she opened the escritoire and laid out her writing materials. She could still feel the imprint of Edward's mouth on hers, still taste him on her tongue. She closed her eyes, savoring the memory of his kiss for a long moment, and then dipped the quill in ink and began to write.

I beg your attention, kind readers, while I share an episode from my past. The events that I shall relate occurred while I was the guest of Lord D., at his hunting box. One afternoon, while D. was riding with the hounds, in consequence of a housemaid telling me there was a litter of kittens in the hayloft, I wandered down to the stables. Only one groom was there, a strong and burly young fellow, with his shirtsleeves rolled up to show sun-browned, brawny forearms.

He had a plain face, but there was such pleasing openness in his expression, such frank and innocent admiration in his eyes as he watched me approach, that I found myself smiling warmly at him as I requested that he show me where the kittens were.

The groom laid aside his broom and led me to the back of the stables, where a ladder led up to a hayloft. "Up there, ma'am."

"Will they be afraid of me?" I asked.

"Belike, they will," he said, and then after a hesitation he offered to accompany me up. He must have known me for what I was, but he spoke to me with such respectful courtesy, as if I were a virtuous lady and not an Impure, that I found myself quite unafraid to be alone in his company and willingly accepted his offer.

The groom ascended the ladder, and I climbed after him and crawled into the hay. It was warm and shadowy up there, beneath the roof.

The groom called softly and after a moment there came rustling in the hay and two kittens emerged. They greeted the groom as a friend, purring, allowing him to pick them up and hand them to me.

I spent some minutes stroking the kittens, before allowing them to escape back into the hay. "Thank you," I said to the groom, and on impulse I leaned across and laid a kiss upon his cheek.

He blushed rosily and assumed an expression of such bashful confusion that I could not help but like him even more. "What is your name?" I asked.

"Tom, ma'am."

"Thank you, Tom," I said, and kissed him again, this time laying my salute upon his mouth.

After a moment's hesitation, Tom returned my kiss, with such sweetness that it provoked a warm friendliness in my breast. You will anticipate what happened next, dear reader, although I shall describe it for you to the best of my memory.

Mattie paused and closed her eyes again, remembering the shadowy coziness of the hayloft, remembering Edward's kiss. If Hoby hadn't made a noise, if Edward hadn't stopped . . .

She opened her eyes and picked up the countess's diary, flicking through the pages until she came to the one she wanted. She read the entry intently. What would it be like to do this with Edward?

Mattie laid the diary to one side and began to write swiftly. *Tom removed my clothes, kissing my skin as he bared it. It was clear that for all his bashfulness he had lain with a woman before, for he knew precisely how to place his kisses to most effect. When I lay utterly naked, he proceeded to give me the most intimate of kisses that a man can give a woman, bringing me swiftly to a state of . . .*

Mattie glanced at the countess's diary. How had she described it?

. . . a state of urgent and voluptuous ecstasy.

She had puzzled over that description when she'd first read it all those months ago. Now she understood what the countess had meant—the fierce urgency, the intense, rippling surge of pleasure flooding through her.

Mattie dipped the quill in ink and continued with the confession: *As you may imagine, dear reader, once I had recovered myself I lost no time in divesting Tom of his clothing and returning the favor, an intimacy to which he most willingly submitted.*

A scene blossomed in her mind: not Chérie and the groom in the shadowy darkness of the hayloft, but herself and Edward, undressing each other, tasting each other's skin . . .

No. The scene dissolved. Mattie frowned down at what she'd written. She couldn't imagine Edward wanting to kiss that most womanly part of her.

But the other way . . . *that* she could imagine: kissing his organ, as the countess described in such precise detail, learning the shape of him with her tongue, learning his taste.

Heat flushed sharply beneath Mattie's skin.

What would Edward taste like?

She shoved the thought aside. If she wasn't already a whore, then inviting Edward to her bedchamber a second time, kissing him like that, would certainly make her one.

She dipped the quill in the little inkpot again and continued the confession: *That wasn't the end of our interlude, dear reader. On the contrary, it was merely the beginning, for Tom was quickly roused again to action and he made himself master of my body at once, possessing me with a most pleasing vigor.*

Mattie glanced at the clock. With a shock she saw that it was nearly time for dinner. Hastily, she gathered the pages she'd written and the countess's diary and thrust them in the hidden cupboard.

∼∾∾∼

Three hours later, she returned to her task, describing Chérie's coupling with the lusty young groom in as much detail as she could think of.

Afterwards, I lay replete in his arms, smelling the scent of horses and the dusty, summer smell of hay, the scent of man, the scent of sex. It was dark and cozy up in the hayloft. I felt as if I had stepped into another world, one where Chérie the courtesan didn't exist, and nor did London salons and gentlemen vying for my attention. Here it was just Tom and me, enjoying each other, with no money changing hands.

His hand smoothed gently down to my hip and then up to my breasts. He shifted, pressing himself against me, asking a silent question, letting me feel his body's eagerness to resume that most pleasurable of activities. I smiled against his shoulder. "Again?" I asked.

"If it pleases you."

Mattie yawned, her jaw creaking. It was only half past ten, but her eyes stung with tiredness. She counted the pages. Four. That was enough for one confession.

It did please me, dear reader, she wrote, *but I shall lay down my pen here and leave the rest to your imagination.*

Chérie.

Mattie yawned again. She hid the pages in the secret cupboard, snuffed her candle, and crawled into bed.

Edward lay awake for a long time, listening to the muffled patter of snow against the windowpanes. All he wanted in the world was to climb out of bed, pull on his dressing gown, and tiptoe along the cold corridors to Mattie's room. He imagined himself standing beside her bed, imagined himself taking off his dressing gown, turning back the covers and sliding in alongside Mattie. He imagined her heat and her softness, the taste of her mouth, her eager response to his lovemaking.

He suppressed a groan and shifted restlessly. Damn. How could he sleep when all he could think about was Mattie? Her hair hanging in curls down to her waist. The astonishing ripeness of her breasts. The way her hips had cradled him while he'd made love to her.

Edward rolled over and punched his pillow, trying to make it more comfortable. He was acutely aware of Chérie's *Confessions,* lying a foot beneath him. He could almost feel them burning through the mattress, full of passion and pleasure, full of sex.

Edward squeezed his eyes shut. He *couldn't* go to Mattie's room, *couldn't* ask her to let him bed her again. Mattie wasn't a prostitute, available for his pleasure whenever he wanted; Mattie was . . .

Perfect. Luscious.

And she's Toby's cousin.

His lust began to fade. In its place was a creeping tide of guilt. What would Toby say if he knew?

But Toby would never know. Toby was dead. *Because of me.*

Edward opened his eyes and stared across the dark bedchamber. The last vestiges of his lust shriveled and disintegrated, blowing away like a handful of dust.

Mattie was halfway to Soddy Morton, her half boots crunching through the icy crust of snow that had fallen overnight, when she heard the sound of a horse behind her. Her heart gave an absurd little kick in her chest. She turned and looked back.

Edward.

He trotted up alongside her and swung down from the saddle. Breath plumed from his mouth, from the horse's nostrils. "Should you be walking in this weather?" he asked.

"It's not snowing."

"It's still damn— er, dashed cold." His gaze fastened on the letter she held. "Is that to be posted? Shall I take it for you?"

Guilt heated Mattie's cheeks. She resisted the urge to hide

the confession behind her back and shook her head. "No, thank you."

The corners of Edward's eyes creased in a smile. "Your daily escape from the Hall?"

Mattie nodded, feeling slightly sick. She was deceiving him—not with outright lies, but with subterfuge. "Do you have business in the village? Don't let me delay you."

"You're not delaying me. It's always a pleasure to walk with you, Mattie."

His words brought more heat to her cheeks. Mattie looked hurriedly away from those smiling eyes. Shame choked in her throat.

"And besides, I would like to ask you about Mrs. Dunn."

"Cecily?" She glanced at him, lifting her eyebrows. "What would you like to know?"

Edward didn't speak immediately. He walked alongside her, leading the horse, his boots crunching in the ankle-deep snow. A frown creased his brow. "Mattie . . . is she on the hunt for a husband?"

"Of course not!" Mattie said indignantly. She didn't pretend to misunderstand the question he was really asking. "Cecy's not pursuing Sir Gareth—or deceiving him! She is precisely as you see her: sweet and kind and . . . and practical." Practical enough to know what she wanted in a husband.

Edward's frown deepened. "Does she truly like Gareth? Or is it his baronetcy she likes?"

Mattie halted. "Cecy isn't after a title or a fortune."

Edward halted too. He regarded her steadily. "No?"

"No," Mattie said. And then she bit her lip. Honesty compelled her to say, "Cecy's first husband died in penury. She couldn't even afford to bury him decently. She said . . . when she marries again it will be to a man who can afford to look after his family. But I swear, she's not on the hunt for a fortune!"

Edward stared at her, saying nothing. He appeared to be weighing her words.

"Cecy is an exceptionally nice person," Mattie said. "Sir Gareth would be lucky to have her for a wife!"

Edward released his breath slowly. It hung in the air between them. "Mattie . . . Gary was engaged to be married, but after Waterloo . . . His fiancée didn't wish to marry a man with one arm."

"Oh." Her heart contracted in her chest. Poor Sir Gareth.

"Mrs. Dunn looks like Miss Swinthorp. Remarkably like her."

"Oh," she said again.

"I don't want Gary to be hurt. To be taken advantage of."

"Cecy wouldn't do that," Mattie said stoutly. "I know she wouldn't!"

Edward didn't reply. He merely looked at her, his eyebrows pinched together in a frown. She had the feeling her words had failed to convince him.

Edward escorted Miss Chapple to the inn, and then went in search of the third and final person on Miss Eccles's list, a Mrs. Starling.

Mrs. Starling lived to the east of the village, just off the pike road. Edward dismounted and surveyed the cottage. This was it: the end of his search. He would deliver his warning to Chérie and return to London, leaving Soddy Morton and Creed Hall and Mattie behind him.

He found himself oddly reluctant to tread down the snowy path.

Edward gave himself a mental shake. He strode down the path and knocked on the door. It was opened by an elderly lady with round, rosy cheeks. Three fat spaniels tumbled out, yapping.

"Mrs. Starling?"

"Yes." She blinked when she saw his scarred face, but her smile didn't falter.

Edward pulled the tattered letter from his pocket and showed it to her, while the spaniels snuffled around his ankles, their tails wagging.

"It's not mine," Mrs. Starling said, shaking her head. "Now that my niece lives with me, I've no need to send letters."

"Your niece?" His interest pricked. "Has she been with you long?"

"Six months," Mrs. Starling said. "Ever since my dear sister died."

"Er . . . could she perhaps have sent this letter?"

"I doubt it," Mrs. Starling said. "But you may ask her if you wish. One moment; I'll fetch her."

Edward waited on the doorstep, while the spaniels sniffed his boots. Curiosity surged inside him. What would Chérie be like? Flirtatious? Reserved and business-like?

Mrs. Starling returned, leading her niece by the hand. "This is my dear Hannah."

Hannah curtsied. She was a plump, pretty girl, perhaps twenty-two years of age, with fair hair and blue eyes and cheeks that were as rosy as her aunt's. Edward wondered what she'd been. A Covent Garden nun? A high-flying Cyprian? An opera dancer? She looked too wholesome to be any of those things—and yet her confessions proved she was no innocent.

"I believe this is yours," Edward said. He showed Hannah the letter, wondering how to speak with her alone. If her aunt didn't know she'd been a whore in London, he didn't want to disclose her secret.

"No, sir. I haven't sent any letters, sir."

Edward narrowed his eyes—and then he understood. Hannah was simple. The intelligence behind those limpid blue eyes was no greater than a child's.

"But I can write," Hannah said proudly. "Mother taught me. I used to send Aunt Starling letters every month."

"You're a good, clever girl," Mrs. Starling said, patting her cheek.

Edward swallowed his disappointment and returned the letter to his pocket. "Thank you, Mrs. Starling, Hannah. I beg your pardon for disturbing you."

Edward handed Trojan to the ostler at the inn, ordered a tankard of ale in the taproom, and climbed the stairs to the parlor Gareth had hired.

Gareth was reading a newspaper while eating a hearty luncheon.

Edward took off his hat and cast in down on the sofa. Chérie could be anyone in Soddy Morton or the outlying cottages and farms. Anyone. *I wish I'd never set eyes on that damned letter.*

"Hungry?" Gareth asked. "Want to join me?"

Edward grunted, and stripped off his gloves.

"I'll take that as a yes."

Edward pulled out a chair with a jerk. The harsh scrape of the chair legs on the wooden floor echoed his frustration. "I'm going to be stuck in this godforsaken part of the country until I die!"

Gareth laughed, choked on his food, and fell to coughing. When he'd caught his breath, he took a deep swallow of ale. "No luck, I take it?"

"It's a damned wild goose chase." Edward combed his hair roughly with his better hand, resisting the urge to pull a fistful out by the roots. "I was a fool to agree to it!"

Gareth lifted his eyebrows, but said nothing.

The waiter brought the tankard of ale. Edward took a long swig and turned his attention to the food on the table. When he'd eaten his fill, he sat nursing the last of the ale. There had to be *some* way of discovering who Chérie was. All he had to do was find it.

Edward drained his tankard and pushed it away. "When are you returning to London?"

Gareth shrugged. "Haven't thought about it." A smile lit his eyes. "I might stay a while."

"Mrs. Dunn . . ." Edward hesitated. Would a friend hold his tongue, or tell Gareth the truth? *A friend would tell him the truth.* "She's looking for a husband."

"Most unmarried ladies are," Gareth said, and picked up his tankard.

"A husband with money."

Gareth's face stiffened. He lowered the tankard. "Are you certain?"

"Her first husband died in poverty. Apparently she doesn't wish to make the same mistake twice." Edward leaned his elbows on the table and stared at Gareth across the ruins of the luncheon. "Mrs. Dunn's a pretty woman, Gary—and a poor one."

"You think all she sees is my money? You think it makes me palatable to her?"

"I don't know. I hope not." Edward met his eyes squarely. "Don't be blind, Gary. Don't make a mistake."

Gareth glanced at his empty sleeve, folded up and pinned neatly. His mouth twisted into a thin, bitter line. "No," he said. "I won't."

Both Gareth and the curate, Mr. Humphries, dined with them that evening. The curate gazed at Mrs. Dunn with open admiration while he ate; Gareth looked at her with mistrust.

Mrs. Dunn noticed the alteration in Gareth's manner. She seemed to shrink into herself as the evening progressed, her cheeks losing their pretty flush. Mattie noticed, too. Edward saw her watching Gareth, watching Mrs. Dunn. Finally, her gaze turned to him. Her eyebrows lifted slightly. He read the unspoken question: *Your doing?*

He conceded this with a dip of his head.

Mattie's lips tightened. She looked away.

Edward cut himself another piece of boiled veal and refused to feel guilty. If Mrs. Dunn was on the hunt for a wealthy husband, Gareth deserved to know.

Gareth chose not to sit next to Mrs. Dunn in the drawing room that evening. Mr. Humphries appropriated the vacant seat alongside her with alacrity. Mrs. Dunn stared down at her hands, clenched together in her lap.

Mattie poured the tea. "Did you warn him off Cecy?" she demanded under her breath as she handed Edward his cup and saucer.

"No," he said, in an equally low voice. "I merely told him what you told me."

Her gaze lifted from the teacup to her face. He saw anger in her eyes. "I didn't expect my words to be repeated."

"You didn't ask me to keep them secret."

Mattie's lips pressed together, as if she'd like to deny this truth. She gave a short nod and returned her attention to the teapot.

Strickland requested another of Fordyce's sermons on female meekness, a choice that Mr. Humphries praised. "I commend you on your selection, sir. Nothing suits a woman more than a proper meekness!"

The choice of sermon didn't appear to give Sir Arthur any pleasure, though. His mouth grew more and more pinched while he listened to his niece read aloud.

"To all other virtues and attainments befitting your sex, learn to join meekness. Meekness is followed with every honor."

Mr. Humphries nodded his agreement to this statement, looking self-important and solemn. Gareth didn't appear to be listening. He was frowning at the fireplace, his mouth as pinched as Strickland's.

As soon as the reading was over, Gareth excused himself. Mrs. Dunn watched him leave, an anxious pucker on her brow. Arthur Strickland barely seemed to notice his guest's departure. He launched into a bitter monolog, praising Fordyce and decrying the tendency of modern women towards foolish and headstrong behavior.

Edward glanced at Mattie. She sat with her hands folded in her lap and her eyes downcast. The speech was aimed at her; everyone in the room knew it—except the curate.

"In *my* day, young women were guided by wiser heads," Strickland declared.

Edward shifted his weight, making the chair he was in creak. *If you think marrying your niece off to Quartley was a good idea, I don't think much of your wisdom,* he told the man silently.

"A proper meekness, a proper deference, are far more to be admired in a young woman than a stubborn and conceited belief that she knows better than her superiors!"

"You are quite correct, Sir Arthur," the curate said. "Quite correct!"

"May I have another cup of tea?" Edward asked.

Mattie cast him a grateful glance and rose to ring the bell.

Strickland continued on his theme after a fresh teapot had been brought in, ably assisted by the curate. Edward had never heard a clock strike nine o'clock with more relief.

"Oh, is that the time?" the curate said. "I had thought it much earlier! Such a delightful discussion we've been having, Sir Arthur. The time has quite flown!" He rose and began an obsequious leave-taking of his host and Lady Marchbank.

Edward lifted his gaze to the ceiling once the man had

gone. *Thank you, Lord.* He tried to catch Mattie's eye, but she was looking at the floor.

"A most worthy young man," Lady Marchbank remarked. "He thinks just as one ought to."

Edward rolled his eyes. He stood and bowed to Lady Marchbank as she made her way to the door, closely attended by Mrs. Dunn.

Mattie followed. Edward fell into step behind her.

"Matilda, a moment," her uncle said coldly.

Mattie halted obediently.

Edward halted, too. Mattie caught his eye and shook her head.

He obeyed the silent message, exiting in Lady Marchbank's wake, but he didn't climb the stairs to bed. He lingered in the corridor. Arthur Strickland was going to vent his spleen, if he wasn't mistaken.

Sure enough, the sound of Strickland's raised voice soon reached his ears.

Edward grimaced in the darkness of the corridor.

Ten minutes later, as the longcase clock struck the quarter hour, Strickland was still berating Mattie. Edward shifted his weight from one foot to the other. He wanted to wrench open the door and command Strickland to stop.

He clenched his hands, holding himself back. He had no right to interrupt. He wasn't Mattie's brother or cousin. He wasn't her husband. Sir Arthur was her closest relative—and if he wished to berate her, it was his right.

I may not be related to Mattie, but damn it, I'm her friend. He took a step towards the door, and halted when he heard the thump of Strickland's cane.

The door swung open and then shut with a snap. Sir Arthur shuffled down the corridor, a tall, gaunt figure.

Edward stayed where he was, in the deep shadows. He waited until the old man was gone from sight, then opened the door. "Mattie?"

She stood beside the fireplace, her head bowed. At the sound of his voice she straightened and turned. "Edward!"

"Are you all right?"

"Perfectly!" Mattie began briskly snuffing the candles on the mantelpiece. "Were you worried about me? I assure you that it takes more than a mere scold to overset me!" Her smile and tone were bright—but he heard the faint catch in her voice.

"Mattie . . ." Edward caught her wrist as she moved past him. "That was more than a mere scold."

"I'm fine, Edward."

No, you're not.

"You are wiser than your uncle," Edward said, pulling her into an embrace. "Don't let him tell you otherwise. To have married Quartley would have been stupidity. Mattie, you *know* that."

She bowed her head so that her forehead rested against his shoulder and sighed. The sound was shaky. "Uncle Arthur went to a lot of trouble for me."

"I know he did." Edward stroked the nape of her neck. "But that doesn't make him right."

Mattie sighed again and pushed away from him. "Thank you, Edward."

He watched her cross the drawing room, feeling helpless.

"Don't judge Uncle Arthur too harshly," Mattie said as she opened the door. "He's a good man. It's just . . . Toby's death has been very difficult for him."

Toby. A tide of guilt surged through Edward. He felt suddenly heavier, as if his limbs were weighted down. "Toby's death is my fault," he said, his voice harsh. "Your uncle shouldn't be taking it out on you."

Mattie turned her head and stared at him. "Your fault? Nonsense!"

"You weren't there. You don't know."

Mattie shut the door. "No, I wasn't there. But I *do* know this: Toby was an adult. He made his own decisions, his own choices. You didn't force him to be there, Edward. No one did."

The drawing room blurred slightly. Instead of Mattie standing with her back to the door, he saw Toby, his face frantic. *Ned! Get up!*

The muscles in his throat clenched. He smelled Toby's blood, tasted it on his tongue.

Edward looked away from Mattie, swallowing hard.

She walked across to him. "You said you made peace with your own death while you were lying on the battlefield."

Edward swallowed again. He nodded, unable to look at her.

"But did you make peace with Toby's?"

He cast her a startled glance.

Mattie's eyes, gray and astute, caught his. He couldn't look away.

Mattie's hand rose to touch his cheek. "Don't hold yourself accountable for his death, Edward."

How can I not?

She must have read his thoughts on his face, for she lowered her hand. "Edward . . . do you think Toby would blame you? Is that truly what you think?"

Edward instinctively shook his head.

"Then why do you blame yourself?"

"Because he died trying to save my life!"

"Then he'd be glad you survived."

They were just words, spoken quietly, but they knocked the air from his lungs, brought tears to his eyes.

Edward averted his face. He squeezed his eyes shut.

Mattie put her arms around him. "Toby would be glad you survived, Edward," she said gently. "*Glad.*"

Edward blew out a shaky breath. He blinked the tears back.

Footsteps in the corridor made them spring apart. Mattie was almost at the door when it opened. "Griggs! Have you come to collect the tea tray? We were just leaving."

Edward followed Mattie into the corridor. Two candles awaited them in the entrance hall. *Toby would be glad you survived.* The words resonated inside him. He could hear the truth of them, could feel it.

He'd be glad.

Edward picked up his candle and climbed the stairs alongside Mattie. The risers creaked with each step they took. On the first floor, their paths diverged. Mattie halted. "Good night, Edward." She held out her hand to him.

He took it. Her clasp was warm, comforting. "Good night." But he couldn't bring himself to release her hand. He didn't want to let her go, didn't want her to turn away from him, to vanish into the gloom. "Mattie . . ." *I need you tonight.*

Mattie stared at him, her eyes dark and wide. She moistened her lips. "Edward?"

His need for her was a physical ache—Mattie's warmth, her company, the joy her body gave him. He swallowed and tried again: "Mattie, may I . . ."

But he couldn't finish the sentence. To ask her would be to treat her as a whore; and Mattie was no whore.

Edward forced himself to release her hand, to step back a pace.

Mattie didn't move. She stared at his face. He felt naked, as if his thoughts were engraved there for her to see, as vivid as the scars. "Edward . . . if . . . if you wish . . ."

He held his breath in painful hope.

Mattie flushed. She broke their gaze and looked at the floor.

Edward realized that it was even harder for her to ask this than it was for him. She was laying herself bare for rejection, for humiliation. He swallowed and took a deep breath. "Mattie . . . may I visit you tonight?"

She glanced at him shyly and nodded.

*C*HAPTER 12

E dward halted outside Mattie's bedchamber, clad only in his dressing gown. Faint candlelight leaked beneath her door.

He tapped lightly.

"Come in."

The smell of Mattie's bedroom was familiar: stale mutton fat. But instead of turning his stomach, the smell made his pulse quicken in anticipation.

Mattie stood beside the fireplace in her nightgown. Her hair hung in long, loose curls down her back. She watched him close the door, her eyes huge and dark in the shadowy bedchamber.

Edward walked across to her. "Are you certain about this?"

She nodded.

He stepped closer, tilted Mattie's chin with one fingertip, and bent his head to kiss her.

The softness of her lips, the taste of her mouth, the eagerness with which she returned the kiss, ignited a fire inside him. He pulled her close, glorying in the fullness of her breasts, in the rich curves of her hips beneath his hands. A groan of pleasure rose in his throat. The taste of her was ambrosia—delicious, heady, intoxicating.

They kissed until he could barely think. The fire inside him was a roaring blaze. Everything was heat and urgency. *I could take her against the wall.*

With that thought came a measure of sanity. Edward stepped back, dragging air into his lungs.

He held out his hand to her.

Mattie's fingers slid into his. Her cheeks were flushed, her lips rosy with kissing.

He led her to the bed, released her hand, and shrugged out of his dressing gown. Then he helped Mattie pull the nightgown over her head, baring her to his gaze. His throat tightened and for a moment he was incapable of breath. She was beautiful. Such a strong, rounded, ripe body. Such creamy skin. Such tantalizingly pink nipples. Such dark and secretive curls at the junction of her thighs. *Venus incarnate.*

He was aware of how scarred he was, how battered. *She deserves better than me.*

Mattie didn't seem to mind the scars. She smiled at him, her eyes shy, and put her hand in his when he offered it to her again. Edward pulled her to him and kissed her, trying to keep it light, trying not to frighten her with the depth of his need, and slid his hands around her waist—smooth, silky, warm skin—and lifted her onto the bed.

She broke the kiss, laughing. "Edward! I'm too heavy—"

"No, you're not." He silenced her with another kiss, this one fiercer. "You're perfect."

He laid himself alongside her on the coverlet, making the bed creak beneath their combined weight, and kissed her mouth, her cheek, her throat, while his hands explored her body. Her breasts had been formed with a man's touch in mind, surely? And the wonderful curve of waist and hip, the ripeness of her buttocks.

He was drowning in heat, in a fierce need to be inside her.

Slow, Edward reminded himself, pulling back from her. His skin was tight, hot. He couldn't remember that he'd ever felt such urgency, such eagerness to bury himself in a woman's body before. *This is what five months' celibacy does to a man.*

He stared at Mattie, panting, trembling. She stared back at him, and then lifted a hand. She traced a scar across his forehead, then a second scar that curved down his cheek until it reached his jaw, her touch so light he barely felt it. He saw no revulsion on her face. "Do they hurt?" she asked.

Edward shook his head. For some reason he couldn't fathom, her light, careful touch had made his throat tighten, as if he was about to cry.

Mattie traced an eyebrow, then touched the corner of his eye. Her fingertip stroked down his face, pausing to outline his mouth, before running along his jaw. "You have a nice face, Edward."

His surprise came out as a grunt of laughter.

She smiled in response. "Can we do it now?"

Oh, yes.

Last time he'd been afraid of hurting her, this time he didn't have to worry; that painful barrier had been broken.

Mattie made a low sound of pleasure when he entered her. She arched against him. Edward's breath caught in his lungs. Arousal surged through him. He squeezed his eyes tightly shut, struggling to hold onto his control.

"Edward . . ."

He opened his eyes and gazed down at her. She was lush and beautiful, with dark eyes and rosy lips and hair tumbled across the pillow. He managed to find his voice. "Yes?"

"This feels good."

Edward laughed. "Yes, it does." He dipped his head and kissed her, and began to move, rocking into her, making her gasp and clutch his shoulders, setting a leisurely rhythm, drawing out their pleasure. *Slowly. Slowly.*

His whole being was focused on Mattie, on her softness, her warmth, on the intense pleasure of making love to her. The rhythm of their lovemaking grew more urgent. He was drowning in a rising flood of sensation, riding the crest of a wave. Everything inside him tightened, spiraling towards the knife edge of climax. He felt Mattie shudder beneath him.

Edward wrenched himself from her, withdrawing before his pleasure overflowed inside her. He almost didn't make it, fumbling for his handkerchief, biting back a harsh groan.

He lay, half-stunned by the intensity of his climax. Pleasure seemed to echo endlessly inside him. His skin tingled and small tremors ran through his body. When he'd caught his breath he turned to Mattie, gathering her close, kissing her temple. *Thank you.*

"Did it hurt this time?" Edward asked, stroking her cheek lightly with his knuckles.

Mattie shook her head.

"Was it all right?"

"Yes." She wanted to cling to Edward, to beg him not to leave her, to hold her forever. With effort, she made herself draw back from him. *Don't make a fool of yourself. He's not offering to love you.* "It was better than last time," she said matter-of-factly. "And last time was much better than I had expected."

Edward grinned. "And how would you know what to expect?"

"Cecy said that it was awkward and uncomfortable and messy."

His eyebrows arched in surprise. "You asked her?"

"Yes."

Edward leaned on his elbow, looking amused. "What else did she tell you?" He picked up a long, looping curl that hung over her shoulder and pulled it gently through his fingers.

"That was all she said, but—" Mattie stopped. Just how much should she tell him? Instinct said she could trust him, especially when he smiled at her like that, his eyes warm, his face shadowed in the candlelight, but . . .

"But what?"

"If I show you something, will you promise not to tell anyone?"

"I promise."

Mattie came to a decision. She couldn't trust Edward with her whole secret, but she could trust him with part of it.

She climbed off the bed, tiptoed across the ice-cold floor to the far corner of her bedchamber, and opened the secret cupboard, reaching for one of the two volumes of *Fanny Hill*. "I read this," she said, walking back to the bed, holding it out to Edward.

"What?" He sat up and took the book and turned it to look at the spine in the candlelight. His mouth fell open. "*Fanny Hill?*"

Mattie nodded, holding her breath. Was he going to be shocked? Appalled? Outraged—

Edward tipped back his head and gave a shout of laughter. It reverberated off the paneled walls and heavy ceiling.

"Shh!" Mattie said, scrambling up on the bed again. "Someone will hear you!"

Edward pressed his face into one of the pillows, burying his laughter.

Mattie hugged her knees. She drank in the sight of his body—naked, scarred, convulsed with laughter. *This will never happen again.* Edward would leave, she'd be alone.

With that thought came a pain in her chest so sharp that it brought tears to her eyes. Her future stretched before her, achingly empty, barren.

Edward turned his head towards her. Amusement was bright on his face.

The urge to cry became stronger. Mattie swallowed. "What's so funny?"

"Your aunt. Boxing your ears because you had a copy of *Sense and Sensibility* and all the time you had *this* . . ." He began to laugh again, muffling the sound in the pillow.

It was such an infectious sound that Mattie's lips twitched

into a smile, even though tears blurred her vision. She gulped a big breath and blinked several times. By the time Edward lifted his head, she had found her self-control.

"*Fanny Hill.*" Laughter still lit Edward's face and glowed in his eyes. "You are an extremely unusual woman, Mattie Chapple."

Her smile faded. *More unusual than you know.*

If Edward knew all her secrets, he wouldn't be amused, he'd be shocked.

Or would he? He didn't seem to think *Fanny Hill* was iniquitous. He was leafing through the pages, grinning.

She wanted quite desperately to tell him, wanted to have one person she wasn't keeping her secret from. What had he once said? Everyone should have someone they could talk to without guarding their tongue.

"Where did you get it?"

"I found it in Toby's room, after . . . after Waterloo, when I was packing away his belongings."

"Ah." Edward's grin faded. He examined the book again. "Toby's." His voice was low, as if he spoke to himself, not her.

I'm Chérie. The confession trembled on the tip of her tongue. Mattie held it back with her teeth. To tell Edward would be to place him in a dreadful position. He'd have to choose whether to betray her confidence or break his word of honor to Uncle Arthur.

She couldn't do that to him.

Edward glanced at her. "You look very solemn."

So do you. Mattie shook her head. She made herself smile again. "You don't seem shocked that I've read *Fanny Hill.*"

"I *am* shocked," he said, but a grin was growing on his face again; he was teasing her. "Deeply shocked! But since you *have* got a copy, we may as well read it. Come here."

She did as he bade her, shyly moving closer to him.

Edward didn't seem to feel any shyness. His arm came around her, pulling her even closer, until she was pressed along the length of his body, bare skin to bare skin. "Listen to this passage."

Mattie rested her head on his chest. Edward began to read the scene where Fanny seduced her lover's manservant. After several sentences she stopped listening to the words and just listened to his voice, a low, deep baritone with an undertone of laughter. She heard the rumble of his voice in his chest, heard his heartbeat. The sound of his voice faded, becoming a background accompaniment to the steady beating of his heart. She rested her hand on his abdomen, felt it rise and fall with each breath, felt the warmth of his skin.

Mattie closed her eyes. Edward's heartbeat filled her head, his scent filled each breath she took. *I think I love you, Edward Kane.*

Edward finished reading the scene. He hoped it had affected Mattie the same way it had affected him.

The pages fluttered closed, scene by scene—Fanny's loss of virginity, Fanny's entry into the bawdy house—until the book lay open at the title page. The publisher's name caught his attention.

An idea burst into life in his mind, as startling as a sudden bolt of lightning. Edward stared at the publisher's name. *I know how to find Chérie.* He'd been attacking the puzzle from the wrong end.

Edward closed the book and put it aside. "Well?" he said, stroking Mattie's shoulder.

Her eyelids lifted. She stared at him, her expression solemn. "Well, what?"

He tilted up her chin, dipped his head, and kissed her, closing his eyes and letting himself sink into the pleasure of the moment—the softness of her lips, the intoxicating taste, the heat flooding beneath his skin, the rising urgency.

He dragged his mouth from hers and eased over onto his side, pressing against her, letting her feel his arousal.

Mattie didn't draw back.

Edward deepened the kiss, reveling in the sweetness of her mouth, in the ripeness of her body. He slid an arm around her waist and held her close while he rolled, bringing her beneath him, settling himself between her legs.

He felt a brief twinge of pain in his thigh. With the discomfort came a familiar flash of memory: Toby standing over him, his voice frantic. *Get up, Ned!*

He bowed his head against Mattie's shoulder, waiting for the black flood of guilt. It didn't come. Instead, he heard Mattie's voice: *He'd be glad you survived.*

Mattie's fingers trailed lightly across his hipbone.

Edward lifted his head and looked at her. In the soft candlelight, she was Venus, with dark, solemn eyes.

The edge of his urgency had faded. Edward pressed a kiss to the hollow at the base of her throat, licking, tasting, and then slid lower, teasing her breasts with his mouth, then her belly, and then slid even lower. He placed lingering kisses along her inner thighs. Her skin was incredibly smooth, like warm silk.

The dark curls at the junction of her thighs drew his attention. He hesitated, then gave in to temptation, stroking with his fingers, opening her, bending his head to taste her intimately.

Mattie gasped. Her body stiffened.

Edward's own arousal kicked up a notch. He bent enthusiastically to his task, holding her hips down, pinning her to the bed. Mattie's scent, her taste, unleashed a deep, visceral response within him. A voice vibrated in his head. *Sex,* it said. *Woman. Mine.* Arousal twisted inside him, coiling tighter and tighter.

Mattie's body clenched in pleasure, her back arching, her hips trying to lift off the bed. A fierce, victorious satisfaction surged inside him. Edward lifted his head and moved swiftly up her body, bracing himself over her, wanting to possess Mattie with more than just his mouth. Her breasts rose and fell with each panted breath.

Edward paused to savor the sight—those ripe breasts, the taut pink crests, the glow of pleasure flushing her skin.

"Edward?"

"Mmm?" He bent his head and pressed his lips to the soft curling tendrils at her temple, breathing deeply to inhale the scent of her hair.

"May I do that to you?"

He lifted his head a fraction. "What?"

"Kiss you like that. Your organ."

Every muscle in Edward's body clenched. He stared at Mattie, incapable of breathing, incapable of speaking.

"May I?"

Edward swallowed. "If you would like to." His voice sounded unfamiliar in his ears, as if someone had grabbed him by the throat and was choking him.

Mattie blushed shyly. "I would."

Edward eased himself off her. His heart hammered in his chest.

Mattie sat up. "Is there any particular way of doing it?"

He tried to answer this question, but his brain didn't seem to be functioning properly. "Uh . . . whatever you want to do is, uh . . . good."

Mattie nodded, her expression serious.

Edward lay back and stared up at the bed canopy, his muscles taut with anticipation. He felt the mattress dip and sway as Mattie moved closer, felt the heat of her knee touching his thigh, felt her long hair tickle across his skin as she leaned forward.

His entire body twitched at her first tentative kiss.

Mattie halted. "Did that hurt?"

"No." His voice was hoarse, strangled. "It was good."

She hesitated a moment, and then laid a second kiss on top of her first. The softness of her lips was pure torture. Edward clenched his hands and began to count the seconds. One, two, three . . .

Mattie began to explore, tasting his skin as he'd tasted hers. A groan caught in his throat. Dear God, her tongue.

Four, five, six . . .

She took him into her mouth. Edward squeezed his eyes shut, fighting for control.

Seven, eight, nine . . .

"Enough!" He sat up, pulling away from her.

Mattie sat back on her heels, dismay creasing her face. "Am I doing it wrong?"

"No, it's perfect." *But I can't last much longer.*

"Oh." The dismay smoothed from her face. She smiled at him shyly.

Edward reached for her, rolling, settling between her thighs. Arousal drummed in his veins. He'd never wanted to bed a woman more urgently than he wanted Mattie right now. "Do you want this?" he asked, panting, hoping he'd have the willpower to stop if she said no.

"Yes."

Mattie lay awake after Edward had gone, staring up at the ceiling, guilt twisting in her chest.

She tried to imagine telling him that she was Chérie, tried to imagine his reaction. Would he laugh, or be angry?

The candle burned down until it was a guttering stub. Mattie climbed off the bed and lit another one. Then she pulled on her nightgown, sat at her escritoire, and began to write. *Edward, there is something I wish I could tell you, but I can't. It's not that I don't trust you, it's that if I tell you, you'll have to tell my uncle—or break your word to him, and I don't want you to have to make that choice.*

She dipped the quill in the ink and continued. *This is what I want you to know: I am Chérie. And I know it is Chérie you are looking for.*

She wrote swiftly, telling him about finding the diary and *Fanny Hill*, about her decision to try to support herself through writing.

I know that what I have done is wrong: writing the Confessions, deceiving my uncle and aunt. But I could see no other way.

I am very sorry, Edward. It was never my intention to deceive you. I wish I could tell you my secret now; I hope you can understand why I haven't.

Yours,

Mattie.

She sealed the letter and wrote Edward's name and the date on the front and put it in the hidden cupboard. Guilt seemed to sit a little less heavily on her.

Mattie picked up *Fanny Hill* from where it lay, half under one pillow, remembering the rumble of Edward's voice when he read aloud, remembering the way he'd turned to her afterwards, his hungry passion. It would make a good scene for one of Chérie's confessions.

She tilted her head to one side, considering this. Perhaps Chérie could read a titillating passage aloud, to inflame her lover . . .

Mattie turned back to the escritoire, pulled another sheet of paper towards her, and began to write.

Edward sought an interview with Arthur Strickland after he'd breakfasted. "I've thought of a way of discovering Chérie's identity, sir."

"How?"

"I shall approach her publisher in London."

Strickland's wispy eyebrows drew together. "You think he'll tell you?"

"I don't know, sir."

The old man grunted sourly.

"I'll leave for town this morning. Within a few days I should know something."

Strickland nodded. He didn't thank Edward, or apologize for the days he'd wasted in Soddy Morton; he seemed to take it as his due.

They weren't wasted days, Edward told himself, as he let himself out of the old man's study. There'd been kittens and gingerbread and kisses in the hayloft—and two astonishing nights with Mattie. And there had been her comment last night: *Toby would be glad you survived.* A handful of words—and yet they had changed his world. He felt lighter this morning. It wasn't merely the aftermath of sex; the crushing burden of guilt he'd carried for the past five months was gone. In place of guilt was only regret.

Mattie had done that.

Mattie.

Her name conjured an image of her: the gray eyes that were sometimes serious, sometimes sparkling with mischief, the lush mouth, the strong, beautiful body.

He couldn't leave without bidding her farewell, without telling her that he'd be back.

Edward climbed the stairs two at a time and met Mattie coming along the dark, drafty corridor. She was dressed for outdoors, a letter in her hand.

They both halted.

Edward stared at her, remembering how she'd looked when he'd last seen her: naked, flushed, her hair tumbled across the pillows. His skin tightened in memory of the intimacies they'd shared.

Edward cleared his throat. "I have to go to London."

"When?"

"Now."

Mattie nodded. He couldn't see her face clearly in the dark corridor. What did she think of his leaving so precipitously? He'd taken her virginity, bedded her more than once. *An honorable man would marry her.* "I . . . er, I should be back by midweek."

Mattie nodded again.

Damn it, what was she thinking?

Edward shifted his weight uncomfortably. He felt as if he was abandoning her, escaping to London while she was trapped at Creed Hall, with its bricked-up windows and freezing rooms and dank, leafless woods. His eyes fastened on the letter in her hand. "Is that to your friend in London?"

"Yes."

"Let me take it. It'll get there faster."

"No, really, Edward, it's not necessary—"

"Nonsense," he said, taking the letter and tucking it into his breast pocket. It made him feel slightly less guilty; he was doing her a service, not simply walking away and leaving her.

Mattie opened her mouth as if she wanted to protest, and then closed it again. She looked down at the floor.

Edward shifted his weight again. "I . . . uh . . . ." He couldn't think of anything to say—and then came a flash of inspiration. He dug in his pocket, pulled out a few coins, and held them out to her. "For gingerbread, while I'm gone."

Mattie's head lifted. In the dim light he saw her cheeks flush. "I don't want your money, Edward."

Blood rushed to Edward's face. He shoved the coins back in his pocket. "I'm sorry. I didn't mean . . ." *I didn't mean you're a whore.* He tugged at his neckcloth. It was uncomfortably tight. "Uh . . . is there anything I can bring back for you from town? A book? Anything?"

"No, thank you."

Edward shifted his weight again. The horses would be harnessed to the curricle, Tigh waiting. "Good-bye."

"Good-bye."

He turned away from her, took a step, and then swung back to face her again. *An honorable man wouldn't walk away.* He owed Mattie more than this. Because he'd bedded her. Because she was Toby's cousin. Because she needed rescuing. "Mattie . . ." He took a deep breath. "Marry me."

195

The words seemed to echo in the corridor, bouncing off the paneled walls, ringing in his ears. Edward wished he could swallow them, could cram them back into his mouth.

"I beg your pardon?"

Edward took another deep breath and said the words again: "Marry me, Mattie."

CHAPTER 13

Mattie stared at him. Her heart began to beat fast. *Marry Edward*. Her imagination took flight, giving her a glimpse of the future: a home, a family, a husband she could love, could laugh with.

But Edward didn't look as if he had the same, happy vision that she did. There was no smile on his face. The line of his jaw was grim.

Mattie's joy began to seep away. "Why?"

"Because, uh . . ."

She remembered what Cecy had said when Edward first arrived: that he wasn't looking for a wife. Suddenly, she understood. "You feel you ought to, because of what we've done?"

His cheeks reddened. "Yes."

Mattie looked down at the floor. Stupidly, she felt as if she might cry. "No, thank you."

"But, Mattie—"

"Have a good journey to London," she said briskly and turned away from him, hurrying down the corridor in the direction of her bedchamber.

Edward came after her, grabbing her elbow, halting her. "It's not just because of that, Mattie."

"What, then?" She tugged her arm free. "Is it because you

pity me, living here at Creed Hall? Because you think I need rescuing?"

She could tell from his expression that it was precisely what he thought.

"I can rescue myself."

"By running a boarding house?"

"Yes!"

"But Mattie—"

"It's a perfectly respectable occupation for a woman."

"Not for one as well-born as you!" And then, in the manner of one clinching an argument, he said: "What would Toby say if he knew?"

Mattie stiffened. "Is that what this is about? Because you feel you owe Toby?"

"Of course not!" Edward said, but his tone was slightly too high-pitched. He was lying.

Mattie took a step backwards, away from him. She folded her arms across her chest. "Edward, when you came to Creed Hall, were you looking for a wife?"

"Well, no, but . . . but I always planned to marry one day and . . . and I think we should suit!"

I do, too. Sadness squeezed in her chest. She shook her head. "I won't marry you, Edward."

"Why not?"

"Why not?" Mattie's face felt as stiff as a statue's. "Because when you marry, it should be someone you *want* to marry, not someone you feel you *ought* to marry."

"I do want to marry you!"

Her eyes met his steadily. "If we hadn't done what we did, would you have offered for me? Truthfully?"

Edward flushed again. "Well, no, but—"

"Thank you for your offer, Edward. But I must decline it." Mattie turned away from him. The urge to cry was stronger, choking in her throat.

"Damn it, Mattie!" Edward caught her arm again. "I'm trying to do the right thing here!"

"I know you are." From somewhere, she found the strength look at him, to smile brightly, to utter a light laugh. "But Edward, you can't force me to marry you!"

He released her arm. "No, but—"

"If I had thought you'd feel compelled to offer for me, I would never have asked you to . . . to do what we did."

"I know," Edward said. "But Mattie—"

"My virtue is intact to the world. There's no reason for us to marry."

Edward frowned at her. "But the boarding house—"

"Has absolutely nothing to do with you." She laid her hand on his sleeve. "Thank you for your offer, Edward, but it's quite unnecessary. Surely you see that?"

He stared at her for a long moment, narrow-eyed, his mouth tightly compressed. "Please think about it."

"I shan't change my mind."

She removed her hand from his arm. Edward caught it. "Please," he said again, gripping her fingers tightly. "Think about it."

Mattie looked at him, seeing his square, scarred face. If he was making this offer from his heart, not from a sense of honor, she'd agree without hesitation.

"Think about it, Mattie. Please."

She should say no, but if she spoke, she'd start to cry. Instead, she nodded.

Edward released her hand. "Thank you."

Mattie nodded again.

Edward hesitated, then bent his head and placed a light kiss on her cheek. "I'll be back in a few days."

Mattie watched him stride down the corridor, carrying Chérie's latest confession in his pocket. She touched her fingers to her cheek, where he'd kissed her.

She managed to hold the tears back until she reached her bedchamber, but once in the privacy of her room, they spilled over. Mattie curled up on her bed and cried as she hadn't cried since her parents died. Outside, she heard the clatter of hooves and carriage wheels. Edward was leaving.

Loneliness enveloped her. Her parents were gone, Toby was gone, and now Edward was gone, too.

Stop it! Mattie told herself. *You still have Cecy. You're not alone.*

She blew her nose and climbed off the bed. Edward had asked her to think about his offer—but no thinking was necessary.

She sat down at the escritoire and pulled out a sheet of paper. *Thank you for your offer, Edward,* she wrote, *but I can't accept it. Truly, you owe me nothing—most certainly not your name. I don't regret those two nights, and I hope that you don't either.*

And then, because the words were churning inside her, she wrote: *I think I love you.*

Seeing the words, black ink on white paper, made her hold her breath for a moment. She wrote them again: *I think I love you, Edward.*

The weight of the words, the way they settled inside her with such a sense of *rightness* told her they were true: she loved Edward.

Mattie took a deep breath. She dipped the quill in ink and continued. *And that is why I can't marry you. Because I want you to be happy. You deserve to marry when you want to, Edward, not like this, because you feel you have to. And you deserve a wife you love, not one who merely suits you.*

She looked at what she'd written and tried to imagine Edward's reaction if he were to read it. Guilt? An even stronger determination to marry her—because he felt he ought to?

Mattie screwed up the sheet of paper and burned it in the fireplace.

At Bletchley, it began to snow. At Leighton Buzzard, Edward was forced to admit that he wouldn't reach London that day.

"Sir," Tigh said, when they entered the outskirts of the town. "We can't go any further."

"I know, God damn it!" he snapped.

They rode in silence the length of the main street. As he halted at the Crown, Edward said. "I beg your pardon, Tigh, I'm out of sorts today." But his foul mood wasn't because of the weather—it was because of the appalling mess he'd made of proposing to Mattie. He'd been more than inept; he'd been insulting.

An ostler ran up to take the horses. Edward climbed stiffly down from the curricle. The cold weather had made his leg ache. He stood for a moment, massaging his thigh.

Snowflakes gusted in a whirling cloud around his head, mimicking the turmoil of emotions inside him: disgust at himself, anger, shame. And beneath those emotions was one that he shied away from recognizing: relief that Mattie had refused him.

He blew out a breath—*And you call yourself a gentleman, Ned?*—and limped into the inn.

Sir Gareth dined with them again. "I shall be returning to London tomorrow," he told Uncle Arthur while they waited in the drafty salon for dinner.

Mattie glanced at Cecy and caught the brief, stricken expression on her face. Cecy blinked several times, took a deep breath, and lifted her chin. Her smile was bright and brittle.

Mattie looked down at the floor. *My fault.* She should never have told Edward the truth about Cecy's circumstances.

A faint sound caught her attention. "Is that . . . ?" She hurried across to the window, pulling the curtains back. "It's snowing again."

Sir Gareth strode over to join her.

They stared out. The snow was coming down fast, the flakes streaking past at a slanting angle.

Sir Gareth turned away from the window. "I'd best get back to the village."

"Nonsense," Uncle Arthur said. "You'll stay with us until it stops."

"Thank you, sir, but—"

"I won't allow a man in your condition to ride down to the village in weather like this."

Sir Gareth stiffened. Color flushed his lean cheeks. "I'm not an invalid, sir."

"It would be a great piece of folly!" Uncle Arthur said. He thumped his cane for emphasis. "No friend of my son will be out in such weather!"

For a moment Sir Gareth stood rigidly, and then he mastered his temper. He gave a stiff bow. "Thank you, sir."

The silence at dinner was even less comfortable than usual. Cecy kept her eyes on her plate. From time to time she blinked, as if fighting back tears.

Sir Gareth only glanced at her once that Mattie saw. His mouth tightened, as if in anger, before he looked away.

She wasn't deceiving you! Mattie wanted to cry aloud. She speared a piece of boiled cabbage with her fork and lifted it to her mouth. She looked from Cecy to Sir Gareth while she chewed, examining their faces—one miserable, one grim. Resolve grew inside her. She'd ruined Cecy's chance of happiness. *Therefore, it's up to me to fix it.*

Her moment came the next morning. Mattie was in sole possession of the breakfast parlor when Sir Gareth made his entrance. Outside, snow still fell thickly.

"Miss Chapple," Sir Gareth said with a polite nod. "Good morning."

"Good morning." She watched as he crossed to the sideboard. "I would avoid the eggs, if I were you. And the toast. The sausages are really the only thing worth eating. Unless you're fond of gruel?"

"Gruel?" He grimaced.

"My uncle says that a bowl of gruel each day is essential to one's health," Mattie said demurely. "He swears by it."

Sir Gareth glanced at her, catching the teasing note in her voice. A smile quirked up one corner of his mouth.

"If the gruel isn't to your taste, have the sausages," Mattie said, more seriously. "They're actually rather good."

"Thank you. I shall take your advice."

Mattie watched as he awkwardly transferred a number of sausages onto a plate. It wasn't until he sat down at the table that she realized he wouldn't be able to cut them up. "Would you like me to cut them for you?"

Sir Gareth hesitated, and then passed the plate to her. "Thank you."

Mattie felt a surge of sympathy for him. It must be galling to need help for the smallest and most mundane of tasks. Every day must be full of mortifications and difficulties.

He deserves to be happy. And so does Cecy.

She bent her attention to the sausages, slicing them into bite-sized pieces. Would it be best to be blunt, or subtle?

Blunt, she decided, handing back the plate. Toby had always preferred straightforward speaking to roundaboutation.

"Sir Gareth?"

He glanced at her, his eyebrows rising slightly. "Miss Chapple?"

She took a deep breath. "It's true that Cecy is poor and that she wants to marry a man who can provide for her, but her regard for you is quite genuine."

The faint smile vanished from Sir Gareth's face. His eyebrows lowered. The polite friendliness was gone, as if a door had slammed shut between them.

"She hasn't been trying to fix your attention." Mattie leaned forward over her plate. "She truly likes you!"

Sir Gareth's lips compressed, a bitter movement. He glanced at his empty sleeve and then pushed to his feet. "Miss Chapple—"

She stood hurriedly, reaching out her hand to stop him. "I know it's none of my business. But please, Sir Gareth, before you judge her, *talk* to her!"

Mattie retreated, leaving Sir Gareth to his breakfast. *Idiot!* she told herself as she climbed the stairs to the sewing room. Her bluntness had misfired. All she'd succeeded in doing was to make Sir Gareth angry.

She busied herself with the gown she was making. *The next one I sew won't be gray,* she promised herself. She built a picture of it in her head while she worked. A gown of colored fabric, blue, or maybe green, with a fitted bodice. No frills or flounces—she was too much of a giantess to suit such things—but she'd have a pretty trim at both neckline and hem.

A small fire burned in the grate, but despite its best efforts the room grew steadily colder. An icy wind rattled the window in its frame and crept in through the cracks. Mattie moved her chair closer to the fire and bent her head over the seam she was stitching.

She was shivering by the time she'd finished the second sleeve. Laying it aside, she went downstairs to fetch a heated brick from the kitchen. On her way back, the low murmur of voices coming from the library caught her attention. The door was open the merest crack. Curious, Mattie pushed the door open a few inches.

Sir Gareth *had* listened to her advice. He sat alongside Cecy on the sofa, talking with her.

Mattie hugged the warm brick to her chest and watched as Sir Gareth said something, as Cecy replied. Their heads were bent closely together.

Mattie carefully closed the door and tiptoed down the corridor.

She was working on the bodice when she heard light footsteps approaching the sewing room.

"Mattie?" Cecy stood in the doorway. Joy glowed on her face. "I have something to tell you."

Mattie laid down her sewing. "I think I can guess what it is."

"Oh, Mattie! He's asked me to marry him!" Tears shone in Cecy's eyes.

Mattie stood and embraced her friend.

"He says it was your doing." Cecy hugged her back, half-laughing, half-crying "Oh, thank you, Mattie! You can't imagine how happy I am!"

Sadness clenched in Mattie's chest. *Yes, I can. If Edward had truly wanted to marry me, I should be this joyful, too.* "I'm glad he listened!" she said, forcing a note of heartiness into her voice. "I'm sure you'll be extremely happy together."

Dusk had fallen by the time Edward reached London. The seventy miles now lying between him and Creed Hall had done nothing to improve his mood. Shame heated his face every time he recalled his attempt to persuade Mattie to marry him. A village simpleton could have done a better job. *How could you have been such a cod's head, Ned? As if your wits had dribbled out your ears.*

But yesterday's proposal hadn't been his first act of stupidity; it had merely been the culmination. His very *first* mistake had been in accepting Mattie's offer to bed her. An intelligent man would have walked away at that point. An intelligent man wouldn't have put himself in a position where he felt obliged to offer marriage.

Edward pulled up outside his lodgings in Ryder Street and handed the reins to Tigh. He rubbed his thigh. "Take it round to the stables,' he said, grabbing his valise and climbing down.

His rooms were on the second floor, above Gareth's. Edward limped up the stairs. The clock on the landing struck six while he unlocked his door. At Creed Hall, they'd be sitting down to dine.

Edward dropped his valise just inside the door, threw his

hat down on the table, pulled off his gloves, then made his slow, limping progress around the room, lighting candles. *How the devil do I fix this mess?*

He could accept Mattie's refusal of his suit and continue his life as he'd planned, down in Cornwall, while she ran her boarding house. After all, Mattie was right: no one but the two of them knew that her virtue had been compromised.

The door swung open behind him. Tigh came in, whistling. The bâtman set down his valise alongside Edward's and headed for the fireplace.

Edward rubbed his forehead and watched Tigh kneel to light the fire. Mattie had said that she didn't need rescuing . . . so why was he convinced that she did? Why did he feel that he was abandoning her?

The fire, once it was burning, filled the grate. Heat began to spread through the room. Edward shrugged out of his caped driving coat and flung it over the back of the nearest chair. He unwound the thick muffler from his throat and imagined Mattie in the drafty, under-lit dining room, wearing her ugly gray gown. To his dismay, he realized that he missed her. He missed the dimples in her cheeks. He missed her gray eyes, sometimes brimming with laughter, sometimes alarmingly astute. He missed her frank utterances and her sense of humor—and he missed her ripe, beautiful body, the heat and passion of sharing her bed.

Tigh materialized at his elbow. "Sir? Would you like to change?"

What I would like is to . . .

To what? Marry Mattie?

The answer was an instinctive *No*.

What then? Should he walk away from her? Abandon her to the future she'd chosen for herself?

The answer to that question was an equally instinctive *No*.

Edward rubbed his forehead again and followed the bâtman into the bedchamber. He sat stiffly on the edge of the bed and extended one leg. Tigh eased the boot off. "Leg hurting, sir?"

Edward grunted, not really paying attention.

Tigh pulled the other boot off and then helped him peel out of his riding coat. Paper crackled in the breast pocket: Mattie's letter. Edward pulled it out. *Mrs. Thos. Brocklesby, Lombard Street.* "Tigh, take this round to the receiving office, please. See if you can make the last collection.'

"Yes, sir."

"Oh, and Tigh . . ." Edward fished in his pocket for a guinea and tossed it to the batman. "Get a copy of Chérie's latest, will you?"

Edward read the confession over a meal of roasted capons and ale sent around from the nearest inn. The beginning was familiar; he'd read it first in Arthur Strickland's study, and a dozen times since. He skimmed to where Lord S. began disrobing Chérie in the folly and slowed to read with his full attention.

He forgot his dinner while Lord S. tupped Chérie in the folly, and then in the brook, and then again on the grassy bank, where they lay bathed in warm, afternoon sunlight. Except that it wasn't Chérie and Lord S. he saw in his mind's eye, it was himself and Mattie. He imagined the coolness of the water, imagined Mattie splashing him, teasing him, laughing, drops of water glistening on her skin, imagined the smell of grass and damp earth and the sounds of birdsong and running water. And—vividly—he imagined the taste of Mattie's kisses, the scent of her skin. He could almost feel her clutching him, her fingers gripping his shoulders as passion took her.

Edward put down the confession. He reached for his tankard and took a long swallow of ale. The room had grown uncomfortably hot while he read.

His food, on the other hand, had grown cold.

He ate, shoving aside thoughts of sparkling brooks and naked goddesses, and reread the confession with an academic eye, searching for any clues to Chérie's identity. He didn't find any.

Edward pushed his plate away and read the confession yet again. Lord S. was an energetic man. He'd tumbled Chérie three times in the space of a few hours.

Edward's thoughts turned to the discreet establishment he patronized whenever he was in London. He drained the tankard and pushed back his chair. Now that his desire for sex had returned and his body was cooperating, it seemed a shame not to pay Mrs. Suffolk and her girls a visit.

Edward had forgotten the scars disfiguring his face. He remembered them as soon as the doorman bowed him into Mrs. Suffolk's establishment. The matron herself bustled into the entrance foyer to greet him, improbably golden curls piled high on her head. Her smile froze when she saw him.

Edward felt his own smile stiffen into something as false as Mrs. Suffolk's. His impulse was to turn and leave, to plunge back into the dark streets, where no one would notice his face. *Don't be a fool,* he told himself, and handed his hat and gloves to the doorman. *You're here now.*

"Captain Kane! How delightful to see you again," Mrs. Suffolk said, her eyes fixed on what remained of his left ear. "It's been too many months since you last visited us."

"Mister," Edward said. "I sold out after Waterloo."

"You were at Waterloo? Such a dreadful engagement!"

Edward returned a noncommittal grunt. He didn't want to think about Waterloo tonight, didn't want Toby's ghost riding on his back.

"Only the smaller salon is open tonight," Mrs. Suffolk said gaily. "Winter, you know!"

She personally escorted him into the salon. Edward blinked and halted briefly in the doorway. The contrast between this salon and the drawing room at Creed Hall was immense. Instead of a few feeble candles, cut-crystal chandeliers glittered overhead. The walls were painted a fashionable shade of primrose, not paneled with dark wood. The furniture was in the Grecian style, gilded and scrolled and upholstered with crimson velvet. A fire filled the fireplace. Flowers and perfume scented the air. In one corner of the room a musician played, the notes a tinkling background to the hum of voices and lilt of feminine laughter.

Mrs. Suffolk glanced up at him. "Mr. Kane?"

Did she think he'd halted because he was shy of his scars? It wasn't that; it was the jarring sense that in stepping into the salon he was passing from one world into another.

Edward shook off the sensation and advanced into the room.

The company was sparse, only three other gentlemen vying for the attentions of the half-dozen girls present—but then, the night was young. By midnight, the room would be thronging with men looking for carnal entertainment.

Mrs. Suffolk escorted him to a sofa near the fireplace and gave him a white silk handkerchief. "I don't need to remind you what to do with this," she said coyly.

No, she didn't need to remind him.

A footman in a wig and livery proffered a tray. "Champagne, sir? Claret?"

Edward chose claret. He sipped the wine while he ran his eyes over the girls. They were all new since the last time he'd visited, but that wasn't unusual; Mrs. Suffolk prided herself on the cleanliness of her wares.

He caught one of them staring at him, a flaxen-haired girl with the rosy-cheeked buxomness of a milkmaid. He saw horror in her widened eyes and parted lips before she hurriedly averted her gaze.

He felt his face tighten. *Coming here was a mistake.*

But Mrs. Suffolk's girls were professionals. Less than half a minute after he'd sat, one of them approached. "Mr. Kane." She settled herself alongside him, plump and pretty, with rosebud lips and glossy brunette curls and a gown cut low over a lush bosom. "Mrs. Suffolk tells us you were at Waterloo."

"Yes," Edward said, and wondered how much of the admiration in her eyes and warmth in her voice was false.

Probably all of it, a cynical voice said in his head.

The girl placed a hand on his thigh. She glanced at him through her eyelashes. "How long are you in London, Mr. Kane?"

"A couple of days."

Her pink mouth formed a moue of disappointment. "Such a shame." She began to stroke teasing circles with a fingertip. If his scarred face horrified her, she was too professional to show it. "Are you familiar with Chérie's *Confessions*?"

Edward blinked. "I beg your pardon?"

"Chérie's *Confessions*." The brunette leaned across him, her hand sliding further up his thigh, and reached for something on the nearest side table. It was a closely printed broadsheet. "Here." She proffered it to him.

Edward recognized it as the latest confession. He experienced a brief and dizzying moment of dissonance, as if Creed Hall and Mrs. Suffolk's parlor tried to occupy the same space for an instant. He shook his head slightly to clear it. "Yes. I'm familiar with them."

"We have them all," the girl said. The teasing circles she was tracing with her fingertip crept higher up his leg. "If there's one in particular you like, I can read it to you . . ."

Edward took a gulp of wine and forced himself to focus. *Forget Creed Hall.*

The brunette had the type of ripe, womanly figure he most liked, but her height was diminutive. He outweighed her by a good ten stone. He'd have to be careful not to be too vigorous or he'd hurt her.

When he'd bedded Mattie, he'd not had to hold back. Her body was strong and voluptuous, perfect. Venus to his Goliath.

Edward shoved that thought aside.

The girl moved even closer to him on the sofa. The soft swell of her breasts pressed against his upper arm. Her hand moved higher up his thigh, a teasing, creeping advance towards his groin. She smiled bewitchingly at him. Her dimples seemed designed to seduce him.

Mattie hadn't used her dimples to entrance him. When she'd touched him it was because she wanted to, not because she'd been pretending. Everything about her had been utterly genuine—her innocence, her shy curiosity, her delight in his lovemaking.

Edward looked at the brunette. He didn't want her. The woman he wanted was a day's ride north.

The girl's hand was almost at his groin. Edward caught it, halting her.

She giggled and pouted, pressing her breasts against his arm. "Is something wrong, Mr. Kane?"

Edward released her hand. "Uh . . . I . . ." He looked around the salon. *What the devil am I doing here?*

"Excuse me." He stood, placed the wine glass and handkerchief on the nearest table, and left.

It was freezing outside. Edward's breath billowed in front of him as he strode back to his rooms. What the hell had just happened at Mrs. Suffolk's establishment?

He wasn't sure.

He crossed Fitzmaurice Place and began to list the things he *was* sure of.

One, he wanted to have sex with Mattie again. Mattie, and nobody else.

Two, if anyone ever read him Chérie's *Confessions,* he wanted it to be Mattie.

A scene blossomed in his mind: candlelight, a wide bed, the warmth and softness of Mattie's body pressed against him, the sound of her voice—that warm, rich contralto—as she read aloud from Chérie's latest confession . . .

Edward shook his head to clear it.

Three, he wanted to be with Mattie. No sex, no confessions, he simply wanted to *be* in her company.

Edward frowned as he turned into Berkeley Street. Had he managed to fall in love with Matilda Chapple? Did he want to marry her? Spend the rest of his life with her?

The answer appeared to be *Yes*.

Edward strode down Berkeley Street, considering what this meant.

He conjured his estate in Cornwall in his mind's eye and imagined strolling through the park with Mattie, imagined her teasing him, imagined her laughing. He imagined sitting in the cozy parlor with her curled up on the sofa alongside him, reading aloud from a novel. He imagined undressing Mattie in the master bedchamber upstairs, imagined making love to her, imagined sleeping with her in his arms.

These visions gave him a feeling of deep contentment, of *rightness*.

Edward's frown deepened. He waited while a carriage clattered slowly past and then crossed Piccadilly. How the devil had this happened? How had he managed to fall in love with Mattie—and not realize it?

Because I'm a cod's head.

Edward grunted, puffing a cloud of white vapor. Yes, he'd proved that without doubt, yesterday. He recalled his proposal—and Mattie's reaction to it—and grimaced.

The question was: had Mattie refused because of how he'd phrased his offer—or because she didn't like him enough to marry him?

Edward had found no answer to that by the time he reached Ryder Street. He mulled it over while he sat in front of his fire drinking brandy, he mulled it over while he prepared for bed, stripping off his clothes, brushing his teeth, washing his face. Mattie liked him—liked his company, his lovemaking—but did she love him? *Could* she love him?

When Mattie looked at him, he forgot he had scars blazoned across his face, forgot his ear was missing—but Mattie would never be able to forget those things. They'd confront her every time she looked at him.

Edward stared at himself in the mirror, seeing the scars, the stump of his ear. *Could you live with this face forever, Mattie?*

"Sir?" his bâtman asked. "Is there anything more you need?"

Edward turned away from the mirror. "No, thank you, Tigh. You may go."

The bâtman picked up his discarded clothes and left, whistling under his breath.

Edward climbed into bed and blew out the candle. His bed seemed very empty. Emptier than it had ever been. But it wasn't just Mattie's body he wanted, it was her companionship, her laughter, her love. She was open and honest and frank. She was intelligent. She was funny.

He remembered her words: *Toby would be glad you survived.*

He remembered how Mattie had traced the scars on his face with a light fingertip. There had been tenderness in her touch, and tenderness was close to love, wasn't it?

If I say the right words, maybe she'll marry me.

He just had to figure out what the right words were.

CHAPTER 14

Edward strode along Piccadilly on his way to confront Chérie's publisher, but instead of hailing a hackney, he allowed himself to be diverted by Hatchards. Inside was the scent of leather and paper and ink. The shelves were crammed with volumes of history and philosophy, poetry and travel—and novels.

Edward selected *Sense and Sensibility,* and three recently released novels. "Deliver these to my rooms." He handed the salesman his card.

"Of course, sir." The salesman's polite smile froze as he took in the scars. He hastily averted his gaze and cleared his throat. "Uh . . . delivery. Yes, sir."

Back out on Piccadilly, Edward hailed a hackney. "Holywell Street." But as he climbed into the carriage, he changed his mind. "But first, take me past Grafton House."

He'd never set foot in the Grafton House emporium before and was rather daunted by the number of items for sale. He recoiled from the displays of muslin and sarcenet and other fabrics, the furs, the frothy lace, the handkerchiefs and fans and gloves, the silk stockings. It was unquestionably a female bastion; he stood out like a Visigoth who'd accidently blundered into the House of the Vestal Virgins—large, uncouth, and most definitely out of place.

Edward's first instinct was to slink back out the door. He lifted his chin and strode across the nearest counter. "Ribbons," he told the shop assistant firmly. "Cherry red ones."

He emerged from that establishment some considerable time later, possessor of not only cherry red ribbons, but a handsome Norwich shawl, a Kashmir shawl, and an ermine muff, all of which would be delivered to his rooms in Ryder Street.

Edward found it hard to sit still as the hackney headed for Holywell Street. He shifted on the squab seat, fiddled with his hat, adjusted his gloves. The nervousness coiling in his belly wasn't because of his imminent meeting with Chérie's publisher; it was because he was unsure what Mattie's reaction to his gifts would be. Would she think he was trying to buy her affections? Pay her off like a whore? Assuage his guilt at bedding her?

He'd propose first, *then* give her the gifts. That way, she could have no doubt as to his reasons for giving them.

Of course, that presupposed that she'd accept him.

He spent the rest of the hackney ride cudgeling his brain for the perfect words of proposal. He still hadn't found them when the carriage drew up outside his destination.

Edward shoved the problem of Mattie out of his mind. If he succeeded here, then he could redeem his word from Arthur Strickland and put an end to this ridiculous search for Chérie.

He looked up at the building. It was narrow and tall, the stone façade pitted and stained from London's filthy air. A familiar alert anticipation tingled over his skin, as if a battle was about to be engaged.

Chérie's publisher, Mr. Samuel Brunton, Esq., was a rabbity little man with an overbite and a receding chin. His eyes, though, were shrewd. "Mr. Kane? Please take a seat. How may I help you?"

"I wish to discuss one of your authors." Edward smiled and tried not to intimidate the man. He didn't want Mr. Brunton defensive; he wanted him expansive.

Unfortunately, expansive didn't appear to be Mr. Brunton's nature. "Which author?"

"Chérie."

Mr. Brunton lost his smile. "What about her?"

"I wish to locate her," Edward said. "To, er . . ." Too late, he realized that he should have spent the hackney ride thinking about how to phrase this request. "Uh, to speak to her."

Mr. Brunton's expression became contemptuous. His upper lip lifted slightly, showing more of his teeth. "You wish to become her client, Mr. Kane? I can tell you now that she won't—"

Edward flushed. "No! You misunderstand me. That isn't my purpose in finding her."

Mr. Brunton drew his lips closed over his protruding teeth. "Then you must wish to request that she stop writing her confessions. Mr. Kane, you're not the first person to make such a petition to me, and I shall give you the same answer I have in the past: Chérie may write as many confessions as she wishes—and I shall gladly publish them!"

"You misunderstand me," Edward repeated. "I merely wish to speak with her."

"Mr. Kane, I have no intention of disclosing Chérie's identity."

"Her address, then," Edward said, beginning to lose his temper. "Please, if I could just write to her."

"I can't help you." Mr. Brunton gave a triumphant smile. "I don't know my client's address. All our correspondence goes through a solicitor."

Edward gritted his teeth together. He took a slow breath. Losing his temper wouldn't help him. "Which solicitor?"

"That is my business, Mr. Kane. Not yours."

Edward indulged in a brief moment of fantasy: he imagined himself holding Mr. Brunton up by his scrawny neck and shaking him until he divulged Chérie's name.

"We are about to publish Chérie's memoir. Perhaps you'll find clues to her identity in its pages."

"Memoir?" Regretfully, Edward let the fantasy go. "When?"

"Two months hence." Mr. Brunton stood. "Now, if you will excuse me, Mr. Kane, I am rather busy—"

A knock on the door and the entrance of a young man in an ink-stained printer's apron interrupted them. "The first few pages, sir." He glanced at Edward, blinked and recoiled slightly, before fixing his attention back on his employer. "You wanted to see them in both fonts."

Mr. Brunton took the sheaf of paper and flicked through the pages. "Excellent." He glanced at Edward and smirked. "Do you wish to see it, Mr. Kane?"

"Is it Chérie's memoir?" Edward pushed to his feet. "Yes, please."

Mr. Brunton handed him half a dozen pages. His expression was one of derision.

Edward read swiftly, blocking out Mr. Brunton's discussion with his employee about print size and font and margins.

Dear reader, I begin my tale with that momentous event in a woman's life: the plucking of her virgin flower. This occurred on my wedding night, when I was a shy and blushing maiden, not yet eighteen years of age. The mixture of anticipation and apprehension within my bosom you can well imagine, for I was quite innocent and had no idea what to expect.

Edward skimmed down the page.

My beloved Joseph stripped off his clothes. I gazed upon him in a mixture of trepidation and awe, and shrank back as he approached me.

Joseph sought to assuage my fear, taking my hand in his and encouraging me to touch his organ. At his urging I shyly acquainted myself with that strange and most alarming part of him. The touch of my fingers on his skin inflamed us both.

Edward turned the page and read further.

Joseph bade me lie down and joined me upon the bed. He soothed my fears with soft kisses upon my bosom, while at the same time he skillfully moved his hand upon that most private and womanly part of me. The sensations that his kisses and the rhythmic movement of his hand instilled within me were astonishing. Dear reader, until then, I had not realized such pleasure was possible!

Edward grunted, remembering Mattie's expression when he'd first brought her to climax, the dazed astonishment on her face. He skimmed further.

"It may hurt," Joseph said, his voice hoarse with passion, and he was correct. I knew a moment of panic as he breached my body and, try as I might, I could not help uttering a cry of pain.

I had no time to mourn the loss of my virginity, however, for my body swiftly accustomed itself to Joseph's invasion. An unfamiliar emotion quickened my pulse. Innocent though I was, I became possessed by a spirit of wantonness. There was a wildness in my veins, a feverish heat. I reveled in Joseph's weight upon me, in his most intimate possession of my body.

Edward skipped to the bottom of the page.

Joseph kissed me afterwards, as we lay in each other's arms. "You were designed for lovemaking," he told me, little supposing that his words were prophetic. "You have the body of Venus, with hips to cradle a man."

Edward's attention was arrested. He reread the sentence.

The body of Venus, with hips to cradle a man.

His skin prickled. He'd said those words to Mattie, hadn't he?

He reread the scene from the beginning, slowly, frowning, taking note of each word Chérie's husband said, each action. It was disturbingly familiar—the way Joseph soothed her fears by inviting her to touch him, the way he drew pleasure from her body with his hand before mounting her—but most familiar and disturbing were those fateful words he uttered: *The body of Venus, with hips to cradle a man.*

A knot began to tie itself in Edward's belly. *No. It can't be.*

"Well?" Mr. Brunton asked, a smirk audible in his voice. "Is it helpful?"

Edward looked up blindly, not seeing him. With a twitch, the pages were removed from his hand.

"I didn't think so," he heard Mr. Brunton say. "But Chérie's next confession will be out next week. A hayloft scene. Perhaps you may find a clue in it."

Hayloft.

Memory flooded through him: the smell of hay and horses, the sound of kittens purring, the taste of gingerbread. And Mattie. Mattie kissing him. Mattie holding his hand while they lay in the fragrant, cozy dimness.

Edward's vision cleared. He saw Mr. Brunton, with his rabbit face and his smirk, holding the first few pages of Chérie's *Memoir*. "The solicitor." His voice sounded as if it came from far away. "Is the address . . ."

Mr. Brunton lost his smirk. "I told you, I won't—"

"Brocklesby. Lombard Street."

Mr. Brunton's face stiffened in shock, and then became blank. "Mr. Kane, I must ask you to leave."

Edward bowed. "Thank you. You've been most helpful."

Mr. Brunton's eyes narrowed in alarm. "Mr. Kane, what—"

Edward turned his back on him. He pushed past the young printer. Anger blossomed in his chest as he strode down the corridor, as he took the stairs down to the ground floor two at a time. She'd used him. Mattie had *used* him.

The porter scurried from his office too late; Edward jerked the door open, almost pulling it from its hinges. The hackney carriage was waiting, as he'd asked. "Lombard Street," he told the jarvey.

He sat tensely on the stained squab seat, while his anger built. He could be wrong. It could be Mrs. Dunn who was Chérie. Perhaps Mattie had confided in her—everyone knew how women gossiped! But deep inside himself, there was no uncertainty. No one but Mattie could have written that virginity scene.

At Lombard Street, he climbed down from the carriage. Mrs. Brocklesby inhabited a handsome, modern house built of Portland stone. The door was answered by a butler.

"I should like to see Mrs. Brocklesby if she's at home," Edward said, handing the man his card. "Tell her I'm acquainted with Miss Chapple."

Within less than a minute the butler returned and ushered him into a warm, cheerful parlor.

"Mr. Kane?" Mrs. Brocklesby rose and held out her hand politely. "You know Miss Chapple?"

"Yes." Edward shook her hand.

Mrs. Brocklesby's hair was an extremely pale shade of red and her eyebrows and eyelashes were so fair that it almost seemed she hadn't any. She was saved from plainness by a pair of vivid blue eyes and a shapely, smiling mouth. "Please sit." She gestured at a sofa upholstered in straw-colored silk. "How may I help you?"

"I . . . uh . . ." Where to start? Not with an accusation. Edward sat, and tried to look relaxed. "I understand that you and Miss Chapple are close friends?"

"Yes. We were at school together."

Edward nodded, not really listening to the words. All his attention was focused on one thing. "Your husband is a solicitor, Mrs. Brocklesby?"

"Yes." Mrs. Brocklesby smiled politely, clearly waiting for the point of his visit.

"He is Miss Chapple's solicitor, I understand?"

Mrs. Brocklesby blinked. "Yes, but if it's business you wish to discuss, you'll need to speak with my husband." She reached for the bellpull.

"No," Edward said. "It's not business. It's about the letters Mattie—Miss Chapple—sends you."

Mrs. Brocklesby paused with her arm outstretched. "I beg your pardon?"

"The letters between her and Mr. Brunton."

Mrs. Brocklesby lowered her hand. "What about them?"

The question was an answer in itself. "You're a receiving office for correspondence between her and your husband and Mr. Brunton." Rage leaked into Edward's voice. "If Mattie were to receive letters from a *man,* her uncle would want to know why. But letters from a woman, a friend—" He made a sharp, throwaway gesture with his hand. "No one thinks twice about it."

"Mr. Kane, I think you'd better leave." Mrs. Brocklesby reached out again and rang the bell decisively.

Edward stood. "She's Chérie, isn't she?"

Mrs. Brocklesby's lips pinched together. She said nothing.

Edward's rage was close to erupting. He bowed stiffly and strode from the room. His footsteps echoed flatly in the entrance hall. He didn't wait for the butler, but wrenched the door open himself.

A messenger boy—from Mr. Brunton's printing house judging by the ink stains on his clothes—ran up the steps.

"You're too late," Edward snarled at him.

Edward walked back to his rooms. It took the best part of an hour. He was limping by the time he reached Ryder Street. He climbed the stairs to his rooms slowly. Rage still simmered in his chest, but he wasn't about to erupt.

He stripped off his gloves and flung his hat on the table. A mirror hung on the wall. Edward scowled at his reflection, seeing the scarred face, the missing ear. *Look at you. You fool! How could you believe she cared for you?*

He limped across to the decanter of brandy. It was almost empty. He upended it roughly into a glass, splashing brandy onto the sideboard. "Tigh!"

The bâtman came through from the bedchamber, a clothes brush in his hand. "Sir?"

"Get some more brandy." Edward fished in his pocket, pulled out some crumpled notes, and thrust them at the bâtman. An ugly hand, missing three fingers. *How could I be so stupid as to think she'd want to be touched by me?*

Tigh raised his eyebrows, but all he said was, "Yes, sir."

"And order the curricle around from the stables tomorrow morning. We'll leave for Northamptonshire at eight."

Dismay crossed Tigh's face. "Not . . . Creed Hall again, sir?"

"Yes," Edward said grimly. He swallowed half the brandy in one gulp. It burned down his throat.

He shrugged out of his heavy frieze coat and threw it over the back of a chair. On the table, alongside his discarded hat and gloves, were two parcels. The books he'd chosen for Mattie, and the ribbons and shawls and ermine muff. "And get rid of those."

"Sir?"

"Throw them out, give them away—I don't care, just get rid of them!"

"Yes, sir." Tigh gathered up the parcels.

Edward turned away. He gulped another mouthful of brandy, remembering the words Mattie had uttered in the library at Creed Hall: *I should like to know what it's like to have physical congress with a man.*

He'd built dreams of affection, of love, when all he'd been for Mattie was the means to an end.

CHAPTER 15

$\mathcal{M}$attie worked through the day, sewing. As the afternoon crawled past, she found herself listening for the sound of Edward's return. He'd only been gone four days, but if his business was brief, if his horses were fast . . .

She shook herself. "Fool!"

It was stupid to miss Edward, stupid to hope that he'd be back today, stupid to look forward to seeing his face again—and yet she couldn't stop it. It was an animal, instinctive thing, utterly beyond her control. *Just let me see him once more.*

At dusk, she lit the candles and continued working. The reek of mutton fat filled the room as the tallow candles spluttered and flickered. When the clock struck half past five, Edward hadn't arrived and the gown was almost finished. It lacked only buttons.

Mattie laid down her needle. It was too late to expect Edward today. *Perhaps he'll be here tomorrow.*

She sighed and rubbed her forehead and went to prepare for dinner.

"Sermon Twelve," Mattie read aloud. Sir Gareth wasn't one of her audience; he'd left that morning to obtain a special license. "On Good Works."

Aunt Marchbank's stiff-backed posture and conspicuously averted face perfectly expressed her resentment at Cecy's imminent departure. Mattie caught Cecy's eye and gave a ghost of a wink. *A few more days and you'll be free of this.*

Cecy seemed to understand the silent message. A tiny smile lit her face before she folded her mouth into a prim line.

Mattie took a deep breath. "If from what has been advanced concerning Female Piety, you are satisfied of its importance and necessity . . ."

She was halfway through the sermon when she heard footsteps and voices in the entrance hall. Her voice faltered for a moment—it *couldn't* be Edward, not at this hour— before continuing: ". . . their gentle ministrations to the sufferers, their stooping so meekly to the meanest of offices of compassion—"

The door to the drawing room opened. Griggs stood framed there. "Mr. Kane," he announced.

Uncle Arthur swiveled in his chair. "Kane? At this hour?"

Edward stepped into the room. Seeing him—the dark hair, the square face, the scars—made Mattie's heart clench painfully in her chest.

"My apologies for arriving so late, Sir Arthur. One of the horses cast a shoe just out of Gripton." Edward made a slight bow. "Lady Marchbank. Mrs. Dunn." His gaze lifted to Mattie. "Miss Chapple."

Her face broke into a smile; she could no more hold it back than she could stop her heart from beating.

Edward didn't return the smile. There was no friendliness in his eyes.

Mattie stared at him, while her joy at seeing him slowly congealed. Why was he looking at her like that? As if he hated her?

And then she understood. *He knows I'm Chérie.* The knowledge was blazoned across his face, as plain to see as the scars.

The floor seemed to lurch beneath her feet. Mattie gripped the mantelpiece to steady herself.

"We've dined," Uncle Arthur said, a querulous note in his voice.

"I ate en route," Edward said, turning back to his host.

Mattie looked down at the book of sermons in her hand. The words blurred, unreadable.

"You were successful?"

"Yes." One short, curt syllable.

Mattie glanced up. Uncle Arthur struggled to his feet, leaning on his cane. An expression of triumph lit his gaunt face. "Come to my study."

"It can wait until morning, sir," Edward said, still not looking at her.

Mattie let go of the mantelpiece. She closed the book of sermons. Her lungs had constricted; each breath was a struggle. "No," she said, forcing the word out through numb lips. *Let's have done with it. Now.*

Both men turned to look at her, one blankly, the other with anger burning in his eyes.

Mattie hugged the book of sermons to her chest. Beneath it, her heart beat rapidly. She took a shallow breath and grabbed hold of her courage. "Uncle Arthur . . . I am Chérie."

Her uncle's mouth opened. No sound came out. He looked like a dead fish, gaping at her.

"I apologize for doing something so . . . so discreditable while living under your roof."

Uncle Arthur's mouth shut with a snap. "You?"

"Yes."

Rage rushed into her uncle's pallid cheeks, flushing them red. "Get out of my house! Get out of it now! This very instant!"

"It's nighttime, sir," Edward said.

"I don't care!" Uncle Arthur cried, his voice shrill with righteous anger. "I won't have such . . . such *corruption* in my house a moment longer!"

Mattie put down the book of sermons.

"Do you hear me, you filthy creature?" Her uncle's voice rose in a quavering shout. "Out! Out!"

"You can't do that, sir." Edward spoke with flat, implacable authority. For the first time in their acquaintance he sounded like an officer, used to giving orders and having them obeyed.

Uncle Arthur drew breath to argue.

"Not at night," Edward said. "Not in winter. It would be un-Christian."

Uncle Arthur's face grew purple while he wrestled with the truth of this statement. "Start packing!" he cried finally. "I want you gone at dawn!"

"Yes, Uncle."

Cecy half-rose, her confusion clear to read. Mattie shook her head. *Don't ally yourself with me.*

Cecy read the silent message. She sank back onto the sofa.

Mattie gripped the mantelpiece again briefly, finding the balance to walk to the door, then pushed away from it. Her uncle struck her with his cane as she passed him, a sharp, stinging blow to her upper arm, almost making her stumble.

"Sir!" Edward said. It was one word only, but his tone made Uncle Arthur flush. He lowered the cane.

Mattie halted when she reached Edward. She met his gaze squarely. "I apologize for not telling you."

His mouth tightened, pinching at the corners. "I read the first chapter."

The outrage burning in his eyes abruptly made sense. He'd recognized the scene, recognized himself.

"Edward . . ." There was nothing she could say to him here, in public. "I'm sorry."

His jaw hardened. He turned away from her.

Mattie heard Aunt Marchbank's voice as she closed the door. "I don't understand. What has she done?"

Mattie climbed the stairs, rubbing her arm. She had deserved the blow. If her uncle had chosen to beat her, she would have deserved that, too.

In her room, Mattie locked her door and leaned against it.

She was shaking, sick to her stomach. *I deserve this,* she told herself, pressing her knuckles to her mouth. *I deserve this.* She squeezed her eyes shut, as if by shutting out sight she could shut out the scene in the drawing room: Uncle Arthur's fury, Edward turning his back to her.

Finally she opened her eyes, blew out a trembling breath, and pushed away from the door. Standing here, feeling sorry for herself, wasn't going to help matters. But her thoughts spun so chaotically that it was hard to know where to start. Mattie turned on her heel. What should she do first? Empty her dresser? Clear out the secret cupboard? Write a note to Cecy? It was too much, too overwhelming—

"Stop it!" Mattie told herself. "Just stop it!" And she inhaled a deep breath and marched across to the escritoire. One thing at a time, that's what she'd do. One thing at a time.

The first letter she wrote was to Cecy. It was the easiest. The second, to Uncle Arthur, was much more difficult. Mattie labored over it for more than an hour, thanking him for taking her in and explaining why she'd embarked on her shameful career, and finally apologizing for deceiving him. *It was not my intention to ever cause you distress, Uncle. I am fully aware how much I owe you—*

Someone tapped on her door.

Mattie's heart lurched in her chest and seemed to stop beating. Was it Edward?

"Mattie?" The voice was Cecy's. "Are you there?"

Mattie hurried across to the door and unlocked it. "Shh. They might hear you."

Cecy was in her nightgown, her hair in a plait down her back. "Mattie, what on earth have you done?"

"It's all in here." Mattie handed her the letter she'd written.

Cecy took it and turned it over in her hand. Her face was troubled. "Is it very dreadful?"

"Shockingly dreadful. Now go! Before anyone finds you here."

"But Mattie . . . will you be all right?"

"I'll be fine," Mattie said firmly. "Don't worry about me. Go, Cecy! If Uncle Arthur should find you here, there'll be the most dreadful row."

Cecy hugged her. "Will I ever see you again?"

Tears choked in Mattie's throat. She hugged Cecy back. "I hope so. If you don't disown me when you discover what I've done!"

No one else knocked on her door while she finished Uncle Arthur's letter. Mattie sealed it and put it aside.

The letter to Edward was the hardest. She wrote it with absolute honesty. When it was finished, Mattie sealed it, wrote his name on the front, and dated it. She fetched the letter she'd written to him five days ago and placed it on top. Explanation, apology, farewell.

The longcase clock in the entrance hall struck midnight, the echo reverberating hollowly through the house. Mattie rubbed her aching arm. If she was to walk to Gripton in time to catch the morning stagecoach she needed to leave soon.

She dressed in her warmest clothes and sturdiest boots. In the pocket of her thick winter cloak, she tucked the only item of jewelry she owned—the pearl necklace her parents had given her on her seventeenth birthday—to be pawned in Gripton for her fare to London.

Next, she hauled the battered bandboxes that contained her belongings from school out from under her bed—translations in French and Italian, stiff little watercolors, sheets of music—and emptied them both. She repacked the first one with the countess's diary, the copy of *Fanny Hill*, the letters she had from her parents and Toby. On top of those things, she laid her hair brush, toothbrush, and toothpowder. Lastly, she crammed in her nightgown and fastened the lid.

In the second bandbox, she packed as much clothing as would fit. When that was done, Mattie sat back on her heels and glanced around the bedchamber. Was there anything she'd forgotten?

What about Mama Cat and her kittens? a voice whispered in her head.

Mattie looked at the two bandboxes. She couldn't carry them both *and* a basket for the cats.

The cats will be all right in the barn, she told herself, rubbing her forehead with her knuckles. *They are only animals, after all.*

But she had promised to take them with her. She'd promised the kittens a home where no one would try to drown them. And drowning the kittens was exactly what Uncle Arthur would order done if he discovered their existence.

Mattie hesitated, and then shoved the second bandbox away. Clothes she could do without.

She let herself out of her bedchamber for the last time, carrying one bandbox, a woolen shawl, and the letters she'd written.

Mattie tiptoed downstairs and placed Uncle Arthur's letter on his desk. He would probably burn it without reading it, but at least she'd tried to apologize.

She left the two letters for Edward on the breakfast table, took a large covered basket from the kitchen, and let herself out the side door.

In the stables, Mattie lined the basket with the woolen shawl and then climbed the ladder to the hayloft. "Mama Cat, I'm taking you all with me," she whispered. "Where are you?"

The kittens woke, making squeaky, sleepy mews. Mattie captured them, carefully shutting each round-bellied little body in the basket. "Come here, Mama Cat."

Mama Cat purred when she was picked up, and rubbed her face along Mattie's jaw.

"It will be uncomfortable," Mattie said, stroking her sleek fur. "But trust me. I'm taking you somewhere safe." She stowed the cat in the basket, shutting the lid against a meow of protest. "I'm sorry, but you'll have a home at the end of this." *We all will.*

She climbed carefully down the ladder, balancing the heavy basket, and hurried back out to the stableyard.

The dark shape of Creed Hall loomed ahead of her. Above, thin streams of clouds scudded in the sky and an almost-full moon shone down coldly. An icy wind whistled over the rooftops and snatched at her cloak. This was it, the moment she'd dreamed of for months: the start of her new life.

There was no joy, no excitement; instead she felt only grief and regret.

"Good-bye, Edward," Mattie whispered. Tears choked in her throat. "I'm sorry."

And basket in one hand, bandbox in the other, she set off for Gripton.

Anger stewed in Edward's chest. He felt as if a coke mound smoldered there, giving off black and stinking smoke. The anger was as much at himself as at Mattie—*Fool for being so easily duped!*—and it kept him awake long past midnight. He heard the clock strike one o'clock, and then two o'clock, and then three, before sleep claimed him. It was almost noon by the time he woke. His head was heavy, his mood foul. He rang for Tigh.

The bâtman bustled in with hot shaving water and a fresh towel. "Good morning, sir."

Edward grunted sourly. He glanced out the window. The sky was that peculiar light gray that signaled snow.

Mattie would be gone by now. She'd probably hired a post-chaise to convey her to London. The writer of Chérie's *Confessions* could afford such a luxury.

Anger kindled in his chest again when he remembered the gingerbread he'd bought for her, the kisses they'd shared. She'd played him, used him—and fool that he was, he'd fallen for it. Her poverty had been as much an act as everything else about her.

Edward picked up the razor and shoved thought of Mattie aside. His stomach growled while he shaved. "Have the curricle sent round in fifteen minutes," he told Tigh. "We'll eat in Soddy Morton."

"I believe one of the horses has been taken into the village to be reshod, sir."

Edward's mood became even sourer. He was too hungry to walk into Soddy Morton—which meant he had to eat here.

"Griggs said to tell you there's a letter for you in the breakfast parlor. From Miss Chapple."

Edward's hand tightened around the razor.

"Shall I fetch it for you?"

"No." Edward said. *You can burn it.* But he didn't say the words aloud.

He shaved slowly, despite the urgings of his stomach, and took his time dressing. No letter from Mattie was going to make him hurry. In fact, it would serve her right if he *did* burn it.

The clock struck twelve o'clock while he made his way downstairs. The breakfast parlor was shrouded in shadows and so cold he saw the ghost of his breath with each exhalation. Edward tugged the bellpull before turning to the table. Tigh was correct: a letter lay on one of the place settings. His name was written on the front, and in the top right-hand corner was a date.

He stared at it. *Damn it.* He didn't want anything to do with Mattie Chapple, didn't want to read her excuses, didn't want—

The date on the letter was five days ago.

Edward frowned, and picked it up. Five days ago?

Another letter lay underneath it, also addressed to him. It was dated yesterday.

Edward hesitated—*Which to read first?*—and then broke the seal on the older letter and opened it. The writing was familiar: Chérie's. His hand clenched involuntarily, crumpling the paper.

Edward, there is something I wish I could tell you, but I can't. It's not that I don't trust you, it's that—

Edward unclenched his fingers. He smoothed the paper, trying to erase the creases.

It's not that I don't trust you, it's that if I tell you, you'll have to tell my uncle—or break your word to him, and I don't want you to have to make that choice.

This is what I want you to know: I am Chérie. And I know it is Chérie you are looking for.

He squeezed his eyes shut for a moment and then reread the sentences. They still said the same thing. "Shit," Edward said, under his breath. His anger was gone. In its place was a sick feeling in his stomach.

He read the letter swiftly. It covered two closely written pages, detailing how Mattie had found the countess's diary, and then later *Fanny Hill,* and her decision to try to support herself through writing. *When I first set pen to paper, I knew I was destroying my reputation past repair should my secret ever be discovered. But I judged the reward—my independence—to be worth the risk. I don't expect you to understand that decision, Edward. How can you? You are a man; you have always had your independence.*

Edward rubbed his brow with hard fingers, feeling the ridges of the scars. He read further. Mattie described how she'd written the first confessions, how the husband of a friend had found a publisher for her, and how, with the publisher's urging, she'd embarked upon a memoir.

I wish I could tell you my secret now; I hope you can understand why I haven't.

Yours,

Mattie.

Edward refolded the letter slowly. He opened the second letter. It was short.

You are right to be angry with me, Edward. You may say that

I have deceived you, that I have betrayed you, that I have taken something precious and private and exposed it to the world—and you would be correct in all those things.

Mr. Brunton refused to accept the memoir without an episode detailing Chérie's loss of virginity. If I hadn't needed to write that chapter, I would never have been so bold—or so desperate—as to invite you to my bedchamber.

But it was more than that, Edward. Much more. You were someone I had dreamed of, but never thought existed. You were the man I fell in love with.

Edward had the sensation that someone had kicked him in the chest. For a moment he couldn't breathe. *You were the man I fell in love with.*

Fell in love with.

Edward squeezed his eyes shut. *Shit.*

When he'd recovered his breath, he read the final few sentences.

I'm not asking you to forgive me, Edward; I know that what I've done is unforgivable. I am very sorry. Please believe that it was never my intention to hurt you.

I hope that you will be most happy in Cornwall and that fortune smiles upon you always.

Mattie.

Edward reread the letter, his attention lingering on the most important sentences.

"Coffee, sir?"

Edward almost leapt out of his skin. He turned hastily, hiding the letter behind his back like a schoolboy caught doing something wrong.

"Or tea?" the butler asked, his face utterly impassive.

"Uh . . . yes."

"Which one, sir?"

"Uh . . ." Edward blinked, trying to gather his scattered wits. "Coffee."

"Very good, sir."

Edward served himself from the dishes arrayed on the

sideboard and sat down at the table and read both letters again. He didn't notice that the food was cold, that the eggs were rubbery and the toast brittle; Mattie's words consumed him. Each one was like a needle being driven into his skin. He'd judged her too harshly, had leapt to conclusions, had allowed his dented pride to fuel his anger.

"I have to find her." His hand clenched around the second letter. "I have to!"

But where had she gone?

He frowned and read the first letter again, looking for clues. Mattie said she was saving to buy a boarding house, that her solicitor had opened a bank account for her in London into which her earnings were deposited.

Edward pushed his coffee cup aside. A bank account in London. That was a good starting point. All he had to do was—

The full importance of the sentence hit him. Mattie's money was in London. So how had she paid for her fare from Soddy Morton?

"Shit!" Edward pushed to his feet so fast that the chair fell over behind him.

He ran the butler to ground in his pantry. "Did you see Miss Chapple leave?"

"No one did, sir," Griggs said woodenly. "She left before dawn."

"But she had no money for her fare!"

The butler's impassive façade cracked slightly. "She didn't?"

"No, damn it, she didn't!" *Shit*. "Send round to the stables. I want my curricle ready to leave in five minutes!"

"One of the horses is still at the farrier's, sir."

Edward clenched his jaw. He took a deep breath. "As soon

234

as the horse is back, then," he said, holding onto his temper. "Have you seen Mrs. Dunn? Where is she?"

"I believe she's upstairs, sir, with Lady Marchbank."

Edward turned on his heel and strode back along the corridor. He took the stairs two at a time and met Mrs. Dunn nearly at the top. "Did you see Miss Chapple before she left?" he demanded, standing in her path. "Did she tell you where she's going?"

Mrs. Dunn looked at him coolly. "What business is that of yours, Mr. Kane?"

"Aren't you concerned for her safety? She could be dead in a ditch!"

Mrs. Dunn flinched. "Dead?"

"Yes!" Edward said fiercely. His hands clenched into helpless fists. "Dead!"

Mrs. Dunn touched the pocket of her gown. "Surely not—"

"It's winter! She had no money for her fare to London!"

Mrs. Dunn fingered her pocket. Edward heard the crackle of paper. "Mattie told me she was going to walk into Gripton and pawn her pearl necklace. From there she'll catch the stagecoach."

"Gripton?" He frowned. Gripton was eight miles distant. A long way on a winter's night, alone. "Where is she headed after that? London?"

"I fail to see that that is any concern of yours."

"I'm trying to help her!"

"Help?" Mrs. Dunn's eyebrows arched derisively. "You?"

Edward resisted the urge to shake her. He took a deep breath, unclenched his hands, and tried to speak calmly. "You are correct, Mrs. Dunn: I am the architect of Miss Chapple's misfortune. Without me, her secret would never have been exposed. But you must believe me when I say I'm trying to aid her!"

Mrs. Dunn looked down her nose at him from her position above him on the stairs. "Why would you wish to help Mattie?"

"Because . . ." Edward took a deep breath. "Because I want to marry her."

Her brow creased. "You do?"

"Yes."

Mrs. Dunn studied his face. She must have decided he was telling the truth, because she pulled a letter from her pocket and opened it. "I don't know where Mattie's going. She says she'll buy a boarding house and write once she has an address." She held the letter out to him.

Edward read the letter swiftly and handed it back. "I'll look for her in Gripton, and then in London. If I fail to find her, will you—"

"I shall give you her address when she writes," Mrs. Dunn promised.

It was past one o'clock when Edward finally put Creed Hall behind him. His frustration had built almost to bursting point. His imagination gave him a dozen different scenarios: Mattie being robbed or abducted or raped, Mattie being run down by a carriage, Mattie lying frozen to death in a ditch.

He sprang the horses as soon as he reached the road. The clouds sat low and gray just above the hilltops. Flakes of snow began drifting down before they'd gone a mile. Edward didn't slacken the horses' pace.

The wind picked up and the snow fell more briskly. Edward squinted, trying to make out the road.

"Sir!" Tigh remonstrated, clinging white-knuckled to the curricle as Edward took a corner too fast.

It's not going to help Mattie if I break my neck.

Edward eased the horses back to a trot. "Keep your eyes peeled for her!"

Ten minutes later he was forced to slow the curricle to

walking pace. Snow gusted in dense flurries, the flakes spinning and whirling, half blinding him.

"We have to turn back, sir."

"The devil we will," Edward said grimly. He drew the curricle to a halt and thrust the reins at Tigh. "Take them. I'll lead the horses."

"No, sir. I will." The bâtman jumped down. "I got two good legs and you don't."

They progressed half a mile, fighting the wind, fighting the snow. A farmhouse loomed out of the whiteness. Edward didn't need the bâtman to tell him they could go no further.

Shit! Shit! Shit!

Where was Mattie? Had she made it to Gripton? Was she outside in this blizzard?

Edward squeezed his eyes tightly shut. *Let her be safe,* he prayed. *Please, God, let her be safe.*

CHAPTER 16

*M*attie glanced up from the seam she was stitching. Outside, a February gale howled. If she opened the window, she'd hear the roar of waves beating against the Ramsgate coast, but here, in her kitchen, all was warm and cozy and scented with the smell of baking bread.

This was it: the dream. Every block of stone, every tile on the roof, every flagstone on the floor, was hers, just as the smell of bread was hers, and the sound of logs crackling and popping as they burned.

She rested her gaze for a moment on the half-grown kittens asleep in their basket, on Mama Cat stretched out beside the fire, then turned her attention back to the gown she was sewing. The fabric was a shade of slate-blue—not too bright a color, in keeping with a widow not long out of mourning.

Her hand faltered as she remembered a wintry lakeshore and Edward uttering the words, *You should wear red.* For a moment she saw his scarred face, heard the baritone of his voice. With the memory came a familiar pain in her chest, a wrenching sense of loss, a grief so intense it closed her throat and made breathing impossible for a few seconds.

Mattie shoved the memory aside. She cleared her throat, blinked several times, and resumed sewing—but instead of blue-gray cloth, she saw Edward's face as she'd last seen it, in the parlor at Creed Hall. It wasn't his anger that had been so devastating; it was the hurt she'd seen in his eyes.

Distantly, she heard the sound of the door knocker, heard Jane, the maid-of-all-work, bustle to answer the summons. A chill blast of wind buffeted down the corridor, bringing with it the salty tang of the ocean. A moment later, Jane appeared in the kitchen doorway. "A gentleman to see you, ma'am. I showed 'im into the parlor."

"Thank you, Jane."

Mattie laid aside her sewing and stood, twitching her apron into place, smoothing the creases. As she left the kitchen, she glanced at the wedding band on her finger, fixing in her mind who she was: Mrs. Brown, soldier's widow, boarding house proprietor.

She sent up a silent, hopeful prayer when she entered the parlor: *Let him be looking for a room.* "Good afternoon, sir."

Her visitor stood looking out the window, dressed in a greatcoat with a multitude of capes. He was gargantuan in the room, his head nearly brushing the ceiling, his height and breadth completely obscuring the window.

He turned at her entrance. For a moment, he was nothing more than a hulking silhouette—and then Mattie made out his features.

Everything stood still. The clock on the mantelpiece didn't tick, the gale outside didn't blow, her heart stopped beating.

Eons passed as they stared at each other, and then her visitor spoke: "Good afternoon, Mattie."

His voice broke the spell. Mattie took an involuntary step towards him. "Edward!" His face was exactly as she had remembered: the scars, the strong, square contours of jaw and cheekbone. She swallowed convulsively, clutching her hands together. "Won't . . . won't you sit down?"

"No, thank you." Edward took a step towards her, his face perfectly blank, perfectly expressionless, and then the mask slipped and fury erupted from him. "Damn it, Mattie! How could you leave like that? In the middle of the night! It was *winter*! You could have *died*!"

Mattie opened her mouth and then closed it again.

"And you left no address!" Edward bellowed. "How the devil was I supposed to find you?"

Mattie looked down at her hands. She twisted the wedding band on her finger. "I didn't think you would want to."

There was a long pause. She heard Edward breathing— loud, harsh, angry—before he turned and walked back to the window. "I apologize," he said in a constricted voice. "I didn't mean to lose my temper."

"You have every right to yell at me," Mattie said, twisting the ring around her finger. "What I did to you was unforgivable—"

"Unforgivable? Do you think so?"

Mattie lifted her head. "I deceived you, Edward. I . . . I *used* you! I wrote about something that was private between us, for all England to read—"

"You rewrote the first chapter." Edward reached into the pocket of his many-caped greatcoat and pulled out a calf-bound volume.

Mattie flinched when she recognized the red marbled covers. She stepped back a pace. "You bought Chérie's *Memoir*?"

"Of course. It's selling well. Everyone of my acquaintance has a copy." He paused, and qualified this statement: "Every man, that is."

Mattie watched in utter astonishment as Edward opened the book and flicked through the first half dozen pages. "Why did you change the beginning?"

Because I couldn't bear myself. The words choked in her throat. She shook her head silently.

"It doesn't read as well." Edward closed the book and placed it on the table. He reached into his pocket again and pulled out a string of pearls. "I believe these are yours."

Mattie stared at him, open-mouthed, speechless.

Edward laid the pearls on top of the book in a neat coil. "We need to talk."

"Edward . . ." She felt almost dizzy, as if the room spun slowly on its axis. "Why aren't you angry?"

His eyebrows lifted. "Should I be?"

"Of course you should! You *must* be!"

A flicker of a smile crossed his scarred face. "Must I?"

"Yes! I deceived you, Edward! You can't hate me any more than I hate myself!"

The smile vanished. His expression was suddenly grave. "I don't hate you."

Tears filled her eyes. She shook her head. "You *must*."

Edward reached into his pocket again. This time he withdrew two creased letters. He looked at them, placed one on the table, and unfolded the other. "Did you mean what you wrote to me?"

Mattie nodded. If she spoke, she'd cry.

Edward walked across the parlor, halting in front of her. "This." He held the letter out and pointed with a scarred finger. "Did you mean this?"

Mattie read the sentence. *You were the man I fell in love with.*

She blinked back tears and nodded, unable to look him in the face, unable to speak.

"Mattie . . ." Edward clenched the letter in his fist. His voice became fierce: "Mattie, how could you—how *could* you write such a letter and then leave!"

She fixed her attention on the floor.

Edward threw the letter aside. He grabbed her shoulders and shook her. "You talk of unforgivable behavior. *That* was unforgivable." He shook her again. "Utterly unforgivable!"

His grip was painful, his voice vibrating with anger—and then his fingers relaxed. "Mattie . . ." he said softly.

She glanced up. They stared at each other for an endless moment, and then Edward released her shoulders. "Marry me, Mattie."

241

Mattie recoiled a step backwards. "You can't want to marry me."

A ghost of a smile crossed his face. "Can't I?"

"Not after what I did to you!"

"I understand why you wrote the confessions, Mattie—and I understand why you didn't tell me." He stepped towards her and took possession of her hands. "Mattie . . . I love you."

Mattie swallowed. She wanted to believe him so desperately that it hurt. She fastened her gaze on the buttons of his greatcoat. "You said at Creed Hall that you weren't looking for a wife." Her voice trembled. "You said you were trying to do the right thing—"

"Forget what I said at Creed Hall."

"No, Edward—" She tried to pull her hands free.

"At Creed Hall, I offered for you because I felt I ought to." Edward tightened his grip on her hands. "But that's not why I'm offering now. Mattie . . . look at me."

It was safer to look at Edward's buttons than his face. When she looked at his face, she became caught, like a trout on a barbed hook.

"Mattie . . . please."

She took a deep breath and looked up, and found herself caught—again.

"This isn't about your virtue. It isn't about Toby. It isn't about rescuing you. It's about you and me, Mattie. It's about *us,* about how good we are together. Mattie . . . I want to spend my life with you."

She stared at him, unable to speak, scarcely able to breathe. The truth was plain to see on his face, it shone fiercely in his eyes, she heard it in the quiet intensity of his voice.

"I knew the first night I was in London, Mattie, and I've had nearly three months to think about it since then. I haven't changed my mind." Edward paused. His grip on her hands tightened. "Have you?"

Stop loving you? Never. She shook her head.

"Will you marry me, Mattie?"

"Yes," Mattie said, and then, to her horror, she began to cry.

Edward made a sound of dismay and gathered her in his arms.

Mattie buried her face in rain-soaked capes at his shoulder, struggling to halt the flow of tears. She couldn't. It was as if a door that had been bolted shut had burst open. All the pain of the past few months came pouring out. "I'm sorry," she said, between shuddering sobs.

Edward held her until the tears finally stopped. The solidity of his body, the strength of his arms, was deeply comforting.

"I'm sorry," Mattie said again. She pushed away from him, groping for her handkerchief. "I hardly ever cry." No, that was a lie; she'd done a lot of crying in the past three months, lying in bed alone in the dark, thinking of Edward.

"Don't apologize." Edward stripped out of the dripping greatcoat and tossed it over the back of a chair.

Mattie blew her nose and wiped her eyes. "I'll ring for some food. You must be hungry—"

"No." Edward took her hand and led her to the sofa. "I don't need anything. Just you."

He pulled her down to sit, settling her within the curve of his arm. Mattie leaned against him, laying her hand on his chest, above his heart. She closed her eyes. Heaven must feel like this.

"I have a special license," Edward said.

She opened her eyes.

"We can marry as soon as you like."

"Tomorrow."

"I was hoping you'd say that." Edward tilted her chin up with one finger and kissed her.

Mattie kissed him back shyly.

Edward made a low sound of pleasure in his throat. He gathered her more closely to him.

An eternity passed. Mattie lost all sense of time and place. The parlor, the boarding house, the storm raging outside, all vanished. The world consisted only of Edward and the sweet fierceness of his kiss.

Finally Edward drew back. Mattie reached out and traced one of the scars that slashed across his face. This wasn't a dream. Edward was real, as real as the ridge of scar tissue beneath her fingertip. "How did you find me?"

"Your friend Cecily gave me your address."

She lowered her hand. "Cecy? Have you seen her? How are they?"

"Extremely happy. You were right. Her regard for Gary is genuine." Edward drew her into the warm curve of his arm again. "She's an admirable woman. Gave me your address as soon as she had it. Your Mrs. Brocklesby didn't. Nearly three months, she gave me the run around!"

"That's my fault," Mattie confessed, resting her head against his shoulder. "I asked Anne not to tell anyone where I was."

Edward was silent for a moment. "Mattie, I tried to write to you so many times." He stroked her hair, a gentle touch. "But I haven't your skill with words. I couldn't say what I wanted to say."

She took hold of his left hand, scarred, missing a finger, and clasped it between both of hers. *My Edward.* "You were very eloquent, just now."

They sat in companionable silence. Mattie listened to the rain gusting against the windowpanes and the gentle *drip drip* of water falling from the capes of Edward's greatcoat; she listened to the soft sound of his breathing, the faint, rhythmic beating of his heart. Joy gathered in her chest, so intense that it was painful. *This can't be real.*

But it was. Just as Edward's hand in hers was real, and his heat keeping her warm.

Her gaze rested on the rain-streaked window, the white-washed walls, the colorful braided rug on the floor. Her own boarding house. It had been a good dream, but the one ahead of her—her future with Edward—was even better.

"May I bring Mama Cat and the kittens with me?"

Edward grunted a laugh. "You have them here?"

She nodded.

"Of course you may bring them." He pressed a kiss into her hair, then pushed to his feet.

Mattie looked up at his face, scarred and infinitely precious. She had to curl her fingers into her palms to stop herself reaching for his hand again. *Silly,* she scolded herself. *He won't disappear if you don't hold on to him.*

"Show me your boarding house," Edward said, smiling down at her. "And then I'm taking you home to Cornwall with me."

Home. The word made her throat tighten, made fresh tears gather in her eyes.

Edward lost his smile. "Mattie? What is it? Is it the boarding house? You don't want to leave it?"

Mattie shook her head, blinking the foolish tears away. She could hand the boarding house with its few boarders and Jane, the maid-of-all-work, over to a new owner without the smallest pang of regret.

"You don't like Cornwall?"

"It's not that," she managed. "It's just, you said . . . *home.* And I want a home with you more than anything in the world."

"You don't mind moving to Cornwall?"

"I'd live anywhere with you. Even a grass hut in Africa."

Edward pulled her to her feet and hugged her. "I think you'll find Blythe Manor much better than a grass hut."

Mattie hugged him back. She inhaled his scent—horse, wet wool, clean male.

Home with Edward.

She could think of nothing better.

*F*IVE *M*ONTHS *L*ATER

*E*dward glanced across at his wife. She cantered along-side him, magnificent in a claret-red riding habit. He felt a fierce sense of possession. *She's mine.* Mattie caught his glance and grinned, dimples springing to life in her cheeks.

They halted on the brow of the hill. Summer surrounded them: the scent of meadows and wildflowers, the hum of bees, birdsong. Edward looked across the pastures and hedgerows to the mouth of the Helford River and the glittering, restless sea beyond.

"I can never decide whether it's more beautiful on a day like this," Mattie said. "Or when it's stormy." Behind her, Blythe Manor could be glimpsed: the mellow golden stone, the gables and tall chimneys, the gardens and orchard.

"Both," Edward said.

The sea breeze lifted a tendril of Mattie's hair and blew it across her cheek. He reached out and brushed it carefully aside.

Mattie smiled at him. It wasn't a mere movement of her lips, it was a smile with her eyes, with her heart. Her love for him shone as brightly and warmly as the sun itself. She leaned her cheek against his hand, a silent *I love you.*

The child nestling in her womb wasn't visible yet. Only the two of them knew of its existence.

Edward inhaled, filling his lungs with the warm, fragrant summer air. Happiness hummed inside him. Not a shallow, fleeting happiness, but a happiness so deep that it was rooted in the very marrow of his bones. "Shall we go down to the shore? And then home."

Mattie captured his hand and pressed a light kiss to his scarred fingers. "And then home."

$\mathcal{A}$UTHOR'S $\mathcal{N}$OTE

Several passages from *Sermons to Young Women* by James Fordyce are quoted in this novel, as are passages from the erotic novel *Fanny Hill; Memoirs of a Woman of Pleasure* by John Cleland. Both *Fanny Hill* and *Sermons to Young Women* were first published in England in the 1700s.

The line of poetry quoted in the first chapter is from *Samela,* by the sixteenth century writer Robert Greene.

Edward's experiences at Waterloo are partly based on a letter by Private Thomas Hasker, First King's Dragoon Guards, and to a lesser extent on the journal of Sergeant Archibald Johnston, Second Regiment of Dragoons. Both men fought at Waterloo, and their writings are some of many letters and journal entries that form *The Waterloo Archive; Volume I: British Sources,* edited by Gareth Glover (Frontline Books, 2010).

$\mathcal{T}$HANK $\mathcal{Y}$OU

Thanks for reading *The Spinster's Secret*. I hope you enjoyed it!

If you'd like to be notified whenever I release a new book, please join my Readers' Group, which you can find at www.emilylarkin.com/newsletter.

I welcome all honest reviews. Reviews and word of mouth help other readers to find books, so please consider taking a few moments to leave a review on Goodreads or elsewhere.

The Spinster's Secret has a prequel novella that explains the origin of the diary Mattie found. *The Countess's Groom* is the story of a young countess trapped in a violent marriage and the servant who risks everything to save her.

The Spinster's Secret also has a sequel novella, *The Baronet's Bride,* which details the events of Gareth and Cecy's wedding night. If you'd like to read the first chapters of either of these novellas, please turn the page.

If full-length novels are more to your liking, I invite you to flick ahead a few pages to read the first chapter of *The Earl's Dilemma,* a Regency romance featuring a former cavalry officer who needs to marry in a hurry and the spinster who's determined to find him the perfect bride.

The *Countess's* GROOM

*O*CTOBER 1762: *P*ART *O*NE

*W*ill Fenmore, horse groom to the young Countess of Malmstoke, watched his mistress as Creed Hall came into view. The Hall crouched on the crest of the hill, a grim building of gray stone with narrow windows and a frowning roof, surrounded by dark trees.

The countess's hands tightened on the reins. The mare slowed from a trot to a walk, and then halted.

Will halted, too.

The countess's cheeks had held a flush of color while they'd cantered; now they were parchment pale. Will saw tension in her shoulders, tension in the rigidity of her jaw.

One more night, he told her silently. *You can do it.*

The countess didn't move.

The seconds lengthened into a minute.

Will wanted to reach out and touch her, grip her arm, tell her that she had the strength to do this. He curled his hands into fists to stop himself.

Another minute passed, and still the countess sat motionless, staring at Creed Hall.

Will's unease grew. *Is this it? Will she break today?* The gelding he rode shifted restlessly, sensing his disquiet.

"He'll be gone tomorrow," Will blurted.

The countess turned her head to stare at him.

Will didn't look away, as a servant should. Instead, he met her gaze. *You can do it, Countess.*

The countess took a deep breath. "Yes," she said. "He will be gone tomorrow." She lifted her chin and urged the mare into a trot.

At the great iron-studded door Will dismounted and helped the countess down from her horse. She took another deep breath and entered Creed Hall—very young, very beautiful, and very afraid.

Will watched the heavy door swing shut behind her. *Someone needs to rescue you, my lady.*

Will was saddling the countess's black mare, Dancer, when his ears caught the clatter of hooves and coach wheels. He knew what it was: the traveling carriage departing, bearing Henry Quayle, fifth Earl of Malmstoke, south to Portsmouth.

For a moment he saw Quayle in his mind's eye: the pomaded, curling wig, the plump and dimpled cheeks, the full-lipped, pouting mouth, the dark brown eyes framed by lashes as long as a girl's. A cherubic face—until one saw the cruelty in the soft mouth, the cruelty in the large and liquid eyes.

The sound of the carriage faded. "Good riddance," Will said aloud. They could all breathe more easily with the earl on his way to the West Indies, the countess most of all.

Dancer flicked an ear at him. She was a beautiful creature, as lovely and slender-limbed as her rider, and as gentle.

Will's heart seemed to lift in his chest when he settled the sidesaddle on Dancer's back. *I'll see the countess soon.* "You're a fool, Fenmore," he said under his breath. "She's a noblewoman, you're a servant. Remember that."

"Fenmore."

He turned. A footman stood behind him in a powdered wig and velvet livery. "The countess won't be riding today."

Will knew what that meant. "He hurt her?"

"Worse 'n usual. Don't look for her this week. She'll send word when Dancer is needed."

Will nodded. When the footman had gone, he turned back to the mare. "I hope Quayle gets the fever," he told Dancer fiercely. "I hope he *dies*."

Like to read the rest?
The Countess's Groom is available now.

The Baronet's BRIDE

CHAPTER ONE

At sixteen, Cecy had married her childhood sweetheart, Frederick Dunn. Two weeks later, he'd been hit by a falling roof tile and she'd become a widow. Now, at twenty-five, she was a bride again.

It was the oddest feeling to be married again, a heady combination of emotions. Joy was predominant, a deliciously buoyant sensation that she'd felt from the moment Gareth had proposed, six days ago. Cecy had tried to conceal the joy from her employer. Lady Marchbank hadn't liked joy or laughter or exuberance. Nor had she liked Cecy's handing in her notice. "Deserting her," in Lady Marchbank's words. Cecy had hidden her happiness, creeping along the dark corridors of Creed Hall, enduring the scolds and the displeasure, counting down the days, hours, and minutes until Gareth returned with the special license, and in the moments when she'd been alone, when there'd been no one to see her—not Lady Marchbank or any of the servants—she'd allowed herself to walk with a bounce in her step, and it had felt as if she might actually become airborne.

Now, on her wedding night, seated at the dressing table in her bedchamber, she felt almost light enough to float out of her chair. *I am married. Married to a man I love.* The joy bubbled up again, and alongside it was sheer, utter relief, because she'd thought it would never happen—a love match—not given her age and her poverty and the fact that she'd been working at Creed Hall, surely the grimmest, gloomiest, most isolated house in England.

But it *had* happened. Gareth was real, just as this morning's ceremony had been real, and the bedchamber was real, and the dressing table she sat at right now was real, and her new name was real. *Cecily Locke. That's who I am now.*

Not Cecily Armitage, vicar's daughter. Vicar's orphan.

Not Cecily Dunn, apprentice apothecary's wife, then apprentice apothecary's widow, and then—for nine grueling years—nurse-companion to Lady Marchbank.

But Cecily Locke, baronet's wife.

Cecily stared at herself in the mirror. *This is actually me. Lady Cecily Locke.*

Disbelief was the third emotion she'd experienced frequently today. A triumvirate of emotions: joy, relief, disbelief.

Cecy pinched herself, an actual pinch, not merely a mental one. *Can this really be true? I'm married?*

But yes, the pinch hurt, and yes, it was true. This was her life now: Gareth Locke's wife.

Her marvelous, miraculous, unexpected life.

Cecy gazed around the bedchamber. She had slept in inns before, but never in a room this nice. A lady's room this, not a lowly nurse-companion's. The candles were beeswax, not tallow, and the bed was piled high with soft pillows and there were pretty knickknacks on the mantelpiece. Outside it was bitterly cold, the longest night of the year almost upon them, but the snug shutters and the chintz curtains and the blazing fire kept winter at bay.

Cecy was tempted to pinch herself again. *This can't be true.*

The buoyant joy surged again, and on its heels, the relief.

Relief that she had a husband she loved. Relief that—for the first time in her life—she had financial security. Money *was* important, and perhaps it was a shameful, shallow thing to admit, but it was *true*. Any orphan who'd lived with an impoverished great-aunt knew it. Any wife who'd been unable to pay for a beloved husband's funeral knew it. And any widow who'd been forced to work for her living knew it.

Cecy thought about Frederick, buried in his pauper's grave. And then she thought about Gareth, who was alive—if somewhat battered. Gareth, with his lean, tanned face and his kind eyes. Gareth, with his amputated arm. Gareth, who'd suffered enough these past months. Protectiveness surged fiercely in Cecy's breast. She wanted to stand between Gareth and the world, to shield him from further hurt, to make him smile, make him laugh, to fill his life with happiness. And children. Lots of children.

Cecy glanced at the wide, soft bed again. Gareth had suggested they postpone consummating their marriage until the journey was over, but she'd refused. Physical congress was part of marriage, and if it was the part a wife liked the least, it was also the part a husband liked the most; she knew that from her brief marriage to Frederick, and she also knew that the act of copulation would be over quickly. A few minutes of discomfort, a little mess afterwards, and that would be it for the night. What wife who loved her husband would balk at that? Especially if it gave her husband pleasure—and if it could bring them the children they both craved.

Cecy closed her eyes and sent up a little prayer: *Please, Lord, bless us with children.* She glanced at the door that connected her bedchamber to Gareth's, and then at the clock on the mantelpiece. Gareth had said he'd knock on her door at ten.

It was only half past nine. Perhaps when she wore the clothes of a baronet's wife, not those of a nurse-companion, it would take her half an hour to undress, but tonight that task had been completed in a matter of minutes—stripping out of the gray dress and the threadbare petticoat, the half-stays and the chemise, and donning her nightgown.

Cecy gave the clock one last glance and turned her attention to the journal she was writing. Not a journal for herself, but for the daughters she hoped to have, so that if she died before they were wed they wouldn't go into their marriages as ignorant as she'd been.

Do not fear the marriage bed, she wrote firmly. *While it is natural to feel shy and nervous, strive not to be afraid. The first time is a little painful, but thereafter it should merely be uncomfortable. As for the act of copulation, it is over swiftly. Your husband will use his hand to position his organ between your legs, then he will push it inside you a few times until he releases his seed in your womb, whereupon he will withdraw. The intimacy of the act will likely embarrass you at first, but you will soon come to regard it as commonplace. It is a little messy, though, so you will need to wipe between your legs afterwards with a handkerchief. Do not be disgusted by this. It is entirely natural.*

There, the sort of practical knowledge she wished she'd had on her wedding night with Frederick.

What else did she wish she'd known then? Advice her long-dead mother had been unable to give her.

Cecy tapped the quill against her lips and thought for a few minutes, and began to write again.

We are formed so that men enjoy copulation and women do not, so don't be disappointed that you don't experience the throes of pleasure that your husband does. A wife learns to enjoy physical congress for her husband's sake. If he loves you and has a kind heart then he will not prolong the act.

Cecy reread those lines, and hesitated over "learns to enjoy." Should she cross it out and write "accustoms herself to" instead? There was no physical enjoyment for women in the marriage bed and she didn't want her daughters to have false expectations. She chewed on her lower lip for a moment, and then wrote: *While you won't experience bodily pleasure in the marriage bed, you will experience emotional pleasure in knowing your husband enjoys copulation, and in knowing that a child may result from your union.*

Cecy glanced at the clock. Still fifteen minutes to wait.

She looked at what she'd written. "It is natural to feel shy and nervous," she read aloud. Advice for her daughters—but at this moment, advice for herself. Because she was a little nervous, and she was feeling shy, and that was *natural*.

"The intimacy of the act will likely embarrass you at first, but you will soon come to regard it as commonplace." Cecy read that sentence out loud, too, and huffed a faint, wry laugh. Embarrassing? Yes, it would be embarrassing this first time, and probably more than a little awkward. But she and Gareth would get past that moment together.

Don't be anxious about your wedding night, Cecy wrote in the journal, to her daughters and to herself. *It is a necessary . . .*

A necessary what? Hurdle? Obstacle? Challenge?

Cecy didn't like any of those words, with their connotation of doing something unpleasant. She wanted a neutral word.

Don't be anxious about your wedding night. It is a necessary event. Every husband and wife must have one.

Like to read the rest?
The Baronet's Bride is available now.

261

The Earl's DILEMMA

*C*HAPTER *O*NE

*K*ate Honeycourt was sitting on the floor of the priest's hole when he arrived. The library door opened and she heard his voice, and her brother's. She started, spattering ink over the page of her diary. James was here!

Her gaze jerked down to the diary in her lap. *I shall, of course, treat James as if my feelings go no deeper than friendship. That goes without saying. But why does it grow no easier? One would think, after all these years, that—* The sentence ended in a splotch of ink.

The voices became louder. Her secret hiding place had become a trap.

Kate dropped the quill and hastily snuffed the candle. The hot wick stung her fingertips. She blinked and for a moment could see nothing. Then her eyes adjusted to the gloom. The darkness wasn't absolute. A tiny streak of light came from the peephole.

"—can't offer you any entertainment," her brother said.

Kate rose to her knees in the near-darkness. The diary slid off her lap with a quiet, rustling thump that made her catch her breath.

"I don't expect to be entertained!" James sounded affronted. "Honestly, Harry, what do you take me for? *You* didn't invite me. I invited myself!"

Kate leaned forward until her eyes were level with the peep-hole. She saw her brother, Harry, the Viscount Honeycourt.

"Don't cut up stiff," Harry said, grinning. "You're always welcome. You know that." He walked across the room to where the decanters stood. "Sherry? Scotch? Brandy?"

"Brandy," James said. He came into Kate's line of sight and her pulse gave a jerky little skip. His back was towards her, but his tallness and the strong lines of his body were unmistakable. He ran a hand through his black hair and turned. Kate's pulse jerked again at the sight of his face, with its wide, well-shaped mouth and slanting black eyebrows. His features were strong and balanced, handsome, but some quirk of their arrangement gave him an appearance of sternness. The planes of his cheek and angle of his jaw were austere. When lost in thought or frowning, his expression became quite intimidating. She'd seen footmen back away rather than disturb him. The sternness was misleading; anyone who knew James well knew that his face was made for laughter.

Had been, Kate corrected herself. James hadn't laughed during the past months and today his face was unsmiling. He looked tired, and as always when not smiling, stern.

Kate clasped her hands together and wished she knew how to make him laugh again. She watched as he walked over to one of the deep, leather armchairs beside the fire and sat. He stretched his long legs out and leaned his head back and closed his eyes, his weariness almost tangible.

"Your timing is excellent," Harry said, a brandy glass in each hand. Late afternoon sunlight fell into the room. The crystal gleamed and the brandy was a deep, glowing amber. "My cousin Augusta has gone to Bath for two months."

James opened his eyes. "I count myself very fortunate," he said, as he accepted a glass.

"So do we!" Harry sat so that Kate could only see the back

of his head, his hair as bright red as her own. "Well? Your letter didn't explain a thing. What's this matter of urgency?"

Kate drew back slightly from the peephole. Should she cover her ears? Whatever Harry and James were about to discuss was none of her business. She raised her hands. To eavesdrop would be—

"Marriage," James said.

Kate flinched. Her heart seemed to shrink in her chest. She'd known this moment must come one day, but that didn't stop it hurting. *James is getting married.* She lowered her hands and leaned closer for a better view of the library.

"Ah." Harry settled back in his chair. "You've found a suitable wife?"

James's laugh was short and without humor. "No," he said, and swallowed some of his brandy.

"You want me to help you? Is that it?"

James frowned at his glass. "My birthday's soon," he said. "You know I must marry before then."

Kate wrinkled her brow. *What?*

"You could let Elvy Park and the fortune go," Harry said in an offhand tone. "I'm sure your cousin would appreciate them."

James transferred his frown from the brandy to Harry. "Would you?"

Her brother, possessor of an extensive estate and a comfortable fortune, shook his head. "No."

"Of course not. And neither will I. I'll marry before my thirtieth birthday, but . . ." James rubbed a hand over his face and sighed. "I wanted— Oh, God, I know it sounds stupid, Harry, but I wanted what my brother had."

He didn't need to explain what that was. Harry knew as well as she did: a love match.

Her brother didn't scoff. "It doesn't sound stupid," he said quietly. "It's what I want."

It was what Kate wanted, too, but she'd given up hope of it years ago.

James acknowledged Harry's reply with a brief, bitter movement of his lips. He said nothing, but drank deeply from his glass.

"Are you certain the will is legal?" Harry asked.

"It's legal." James's smile was humorless. "Edward tried to find a way around it, but the lawyers said there wasn't one. And then he met Cordelia and it didn't matter." His face twisted. "Oh, God! If only he—"

For a moment Kate thought that James might cry. The notion shocked her. Even after the tragedy last year, when a carriage accident had taken the lives of his father and brother and sister-in-law, she'd not seen James lose control of his emotions. His face and manner had been composed, but his eyes . . . She'd wept in the privacy of her bedchamber for the silent grief in his eyes.

James shook his head, his expression bleak, and swallowed the last of the brandy. "I never expected to inherit Elvy Park and—and everything else. Never wanted to! But damn it, Harry, I'm not going to give it all away now that I've got it."

"No." Harry sighed and got to his feet. He walked over to the brandy decanter. "More?"

James nodded.

Kate's knees began to ache from kneeling on the hard floor. She shifted slightly and wished she'd brought a cushion in with her.

"You've got two months to find a bride," her brother said, as he refilled James's glass.

"Yes."

"So what the devil are you doing in Yorkshire?" Leather creaked as Harry sat down again. "The Season has started. You should be in London."

"Débutantes." An expression of distaste crossed James's face.

"What's wrong with débutantes?"

James swallowed a mouthful of brandy. "*You* don't get mobbed by them—and their mamas."

Harry laughed. "Of course not! I'm not half so well-favored as you."

Much as Kate loved her brother, she had to admit he was correct. Poor Harry had the Honeycourt red hair and freckles. James had no such flaws, unless the stern cast of his features could be called one. He'd always been handsome, but in his uniform, with his grin and his slanting black eyebrows, he'd been astonishingly so. She had heard—with no surprise—that he'd cut a swath through ballrooms in England and abroad, despite being a younger son with no title or fortune.

That status was a thing of the past, as was his military career. James no longer wore a hussar's colorful uniform. His riding-dress was somber-hued, the breeches dun-colored and the coat a dark brown. The clothes were elegant and expensive, as befitted an earl, but not dashing. Even so, he looked finer than any gentleman Kate had ever seen.

James's appearance wasn't the only reason débutantes and their mamas sought him out, but Harry didn't mention the earldom or the fortune. "What's wrong with débutantes?" he asked again.

"I could have my pick of a dozen of them," James said, frowning at his brandy.

"Only a dozen?"

James looked up. His mouth curved into a reluctant smile. "All right, I could have almost any débutante I wanted." The smile faded. "But I don't want one."

"Why not?"

"I don't want a chit straight out of the schoolroom."

"Why not?"

James shrugged. "They giggle too much."

"Nonsense!" Harry said. "A young and pretty miss would be just the thing."

"I can get young and pretty from an opera dancer," James said, exasperation in his voice. "We're talking about a *wife*."

"So?"

"So, I want a wife whose company I can tolerate. Damn it,

Harry, I'll be spending the rest of my life with the woman. I want her to be someone I like!"

"And you can't like a débutante? Come on, James, that's a bit steep."

"Remember Maria Brougham?" James asked, swirling the brandy in his glass.

Kate had heard the name before, but she couldn't recall the context. Harry clearly did. He nodded. "Those eyes," he said. "That mouth. And her breasts!"

"Yes," James said. "Exactly. And look at her now. She's become a regular Devil's daughter. Poor Edgeton lives in terror of her tongue."

"She's still beautiful," Harry protested, while Kate realized who Maria Brougham was: the Duke of Edgeton's wife. A woman with the figure of a Venus and face of an angel—and the sharp tongue and uncertain temper of a shrew.

"Certainly," James agreed. "But would you want to be married to her?"

"No," Harry said. He tapped his fingers on his knee. "I offered for her, you know."

Kate's eyes widened. Her brother had offered for the waspish Duchess of Edgeton?

James grunted as he looked at his brandy. "So did I."

Kate blinked, astonished. She wasn't sure what surprised her most; that James had proposed, or that Maria Brougham had refused him. How could anyone refuse an offer of marriage from James?

"She held out for a duke," Harry said, his tone faintly resentful.

James glanced up. A hint of a smile touched his mouth. "For which we should both be thankful."

Harry made a brief sound of agreement.

James eyed him, and Kate watched as his smile widened. "I remember you fought a duel over her."

Harry cleared his throat. "Mmm."

"Some slur on her appearance. What was it? Her lips?"

"Her eyelashes," Harry said, shifting uncomfortably in his armchair. Kate stared at the back of his head. Her brother had fought a duel over the Duchess of Edgeton's eyelashes?

James grinned, and Kate's breath caught in her throat. She hadn't seen him look like that in a long time. "Her eyelashes."

"*You* fought a duel over a pair of *boots*."

James's grin faded to a reminiscent smile. "So I did. I'd forgotten. Lord, what a young fool I was."

"And you broke Camden's jaw over that opera dancer."

The amusement left James's face. His features became stern once more. "Bella," he said. "Yes, I did." He looked at his brandy and swirled it gently in the glass. "He hit her, you know."

Harry nodded.

"I liked Bella," James said. "She was . . ." His voice trailed off.

"Expensive."

James shrugged a shoulder. "Worth it."

"If you say so."

James looked up. His brown eyes seemed very dark and his mouth was almost smirking. "I do," he said, and something in his voice made Kate's cheeks flush hot.

The library was silent for a moment, apart from logs shifting in the fire. Harry cleared his throat again. "So, not a débutante?"

James's face became blank. "No," he said. "A woman whose character is formed. I want to know what I'm getting. I have no wish for a wife whose company will grow irksome."

"And you want my help. That's why you're here, isn't it?"

James looked at Harry. It seemed to Kate that he didn't wish to speak. "No," he said finally. "It's not."

"Not?" Harry sat up straighter, his tone baffled. "What then?"

James frowned past Harry at the wall. It was as if he stared directly at Kate. She shrank back in the priest's hole.

"I'm here because I want to marry your sister," James said.

Harry choked on his brandy.

Kate jerked back, knocking over the candlestick. She reached for it desperately, blindly, and missed. The muted clang went unheard beneath Harry's coughing.

She knelt in the dark, unable to breathe, while the candlestick rolled across the floor of the priest's hole. James wanted to marry her?

"You want to marry Kate?" Harry said, when he'd regained his breath. "Why?"

Yes, why? Kate leaned closer to the peephole again and looked at James's face. There was a crease between his eyebrows. His lips were pressed tightly together.

"Because I think we should deal tolerably well together."

She closed her eyes. *No.*

"That's no reason to marry," Harry said.

"I have to marry." James's tone was flat. "And I like Kate better than any other lady of my acquaintance. I *know* her. She's not going to turn into a shrew on me."

"But you don't love her."

For a brief, foolish second there was hope. James's words extinguished it: "Of course I don't."

"James . . ." Harry sounded worried. "You're my best friend and I'd be pleased to have you for a brother, but—"

"You think it's a bad idea."

"I want you to be happy. Both of you. And I don't know whether this . . ." Kate opened her eyes to see Harry shaking his head.

"It's the only choice I have left. Damn it, Harry, if it must be a marriage of convenience, then I want a wife I can tolerate." James's voice was hard and his expression would have sent a dozen footmen scurrying for cover.

Tolerate. Something in Kate's chest clenched miserably.

"But would you be happy?"

"Happy?" The word sounded bitter in James's mouth. He shrugged. "Why not?"

"Would Kate?"

"She'd be mistress of Elvy Park. She'd have a title and a husband who respected her."

"Respect," Harry said. He shook his head. "Respect is all very well, but—"

"But?"

"But . . ." Harry shifted in the armchair. Leather creaked. When he spoke, he sounded uncomfortable, embarrassed even: "Shouldn't a happy marriage have an element of . . . of passion?"

James's mouth tightened. "Many women would prefer a passionless marriage."

Not I. Spinsterhood would be preferable to such a fate.

Harry stiffened in his chair. "You don't believe the marriage bed should be pleasurable for both parties?"

James clenched his jaw. "Damn it, Harry, don't lecture me!" His grip tightened on the brandy glass, becoming white-knuckled, and then his anger appeared to ebb. His face became devoid of expression. His voice, when he spoke, was flatly neutral: "You think I can't give a woman pleasure, even if I feel no desire for her?"

Harry put down his glass and leaned forward in his chair. "I've no doubt you can. But would you be happy doing so?"

James lowered his gaze to the brandy. A muscle worked in his jaw. "One woman is like another in the dark," he said.

"You really believe that?" Harry's voice was disappointed.

James looked up. His eyebrows drew together in a savage frown. "Damn it, Harry," he said fiercely. "What do you want me to say? I have to believe it!"

Harry was silent.

Weariness replaced the scowling anger on James's face. "If I could marry for love, I would," he said. "But my time's run out, Harry, don't you see? I have no other choice. I've thought about this seriously. I don't love Kate, or desire her, but I *like* her. If she married me I'd see that she was happy; you know I would."

Harry sighed. "Very well," he said. "Ask her. I don't know what her answer will be."

James looked momentarily startled. "You think she'll refuse me?"

Harry shrugged. "She's refused several offers."

"Really?" James's eyebrows rose. Kate was stung by his surprise. Resentment stirred in her breast. He needn't be so astonished. He wasn't the only man to see some use in her as a wife. "Such as?"

"Reginald Pruden proposed when she first came out."

"Pruden?" James laughed, but there was little amusement in the sound. "Dear God, no wonder she refused! The man's a pompous ass." He drank a mouthful of brandy and then shook his head. "Pruden." His upper lip curled with scorn.

"And . . . oh, there was Sir Thomas Granger, five years ago."

"Granger? Don't know the man."

"You haven't missed anything," Harry said. "He's a local baronet. Resembles a peahen."

The description should have made Kate smile—for Sir Thomas Granger *did* resemble a peahen—but instead she shuddered with memory of that proposal: Sir Thomas clasping her fingers with a plump, damp hand and leaning earnestly towards her, and then, when she refused him, flushing with rage and calling her a bran-faced dowd who set herself too high.

James laughed again, a humorless sound. His voice held pity: "Poor Kate." He looked at Harry and swirled the brandy in his glass. "Do you class me with Pruden and your baronet?"

Harry shook his head. "Of course not."

"So why should Kate refuse me?"

Why indeed? James Hargrave, Earl of Arden, was a prize on the marriage mart. His wealth and title made him one of the most eligible men in Britain. And he was handsome. He could have his pick of ladies. His offer was extraordinary.

I should be flattered. Why, then, did she feel so wretched?

Harry shrugged. "I don't know. I'm just saying, she might. Kate has a mind of her own. You know that. She's not some milk-and-water miss."

"She would have jumped at the offer eleven years ago," James said, raising his glass to his mouth.

Kate flinched at this comment. Hot humiliation rose in her cheeks. The memory of that girlish infatuation was hideous. It made her cringe to think of it.

"Do you think she's still partial to you?" Harry sounded surprised.

"No." James shook his head and swallowed a mouthful of brandy. "She treats me the same as she does you—thank God! Having Kate making sheep's eyes at me all the time would be dashed uncomfortable."

Harry grunted agreement. His tone, when he spoke, was unexpectedly glum: "When will you ask her?"

"Tomorrow," said James, looking as if the brandy had left an unpleasant taste in his mouth. "Unless you have an objection?"

"No." Harry was silent for a moment. "I suppose I should wish you luck."

"Thank you," said James. "But I doubt I'll need it. Kate's been on the shelf for years. Of course she'll accept my offer." His voice was even, toneless almost, and his face was without expression. He looked trapped, Kate thought. As trapped as she was in the dark priest's hole.

When the men had gone, Kate fumbled for the tinderbox and lit the candle again. In the flickering light she stood the goose feather quill in its holder and tried to blot the spattered ink. It had dried. The page was ruined. Not that it mattered; no one but herself would ever see it.

Kate gathered the diaries together. There were eleven of them, one for each year she'd been using the priest's hole. She picked up the earliest one and opened it at random.

Her handwriting was young and unformed, the entry hastily written. *He's coming again. I am determined to treat him as if he is nothing more to me than an acquaintance. No one must know of my feelings for him.*

She closed the diary. She'd been seventeen when she'd written those words, seventeen and desperate not to make a fool of herself again. Her pretense had worked. James didn't know, and neither did Harry.

Kate made a pile of the diaries and sat looking at them. What was she to do? She was no longer in the throes of a foolish infatuation, stammering and stuttering whenever she spoke to James and blushing hotly if she met his eyes. That youthful passion had long since matured into something deep and lasting. She loved James, and would do so until the day she died. There was no other way it could be.

He was going to ask for her hand in marriage. What would she say? What *should* she say?

Kate touched her mouth lightly with a fingertip, imagining James kissing her. She wasn't a complete innocent. She knew something of what the marriage bed entailed: kissing, and much more intimate acts. To do those things with James would be marvelous beyond anything—except that he wouldn't really want to touch her. He'd do so because he had to, because it was his duty, not because he desired her.

And why should James desire her? She was too tall to be considered feminine, and quite plain. The natural curl in her hair might be the envy of other ladies, but the color was a garish red and was accompanied by that worst of disfigurements, freckles. Looking as she did, it was inconceivable that any man would feel passion for her.

Kate closed her eyes. She wanted nothing more than to marry James—only not like this, without his love. He'd said that one woman was like another in the dark, but he was wrong. He might be able to imagine away her hair and her freckles, but darkness couldn't give her a voluptuous figure. He would touch her and, even if he couldn't see her, he would know that she wasn't the woman he wanted in his bed.

She couldn't do that to him. Or to herself.

Kate opened her eyes. She reached out and picked up a diary. It was dated 1813. Three years ago. She flicked through the pages. *James has sailed to Spain again with his regiment. I am so afraid . . .*

She closed the diary. Eight years he'd served in the 10th Hussars. She touched the calfskin cover lightly with her fingertips, tracing the date and remembering the changes she'd seen in him. It had been more than the uniform. He'd become quieter, more serious, although he'd never stopped laughing. The loss of laughter had occurred in the past nine months. Perhaps it had something to do with the action he'd seen at Waterloo, which she'd heard had been bad, but she thought mostly it was because of his father and brother. Grief could stop a person laughing, and so could responsibility.

She wanted James to laugh again, and she wanted him to have a wife he loved. Not someone he could tolerate, such as herself, but someone he could love. Someone who would make him happy.

When he asked her tomorrow, she knew how she would answer.

Like to read the rest?
The Earl's Dilemma is available now.

$\mathscr{A}$CKNOWLEDGMENTS

A number of people helped to make this book what it is.

I would like to thank my editor at Entangled Publishing, Erin Molta, for her work on the first edition of *The Spinster's Secret,* and I'd like to give a big thanks to my copyeditor, Maria Fairchild, and my proofreader, Martin O'Hearn, for their work on this (second) edition.

The cover and the formatting are the work of the talented Jane D. Smith. Thank you, Jane!

And last—but definitely not least—my thanks go to my parents, without whose support this book would not have been published.

Emily Larkin grew up in a house full of books. Her mother was a librarian and her father a novelist, so perhaps it's not surprising that she became a writer.

Emily has studied a number of subjects, including geology and geophysics, canine behavior, and ancient Greek. Her varied career includes stints as a field assistant in Antarctica and a waitress on the Isle of Skye, as well as five vintages in New Zealand's wine industry.

She loves to travel and has lived in Sweden, backpacked in Europe and North America, and traveled overland in the Middle East, China, and North Africa.

She enjoys climbing hills, reading, and watching reruns of *Buffy the Vampire Slayer* and *Firefly*.

Emily writes historical romances as Emily Larkin and fantasy novels as Emily Gee. Her websites are www.emilylarkin.com and www.emilygee.com.

Never miss a new Emily Larkin book. Join her Readers' Group at www.emilylarkin.com/newsletter and receive free digital copies of *The Fey Quartet* and *Unmasking Miss Appleby*.

$\mathcal{O}$THER $\mathcal{W}$ORKS

THE BALEFUL GODMOTHER SERIES

Prequel
The Fey Quartet novella collection:
Maythorn's Wish
Hazel's Promise
Ivy's Choice
Larkspur's Quest

Original Series
Unmasking Miss Appleby
Resisting Miss Merryweather
Trusting Miss Trentham
Claiming Mister Kemp
Ruining Miss Wrotham
Discovering Miss Dalrymple

Garland Cousins
Primrose and the Dreadful Duke
Violet and the Bow Street Runner

Pryor Cousins
Octavius and the Perfect Governess

OTHER HISTORICAL ROMANCES

The Earl's Dilemma
My Lady Thief
Lady Isabella's Ogre
Lieutenant Mayhew's Catastrophes

The Midnight Quill Trio
The Countess's Groom
The Spinster's Secret
The Baronet's Bride

FANTASY NOVELS
(Written as Emily Gee)

Thief With No Shadow
The Laurentine Spy

The Cursed Kingdoms Trilogy
The Sentinel Mage
The Fire Prince
The Blood Curse

Printed in Great Britain
by Amazon